MW01042957

NEVER AGAIN

DOUG NUFER

BLACK SQUARE EDITIONS NEW YORK 2004

NEVER AGAIN

Copyright © 2004 by Doug Nufer
ISBN 0-9712485-6-7

Published by Black Square Editions, an imprint of Hammer Books, 130 West 24th Street, Suite 5a, New York, New York 10011. U.K. offices: Four Walls Eight Windows/Turnaround, Unit 3, Olympia Trading Estate, Coburg Road, Wood Green, London N22 6TZ, England

First printing June 2004
ALL RIGHTS RESERVED
Library of Congress Cataloging-in-Publication Information on file
No part of this book may be reproduced, stored in a data base or other retrieval system, or transmitted in any form, by any means, including mechanical, electronic, photocopying, recording, or otherwise, without the prior written permission of the publisher.
The author is especially grateful to Harry Mathews for his encouragement and support throughout the years, to John Yau and Kenneth Goldsmith for setting this book of severe restriction loose upon the world, and to Jeff Clark of Quemadura and John Oakes of Four Walls Eight Windows for their work on this edition. Nico Vassilakis and the Subtext Reading Series first helped me present versions of this publicly, as did Anna Mockler, in *Never Again Reviewed*, which she and I performed at the Seattle Poetry Circus. Warren Motte, Philip Wohlstetter, and the members of the Oulipo have given me invaluable advice, either directly or by example.

Never Again has appeared on ubu.com and, via an excerpt from an earlier version, in the anthology *clear-cut* (Seattle: sub rosa, 1996).

Designed by Quemadura
Printed in the United States on acid-free, recycled paper

FOR KATHLEEN

1

WHEN THE RACETRACK CLOSED FOREVER I had to get a

job. Want ads made wonderlands, founding systems barely imagined. Adventure's imperative ruled nothing could repeat. Redirections dictated rigorously, freely. Go anywhere new: telephone boiler-rooms, midnight grocery shooting galleries, prosthetic limb assembly plants, hazardous waste-removal sites; flower delivery, flour milling, million-dollar bunko schemes. Do anything once; then, best of all, never again.

No more gambling, horseplay, poker. Hyperordered strictures posit antipredictability, perhaps.

"References?" Herr Trollenberg interviews, cocked brow adjusting monocle glinting somber intent.

"Certainly."

Application blanks require plausibilities, employment doyens earnest applicants, fictions facts.

"William Henderson, Universal Export; Niles Whitehead, Schweppes Flypaper; Sneed Moot, Hunsuck/Moot/Flagwipe; Harley Bloom, Celibate Communuchations; Dr. Sydney Culpepper—"

"Mr. Raymond!"

"O.K."

Phony resume misrepresents George R., 39, divorced, remarried, kids; Foreign Legion, MBA Marketing, BS Economics, appropriated universities fronting posts commensurating mendacity.

"Fice-president, Vhales, Paratron Intercetational?"

"Cetations. Orca brokering. Aquaria, marine rodeos, Hollywood. Tremendous seller's market."

"Fending machinegunner, FoMoCo, Edsel Longdivision?"

"Common antiques. Dinosaur V-8 fossil-fueled premiums. Autoclubs, collectoral collages, gaspump themeparks."

"Mint?"

"Unused."

"Hmmm, caveat emptore," mumbling. "Porter, Vax Museum!"

Duties included mold preservation, mustache touch-up, anticandle eventuation, maniac proactionary vigils viz. sexdoll fetishisms, cathode monitoriums, lollipop fear-reassurance, hunchback impersonations.

Bigger lies fly hire? Entrenchantly fatuous ad-libs pique counterapplicationary formulae, inverting title-position hierarchical privileging. Heretically, lessened discomplishments premiere greaters, resisting progress. Troll deliberates. Protection's panic button? Applicant's attire connotes acquiescence, corporate-incorporation. Polite-toned conversing encodes dress. Well-spoken assertiveness forwards tempworker compliance, reallocating proportional cares. Tempagent's loyalty pinions: Das Ferm oder Der Vorkfarce?

Reliability commands responsibility. Trial ethics ideate intermixable tolerances. Businesses dun personnel, affording prognosticated risks.

"You vant vot?"

Forbidden kneejerks cue; free beer, instant gratification, effortless effort, monkey's paw nonbacklashing wish-fulfilled deliverances. Rather, employmentality affirms standardizational blubbering inre collar bleaching (white/blue), salary leashing (short/tight), benefit fleecing (bald/fuzzed). Backgrounding whitenoise annoys. Recession-minded exigencies pressurecook thought. Steely lips acclaim eye-lazered consequentiality, commanding reply.

"Opportunity."

Tilt? Nodded acceptance unclogs processional drainpipe. Headtalk gestures convey protodocuments: workpass, memo allocating stingy directional information.

"Report 8:30."

$6.50/hr answers unasked interrogative. Duration?

"Ve'll see. Veeks."

Among serious wackos, ordinary sober eccentrics hardly rate peremp-

4

tory heave-ho. Handshaken thank-yous prestyle orderly's retreat. Deference uber alles.

Ratty glances deface waiting-room youngerlings learning hypocritical deceits enate magazines, sweating runaway apathy. Dressed, cleaned, cool-heeled musicians, artists, hacks, fuck-ups, Janes, Johns belong Paris, Kauii, Venice, SoHo because they'all're special.

Decades older, 39-year-old leapfrogs polywogs. Assignment: Overseer, Redline Abatement Vault, Transpacific National Bank. Objective: Burma. Entice Asians into dejunkied tenements via liponym (cull non-Asian surnames), purging loan-aps.

YESTERDAY'S TOMORROW TODAYBREAKS, establishing management toady rank authority's half-assed accountableness, carelessness. Age's virtue installs otherwise-unqualified supervisor, but nonjob's cirrus-status desubstantiates task's resolution.

Samoan factor complicates mission. Teen gang profilings overshadow rival ethnic delinquencies, mixconstruing Filipino cannery syndicate mayhem, Chinese watertortures, opium tongs, postwar's abase vengeances interalienating Vietnamese, Laotians, Montagnards, Cambodians, Hmoung-others (essentially, non-Japanese orientals). Unstated jargon slates conquer/divide ghettoization modules platting African-American exile.

"Diversify," corrects apologist.

Provisional cullsquad scoutmaster briefing interjects clue-in terminology, public-address cistern's anti-giardial chlorine.

Russel Nakagawa, cleancut Nisei baseball fan, compassionately buttresses Charles Pickford's teamspeak. Superanglo exec-seminar cant swirls innocent corruptions justifying greed's underlying heartfelt paternalism. C.P. counterwinks Russel's admissive shucksing, humoristically ass-backing lest neo-employed tempster unpeel indiscriminatable civil right's facemask.

Underseated, toilers moil meanly. Para-employed placements file shufflings. Individualistic famines fantasize idling's idyl, waging workaday's lickspittle pittance.

Ordinarily, funds greenlight extrafunds; representatively, collateral's easysleaze guarantees rejection. Speedlabs, coca popstands, greenback laundryrooms, nefarial etcetera forebode sheriff's foreclosured posse. Mortgagors reshade black/white affluences denoting business-as-usual rubberstamp.

Overlapping instructions tether initiative, complicate supervising's easiness. Blurred accountability expresses month-old takeover confusion renominating TPNB (nee' Sasquatch Bancorp), currently B-o-A subsidiary. Triplicate stationery's letterheads confound drawers, self-inker hazards compel trialballoon blottering, phone-IDs splice trinomials. New-hires, tempists, unbenefited crewlings abound; retiring pension-treaded staffers rotate humanity spares. Pitbosses duck pendulum.

Namescanners scour barrio lien futures. Batteried Walkmen leak clashing Nirvanas' rhythmic poundings, avert authorizational muzaks. Henry Margashack, Cynthia Pugh, Christine Balder badgily number-name breastpasses. Henry's fingernails're longest. Guitarist tendoncies freakishly handsell narrow-gauged ring-sized digits. Cynthia's unbraed, spikey nipples symmetrate nosepins. Manlike crewcut crowns; midriff-bared navel encrusts lintal crud. Christi redheadedly flips ponytail, repeatedly backpushing hornrims ascrunch. Busy yawns yoke nonunion oxen.

Outputting's subaverage sag evokes substitute teacher hazing rituals. Intimidative slowdown's deceitful clumsiness charms, prolonging estrangement as tapes forestall conversation.

Pouting repulsers attractively invigorate casting-couchpotato mashering. Doubledate scenaralio satyricates. Backseat lap sitting apes Yulelogged office party's bacchanalian abandonings drunkly blundered ruts. Crashpad Romeo duel enscrews, sordid proximity reheating rawly wangled meatpie mincefillings fissured amid filo-layered wallboard tympanically reverbing ruckus.

Realistically untransposed, cullions amass jerkloads. Dull chores sometimes cultivate flattering self-images, battle-ribboned fanciful cicatrixes demarcating angst. Naivete indemnifies foolish defiance.

Secretary sweeps out-basket.

Composing token burden, brevet corporal's minimalist hand-ins might also rankle esprit d'corps. Bossman's daydream off-fucking spurs nerve-ridden snits. Elsewhere-presided, martinet impersonation manages efficiently (goodguy persona's ineffective); herever, friendly manners, industrious attitude, businesslike wiseguy cracking succeeds.

Pee-bound self-excusing leavetaker HM saunters restroomward, savoring unsmoldered cigarette, cloth-bound *Cigarettes*. Midmorn addictions espressify adulthood's strapless privilege versus junior high's strap-on obedience.

Women continue.

"Coffee anyone?" disestablishes once-held pecker ordering.

He-man gofer?

"Double-short latte, pain au chocolate."

"Triple-creamed mocha, almond croissant."

Stuporvisor wobbles outward, passing cubicled blurs immuring hive-minded workerbees, uncrowned queens. Binged slid-shut elevator innocuously de-levitates, alighting downwind acrid steams, pastry-balanced butterings, almondian creams. Orders overlap unit's foursome (HM's unrequested portions appended), distending huge bag's protean comeuppance.

Retracing stirs bees. Swarm-drawn organizettes strop stingers, zingering impudence's cornucopia. Stylish audacity, panache, come-what-may spinners gyrate countertimeclockwise, defying roulette's revolvered gravity. Officious regulationists chowdown grease-nutted non-French doughs, industrially urned non-Italian java.

"Buncha feinschmackers," jabbers.

Feast-scale repast strews obliviously underneath capletters spelling offense: FOOD/DRINK/SMOKE PROHIBITED. Compu-copiers interdict room-shared snacking, superinvoking pristine environeeds. Liberties main office's papermates indulge're denied tempstaff, foreman comprehends. Delight pollutes guilt. Deficient wage's squandering ennobles unselfishness.

Solidarity enhances morale, reinstigates saltmine spelunkering.

"Harrumph!" toe-tapped designating.

Evidence condemns ex-post-facto: styrofoam beads, powdery finger-dust, fleshly smeared formica, breathable sweetened atmospherous particulata. Airblown contaminators doubtlessly windvade mechanisensors, altering delicate chemistries. She's correct. Wienerking's hotdogging endangers operational sensitivities.

"Sorry."

"Xerox specifically warned, contami—"

"Mea culpa."

Abject groveling unsettles wrath. Roiled angers displace, redouble, mysteriously reintensify. Glib contrition rings wrong? Passive-aggressive lassitude baits shark-attacked retaliation. Manpower-eater jaws self-righteously snap.

"Repairs cost thousands!"

"Heart bleeds," underbreaths.

Giggles unstifle, tempting shoutrage. Outnumbered spike-heeled toothcutter slinks offstage.

"Uhhh-ohhhh," milks yuks.

Gleanwhile, scurried wiping, trash concealments, grimescene fleck removals precomb Mac Arthurian beachlanding. Bag-crammed refuse eludes wastepaper's circularfile (disimplicating mess's transgression). Ingenues radiate productivity. Document-piled efficiency deletes antipathetic slackusations. Per-agreement compilative nomicultural investigations unstack in-basket, towerstack outgo.

Ogre, stormtrooper twintrude.

"Ready," perkily welcomes.

"Rules exist," stonetableheads preach, "preeminently—" goggled sniffing can't affirm sugar traces. Aimless fingerpointing merely visualizes refuse's prima-facie wastepapers.

"Problem?" rallies subchief.

"Eating's off-limits. Insubordination's categorically inappropriate."

"Pardon?"

"Miz Saludo observed four persons disobeying restrictions, stomached snickering insults—"

"Kindly give proof."

Grins freeze. Ballsy ploy knocks protocol, teetering King Charly's mountaintop hegemony.

Tattler lunges purseward.

"Scram toots," Christy stiff-arms.

Contact braces tableaux.

"Gotta warrant, babydoll?"

Sequestered allegements muddle vigilante moralists. Theft's casemaking disapplies. Marijuana smoke's likewise unwhiffable, defeating probable-causeways' paralegal contraband seizure. Satchels hide plunder, loot, narcotics? Garbage. Incineratable incriminations'd confirm caper. Napkin-wad inferences lie stashed: constitutionally protected.

Speciously espied gluttonies underpin emergent conflicts between corporationists, discorders. Clean-up's carpetbag rugsweep stashing waste renders accusations untenable.

Fish-hook extrication's easier. Unprovable charges damn accusers. Command-chain twistily chinks unlinkable apologies. Eagle-eye's knowledge complicitly echoes headman's proclivity: believe worst.

"Falsely" slandered noshers appear guilty unless charge's refuted. Deep-seated disaffections throb. Puny sin's inconsequentiality compounding contradictory Republican-held worldviews anent bill-of-rights privacy precedence emphasizes oppression. Suspended lectures forecheck lawyerly hockey defenseman reiterations. Eye-contact dominations emulate dogfight etiquettes. First-spoken interruption's weakening potentially registers wimphood?

"Apologize!," first-strike advantage's mine.

Adversaries harmonize ominously sucked-up breaths. Their departure chastens victory-minded rights advocates. Retributions'll appreciate exponentially, dwarfing normal rollovers.

Formerly committed sorters skitter carelessly, heaping willy-nilly yesses heeding shiftable confabulations respecting nomencultural numerology, concrete noun suggestions, fetched allusions, funny syllables, eeny-meeny-miney-mo. Minutes tumble lunchward.

Noon evacuates working-pooled secretarial strokers, suited mandarins. Errands untangle genders (brownbagger ladies, liquidlunch gents). Pre-fired jobsighter surveys alternatives illustrating optional choicelessness: cafe-carts, messengers, taxis, letterluggers, windowcleaners, leafblowers.

Comparatively, irony enlivens bankster drudgery. Monolithic institution's drab foilhood targetspots sportively flingminded dart-throwers. Edgewalking stress recommends officework, re: parasite interdependency breakdowns analyzing host/guest needs. Behemoth scratching plague-infested fleas romantifies mites' mightiness. Dumbo tasks institutionally insure hide-thickened surface.

Postnoon returner X-rays floorstaff's skeleton. Skullheaded executrix wields envelope's orthographic hatchetjob: Gorge Ramond.

"... decision, unfortunately, precludes continuance ..." rejectionspits minced tidings.

Lowkey upperlackey, well-warned, tactfully ushers axed ex-supervisor closetward. Bricabrac's prepackaging de-necessitates reentry. Paperbacks (Perec's *Disparition*, Katchor's *Knipls*), soundtapes (Negativland, Bikini-Kill), combs, rattlings, material sundries underdefine quirk-sketched dog-impounded lost'n-found cohorts. Waiting hereabouts provokes impatience.

Gatekeeper's glanceblown acetylenes pantomime may-I-help-yous that'll tickerset tresspassing's countdown. Henchmen loiter nonchalantly.

Shrug countersigns impasse-word's unsaid "git!" Callbutton brings bingabonged elevator's all-aboard.

Lobby's desolate, excepting Buddhist securitygod. Benchless marble-lined temple stone propitiates riff-raff disaccommodation's, excommunicating unsuitable humus beings. Freed bankculler exeunts.

11

Presently, gals upstride, unrecognizing co-worker herewithin sidewalk's chaotic context.

"We're canned," reintroduces.

Kaffe klatch kaputted livelihoods, however chinzy. Kiss-and-make-up's lascivity countercurrents commiseration.

We-word royally presumes this as-yet unconfirmed blanket firing; schmooze incorporating jingoistic anticorporate lingo effectively babbles, stymies cameraderie.

Credibility graduates. Misanthropic, disenchanted, resigned, C&C agree upon powwow, should pink slips accost them.

RENDEZVOUS PROPOSAL CURDLED BELIEF: Grinder's

Meatery. See-yas foresaw belongings retrieval. Pointlessly consulting wrist, untimed jetsam intuitively schedules yet-to-be meetings. Shammed appointments' pretext deactivates pedestrian alarmists, regarding loiterer's stumblebum streetcorner idling.

Flight-for-flight's-sake rationale hypotheticates audits, foundation inspections, medical digging: things preferably escaped.

Solution's salon contains stools, foot-rail, polished mahogany, ceilingwhomper ventilator paused o'er exiguously intricate tile patterns stalking Gestalts. Mishmashed Zeitgeists addle troubled accounters factoring 20-year-old soundtrack reprising swarmy film-trended lostalgias, fixture-appointed detailing reinfecting age-old boardinghouse reachbacks circa Tamed Frontier era, horseshit forgiven.

"Deschutes," establishes residence. Propriety's hourglass inverts, gravitating desire.

Supposer worries: loanbusters subsequently re-manacled? Neo metronome drums slaves' exerting.

Buying brew, customer kiboshes bartender/dishwasher query opportunities, substituting sopuppertunity persona-non-applicara microlabel hypernomially. Drink entity's identity barcodes well-stooled ciphers.

Whethertheless, unapplicability fantasizes-up employmental placemats. Here's workplace postulates Edenhood; by-and-buy, lesser Eden supermerges. Bouncers watch heartbreaker waitresses. Backscenes kitcheneers stain ugly lusts, ogling seamy swished static-electric thighs thunderscoring Adams' essential Evelessness.

Firmamentally, sportsticker transits backbar, glittering fabulous odds. Obscure boxing match televises abreast suds-trade lumenette's contemporary odalisk (frat posterbabe). Well-known athletes guzzling on-premesis photogenuously aggrandize depressing familiarity. Bargone concluder's non-repetitional pulsion harkens Porterian inversion: everything goes.

13

Marketfree brokers enter, wakesurfing NYSE. Handicapping's characteristics forge ironclad tautologies boringly galvanized. Offwork securities swappers compute number-called aboveboard's raptures: CLEVELAND -7 San Diego .... METS 6 1/2-9 Astros .... Albuquerque even-6 EDMONTon .... HOMECAPS [idiotcue] .... Serbia invades BOSNIA .... CUBS lose .... SEAHAWKS -29 Miami ....

Knicknaming baffles, muddling disciplines/specialties. Disclarity paracodes insider-tipped chestnuts? Ex-punter dissembles: mascots mean patsies.

Hush crossripples babble. Stockbroker bloodhounds detect air's reflushed surfumes: nonwaitresses, ergo available. Immediate occupancy desired.

"Fuckers," slaps tabletop.

Unshouldered bags claimstake no-man's-land abutting ex-super's stool.

"Cheapskate pricks," prods kindness.

He-mensch conveys bartendered requests, destools, tablehops. Bigshot gesture tweaks stags.

"Margashit."

Treacherous co-conspirator ratted. Two-on-one bushwack consecutively isolated temployees, solemnizing slime-honored police extractions. Liewitness testbaloney inveigled attributions pinning donkeytales blindly, offering squealer amnesty. Whereas ladies-first prioritization anteceded surviving crewmember's disreputation, 'Enery must've pinned'm.

Cyn contemplates dancer re-enlistment: Deja-Vu. "50 Gorgeous Showgirls," billboard pastie-faced renderings ubiquitously remind ex-dancers —flashbacks featuring minor stripping, G-string tablehumping, majordomo peek-a-boob buggywhip, cigar-rat smokiness, lowlife stareworts fungal colonizations, fiercely remonstrated customarital relations, draconian houserules, unwelcome homelives, all-around shitty existences.

14

"Gimme McDonalds."

Monthlike weekspans counterbalance supposed advantages: liposuctioned salary's bloated deductions (bouncer kitty, cabaret licentiousness fees, taxicab fares), exposing short-lived illusion.

"Sex-descrimination employers?" male diddles.

"Georgy-porgy! Mistertwister? Audience's likelier."

Father-aged rogue mopes.

Twenty-three-year-old calibrates mankind, hypersensing prickly innuendos wherever men're introspective, morosely emotional, mordantly solicitous, or flat disingenuous.

"I'm your basic burned-out racetracker," disarmingly redefines. "Racetrackers're audience-participators."

Fleshdancer's cynicism sloughs-off girlfriendly eye-rolling. Acquiescent repose sleepily anticipates autobiographer's self-aggrandized humilities.

Ego cogitates autobio summation: upper-middleclass swaddlings cushioned momma's boyhood, coddled softspun affectations, romance-tranced boundless bounties within graspiness's wonts. Schooling preset bratty confidence's jerrybuilt ramshackle dreamhouse; lumber-graded D-efforts framed honor-roll facades. Postgraduated bullshitter naively grazed business minefields. Self-maker enterprises appealed; ground-floor subservience appalled, engendering wildly metacommercial flings. Venture vultures undoubtedly drooled. Preswooped-upon carcasses shortlisted Lionel Roundhouse Shoppe, Hellmark Greetingcard dealership (trademark-infringing, said Hallmark's legal jackals), fishmonger consultancy (offishally, albeit fraudulently, licensed). Credit flame-out disenfranchised flame-broiled burgerbar's last stand.

Restless successlessness damaged childhood sweetheart matrimony. Defunding's recurrances miscarried pregnancies allegorical, actual. Chilled passions, disaffected youthful yens killed love.

Tailspindling mutilations unfolded. Coke-fueled sexploit wildings re-

15

constituted updated French postcard ooh-la-las. Drugstore vigors sped metabolized concupiscence, pre-valium let-downs. Rechemistrated dissolution recital resembles tinhorn preacher's preconversion sermon whereonto self-proclaimer gloms victimhooded glory. Boastmaster lulls dolls. Companionship nearly napsizes before *Daily Racing Form* salvation's confession.

Barmates inch forwardly.

Months spent dissecting results, memorizing odds-ratio expectancies, examining strident methodologies, dry-running theoretocracies preceded live-action bets. Thereafter, defeats counted, yet paper losses' insignificance duplicated "legitimate" entrepreneuralistic outcomes. Pre-suffered bankruptcies wistfully reframed gaming's seriousness. Wildcatter biz endeavors forewent so-called irresponsible gambles. REGULAR-type investments were riskiest; study-gathered infotrawling's risk-managed analytics, otherhandedly, prefigured shrewd prudence. Furthermore, losing's commonness liberated tight-fisted reluctance.

'79–'80's season inaugurated some sorta breakthrough. Openings'd pre-emerge paratelegraphically! Insightful glimpsing caught sparklit ideas! Guesswork's essentiality deserted fling-prone fliers, implanting horsechip softwares's intuitive databank which'd amassed experientially, experimentally, expedientially. Hours-long racestat scanathons' magical kiss defrogged prince.

Flashlit finishline photos previsited ponypicker's ken, exhibited *Twilight Zone* fidelity, if sub-100% certainty. Converting +/-50% fat payoffs, though, amply over-reimbursed outlaid wagers. Unlike sixties 30-minute teledrama morality squelching jackpot visions, such windfalls brought money-backed self-confidence's brass-assed, platinum-plated expectations guarantee.

Skeptics behold guy nursing beers, ill-affording peanuts. Wallstreeters background erstwhile bettor: shoeshines blazing, money-hung codpieces, handsome come-ons.

Longacres' closure poetically justified gambling's caesura. Cross-examiners further doubt testifier's bankroll staying capability. Tempjobbing's nadir chosen? Self-sufficiency's apex drooped!

"Y'see ..." Contributing discouragements intervened. Getting laid's paradox, fr'instance: singleminded dedication meant monk's fervor, unrequitable romances contradicting sensual highroller image.

Ultimately, money talked, bullshit walked. Cavalierly treating raw greenbacks (twenties, fifties, one-hundreds) fatigued caginess. Untightened monetary grasp replaced prudential gamesmanship. Money's derivative nature (buying-power valuing dollars) underwent reprioritization. Currency symbolized itself, dismissed conspicuously consumed goods standardly ranking self-worths.

Evaluation literally actuarialized. Hamilton-, Franklin-, Grant-headed simoleans re-accounted accomplishments' integrity. Pressure's stream rediverted alcohol's liverbank erosion, strengthening "courage," ruining nerves. Thus, nerve-racked monotony destroyed horseplayful urge.

Explanation's largesse strands listeners, who're blatantly admired. Buckaroo stockbrokers hump stool-spun bullrides.

"Purity's addiction," toasts escapists needing maze.

TRANSPAC BANK'S EXIT CONFIRMED tempestuous rap excluding additional agency-sanctioned assignments; blacklisting confirms art's delusive conceit sassing others' comprehensibility failures, forgiving one's own. Reasonable expectation dictates unremitting rejections. Boorish seersucker suitcoat outfits jobseeker. Eluding tempagent-mediated compuscreenings, snazzily attired longshot specialist takes direct action: classifieds, wherein worst-taste scenarios inveigle multi-dozen hungry droolers, tendering bitter sweets.

"6.66/hr. grndflr. opty./ltd.bfd." cattleprods stampede. Unrealistic insistances blythely decree undegreeable techschool diplomas, verifiable experiences slavishly mimicking these ad-stated elementarily stupid activities (ladeling molten metals, foiling lava, inhaling toxic ethers), preferring non-preincarcerated noncombative military veterans, minority ethnicities preapproved.

Preposterousness lures unqualified applicant wearing crapshooter's jacket. Industrial-strength hellfires? Beastly wage? Jobhunt anthropology discovers absurdist glee's perverse rewards. Trudging drudges astonish lone bicyclist, hereas unmotored transport corroborates suitcoated interloper's dilettantism amongst jalopy-taken, flivvered, bussed hordes.

Unemployment compensation punchcards excuse serfs' futilism: filling unfillable jobs-sought column insures incoming dole check's validity. Food/shelter basics cannot rationalize DeMillean extras' queue.

Breadline lottery fever infests gallows-humored shufflers lucidly debating Quixote v. Panza standpoints referencing shit-waged labor, impossible dream. Goal's paltryness exonerates non-attainment.

Self-deployed adventure capitalist incants underbreath chant recognizing herein's prime-directed systematic fancy: present's participation bans thereafter's destiny. Hardcase exploited Parliaments, Kools, Luckies strike menthol solidarities smoking unquittable deadends.

"S'pose dey scabbin'?"

18

"Local's doin' da lapdog."

"Wha? Workman's comp, 'dustrial 'demnity, fuckin' turkey fo' Thanksgivin'."

Laid-off forger briefs throng, attributing trickle-down generosity snidely. Youngish grandfather-type basso profundos vulcan mystique. Death-defying spillages enlivened drabness. ER excursions toured paininsulas, ailands, frightseeing tractions—expenses paid (minus whopper deductable). Terrifier's gritty spinetinglers ennoble grunt gig's pathetic attraction. Apply-minded braves smirk "dat-so?" Smoke-signaled diatribes display warpaint.

Scars brag. Paramortal wounds stipple cheeks, chests, bellies. Coarsely sewn lacerations reorder sissors/paper/rock hierarchies. Shards riposte blades, bulletholes parry slices, sawmill run-ins trump lawnmowered mishaps. Everybodies' anguishes memorialize pains overtaken, undergone.

"Burns burn."

Bassnote clefhanger muffles trebbling lookie-heres. Burning's glass-magnified concentrations excruciate. First-degree universally felt sunburns, secondclass stovetop blisterers constitute stepladdered wounderstandability foreshallowing 3D's skyhigh agony.

Ore-liquifying temperatures reconceive epic hells. Dantely, forgemaster uplifts pantleg. Wrinkled, charred orange pinkness unblackens natal brown. Hairless crenels' rubbery sheen, warping musculature, sagging rehinged artificialities approximate indistinguishable knee. Thigh-to-toe skin grafts' patchwork vinyl waders seemingly replace flesh.

"Counta bein' stinko," sank job-injured claimant's lawsuit.

"Employee shall forfeit disability coverage," conditionally began millworker contract's substance-abuser 8-page exclusion clause section, followed by 8-line perk section's November turkeys, Easter hams, unstinting shebangs.

Simultaneously, corp. reorganization bankruptured unionmade truss. Chapter Eleven's takeaways de-instituted skill's wage-tied recognition, lowering payroll. Debt reshuffling buffaloed civic-blinded assessments dropping taxes companies not threatening emigration must pay. Relocation's south-of-the-border scare somehow cemented localcification, awarding steelmill's industry public service medallions neck-ribboned onto chestless, wobbled guts. Mexicali blackmail finessed mill's perpetuity. Courtroom upholdings preinstated corp-friendly rulings, classically canonizing sainted partnerships damning churchmouse poverties.

Microeconomic aftershocks quake, splitting earth-shattering gape: waistband pistol? Ex-plaintiff protrudes undeniable butt, hernialike subcardigan, recalling Mae West's hard-on wishes, wrongly.

Threshold's dilemma dawns red sky overhanging applications' preprocession. Magniprint questionnaire's obstructive idiocy nitpicks brain; detailed schoolyear, work-dated probes importune. Thinking jams. Howto books inadequately advise tipsters confronting imminent workstation violence (step one, yell, "Waaaaah!;" steps two-ten, skidaddle!).

Officiously tidy lady sharpens schoolbus-yellow # twos. Hulky illiterates bite tongues, wrestle pencils. Long-standing forge-burnt gunslinger imaginatively strafes room. His "sidekick" procrastinates taddling; weapon's drama-principled spotting plots catharsis, counsels cowardly fatalistic surrender. Object lesson CEO headshot begs justifiability, assuming psycho's sanity.

Justice's deliberator counterweighs: fusillade chaotics ensure omnidirectional peril, recommend heroic tattle. Besides, after-the-fact accessory charge fixes cowardice's vagrant morals.

Observing linear orderliness, stoolie scribbles suspicions, hastily describing gunsel—inserting vita acta dating school-termed brackets. Ignorable drek masks crucial intelligence.

Secretary's dogpiled reshuffle buries crimespotter's shakily scrawled claxon.

"Maam?" ahems urgency vainly. Pretensed omission necessitates recollected apform.

"Y'all gots t'be top," flirts at whistleblower's overeagerness.

Inverse-aligned boldface print jolts, buckles jelly-kneed reader. Botched jackrabbit boundaway stalls would-be victim awaiting excuse's reprieve. Silence gives grim answer: glazed-eye, dank brow's fiend mien. Lock-'n-load determination projects blood rays. Tension foreplays lead ejaculation.

Plant manager's door whooshes upspun papery leaves clearing desktop. Whirling honcho joyously bellows high-pitched, long-winded directions. Exultant buyer's attitudinal conceitedness overweeningly pumps head's multi-gallon hatsize, conferring baby-scaled macrocephalic dimensions, seeings how he's scarcely 5-2.

Nasal-toned bellower blinks demi-recogniton. Hits dirt.

Blasted steampipe squeals heat. Open-fire avenger jostles mid-stampede, steadies "house cleaning" aim (hyperextending business-termed euphemistic abuse). Panicked escapees palpate hailed skull-fragmented matter, sundry organ confetti; stumble gasping liquid, clotted vapors. Big caliber dumdums excavate fleshes. Red's brutally bland oxidized browns repaint DutchBoy-coated interior's ecru/beige nondescript blandness. Slithering, diving, writhing unshot fortunates flit.

Banged yells connote wounding? Predeath moaning resignations shroud steamclouded umbral mists' dreamy pointillism. Hard-edged pistolshot cracks attack flatly declare defiant nonresonance. Discrete small explosions interrupt blown pipe's onrushing furor. Annihilation's punctuality crisply disenchants comics' KABLAMMO-style mayhems.

Bewilderment storms yard. Smoke-white nimbus postscripts skywritten cryptograms telling fires' potential spread. Killing-identified sounds intermingle manufacturing's droning.

Bike unlocks. Air-packed tires celebrate life's flimsiest joy: continuing.

21

MURDER/SUICIDE CLOGS evening reportage channel-to-channel. Squelched inquest outcome likely, headline syntax automatically writes, ex-steelworker's pathological disgruntlement predicts. Shootist doctor's records chart depressive-bent motives. Although there's an unsigned tipsheet foretelling massacre, newscasters omit taglines 911-ting stoolpigeons.

Primecut slaughterhouse photo-op droolingly re-inspects kill-site decapitation—beautiful factorial bowels entrailing scenically compelling tubal superstructure disrupted, leaking, gnarled. Visual evisceration counterpoints anchorperson chitchat.

Bambi: "Gee, that's tragic."

Dirk: "Times have gotten tougher."

On-camera mush inspires televiewer's grossly hatched off-camera unspeakable egging. Bambi's, "Kamikaze victims, *Newsweek* coverbait?;" Dirk's, "Blue Cross'd needa shield," inwhich solitary instances're trendily uplinked, configuring apocalyptical topicality.

Nonesuch blather would conceivably ensue. Presspassholders eulogize innocents' finales, confine lunatic's self-made blame.

Watching vidiotic retelling, immaterial witness relaxes. Poolhall setting undertones shilled crimestories nobody else watches. Gameface focuses circle felt-topped greens. Softly controlled strokes, rumbled clicks, pocketed clunks soothe vexed dendrites. "SilentRadio," omnipresentational backbar's sportsline ticker, repeats pointspreads under/over wall-mounted billiard tools quaintly decorating Belltown Billardhall's upscale authenticity. $40 California Meritage glass-pours underlining assorted cuesticks, cuestick cases, chalks, bridges, ballracks, cueballs, full ball-sets probably outsell functional paraphernalia.

Ticker-lit points interwork news bits lagging bodycounts. Paraguayan earthquake toll, Cypriot ferry crash, Siamese twinjet shipwreck, Israeli/Palestinian guns/rocks face-offs, desultory "fallen-arrow" slayings' spreely discharged gravity-prone bullets finding untargeted skulls preamble forge-marred avenger's promenade. Summation's curtly trundled phrase twinkles casualties "2-3," paraphrasing odds-like ratios.

Murders' spectator fears post-mortive interrogation'd cramp mobility, feasibly implicate otherwise-uninvolved murderer's observable companion. Considering I'ven't been fingerprinted (therefore remain hopefully dragnet-proof), AM's bloodfest cranks anti-vagrancy winch.

Work's alibi potentiality stimulated itchy-fingered jobgrab. Seeking vague date-placed locality sequestering myself, death's evader hit-up variably graded restaurants—enthusiastic efforts pursuing grubby labors.

Several kitchens nixed abnegatory galleyslave impressment bid. Despite lowliness, dish bussing/pot licking positions stood unavailable. Secondhand connoisseur multitudes already'd uptaken leftovers' first-scrape privileges. Untraceable saliva wines marinating demi-eaten clumps enticed ravenous dozens wanting edible drool. Winter's approach, too, antishly motivated grasshoppers that'd postponed working's call.

Undeterred seeker persevered. Overwhelmingly ratified negatives commensurated apocryphal Q/A sessions starring streethanger stag Q's "Fuck?," non-streetwalker female A's "Beat it!" Diner-to-counter-to-cafeteria, chowderhead journeyed scumward, disdaining reality's grimmest clue: nonoption. Policymakers conferred doormat-status democratically. Midafternoon's hunting grounds flushed grousing asst.mgrs., peacocking chefs, lounging impresarios citing all-Latino crews' language barriers blocking English-speaker.

"Habla español?"

"Un poco."

"Olvídalo."

Bothersome hustlers, hat-in-hand beggars, avuncular purveyors swarmed bullshitting poohbahs whose haughty brush-offs resonated previous lifetime setbacks (mild, mediocre, heinous). Digressively, self-esteem's swoon mucked benthosian sediments' stalk-eyed needleteethed

23

monsters: spiteful ex-girlfriends, remorseless creditors, bloodthirsty gradeschool rulersnappers, paranoiac bossy rebukers.

Defeatism's funk snowballed melting. Jobcaster fishing expedition's skunking cheered nondrinking barhopper, delivering me, job-unencumbered/cop-undetained, hereunto ordeal-ending shallow binge (3-4 well-intended drinks preliminating procrastinated decisions).

Pool's plush ivory clamor, staid mutual self-respects, hallowed silences mollify. Nineball's triangle-set diamonds, snooker's sphered rubies, eightball's black pearl glow invaluably, reflect unmarketable resilience greater than Jupiter's moons. Billiards' sight-based, sound-enhanced priceless appealingness, counterargumentatively, sells gametime's jacked rates upscalers readily remit.

Auxiliary enhancements exude: ristorante cucina cuisine infumes grilled oven-belched reek. Garlic's perpetual fry bakes toasted sautees. Expensive pastas cheaply undercut "gourmet" pizzas, ten-dollar hamburgers' ersatz-themed associations (Cajun, Tuscan, Micronesian . . .).

"Double-tall Americano," precaffeinates boozing. I'll pluck all-due assiduous job-strumming overture ere saying "double-rum maraschino."

Hopper hues compositionally situate lone-stool sitter, barkept laconic tidying, solitaire poolplayers. Peaceful, romantically depicted bored delirium suddenly ruptures. Bantering kitchen bantams cockfight—spurred yelp, pecked hiss (animalistic outrages're applicable).

"Routine?" newcomer intones.

"Lithium," unsmiling bartender betrays someone's mental ills.

Balkan imprecations stab atmosphere's mellowness. Punch-'n-Judy torsos stage shadowboxed fistfought feints resolving redlit antagonists basking under heatlamp suns. Quadruple order-up! bells bong unheeded; bartendress cowers, hungerers suffering cooks' forcefed delay.

Aproned Greek insulting T-shirted non-Greek younger thesbian prompts massively aped retaliations emoting hammy accent/lingo/mannerisms. Spotlight's poseur improvises workshop-quality skits which're reportedly drug deprivation-inspired. Upstaged unwilling co-star's ionic non-ironic retort cleavers meat. Danger's antitheatrical sharp steel props scatter helter-skelter.

Bartender's chorus sotto-voces ancient strife's strophe: filthy dishes. Chefly penchant repudiates plate washing's low chore; chiefly, chorine trills, "So's Demitri can chomp Andrew's bum."

Owner's absenteeism elongates spat, calibrating pepperoni's heatloss wasted fearing noisy fighters.

"S'cuse," meddler walks around.

Disputers arrest themselves, regard—agog—patron's intrusion.

Sleeves uprolled, sneakers gripping mat, understudy partakes center-staged slimelight. Scrubber assembles raspy-padded soap sudsers, peaceably scours stove's aluminums, alloys, ironcast warhorse skillets.

Rechanneled invective loonily unites goons. Greek/pseudoGreek co-deploy guardhouse challenges countermanding sink's incursor.

Interloping customercenary lathers beef-cutter serrated carving knives. Sinkload overflow cancels weasely whines, barmistress avers, geometric clarity disproving germ theorums culturing unsterilized dinnerware.

Upset scenaerialist remounts trapeze-acted melodrama; greencard-holder spectates. Everyone mentally clips figurative safety-net's guylines.

"Chas, help!" hails returning owner, quickly exonerating Demitrios Spanikopolas, heroizing sink stand-in.

Interrupted histrionics captivate stately, plump Chauncy B. Huber-mayer. Doubletakes hang airheaded artiste's swansong diva swandive.

"Sheba dear, l'exchequer, sil vous plait."

Boom-lowered stillness accentuates faucet drip, shot scratch, breath pant.

"Andy," musically tuned coda appends check-written drum solo's dot-lined rip, "philosophy's consolation."

HANDSHAKE'S HEGEMONIAL RESTRUCTURING installed mutually agreeable pact: he-cooks/I-wash. Swaggered off-key whistling fit D's newfound regality, projected dreary reign forecasts.

Hours hence, dishwasher understands kitcheneer's mutiny. Dimi boasts vanquishing "candy-pants sissy" helpers, "dose pretty's y'please dilly dalliers." Schmaltzily hummed sitcom themesongs rousted sentient humanoids. Bewitched mayberry petticoat junctions rerun revelry's hillbilly eternity.

Amidfloor, C.H. hobnobs. Backslapper razzes chums, warmly greets unfamiliar customers, generally hosts party. Behind bar, late-model Mondavi Reserve Cabernet Sauvignon hyperventilates, cruising top-down, convertably coaxing beer-drinking, single-malt scotch dreamers hypothesizing "smoother" palate ride. Overpriced underaged wine symbolizes neo-pool's hallmark, resonating 80s-era jingles morally elevating greed-fed sponging acquirers, typecasting youthfully vigorous, career-tracked, self-assured worldbeaters (who, 1990s, relinquished middle-management sinecures). Upscaled survivalists, heresoever, continually thrive, comfortable amusements undivided.

Eleven O'clock Newshour Showtime soundlessly reflashes gunshot scenes montaging announcements, sanguinely pictured horrors, stern-faced splattercasters, mugphotos, police-sketched portrait. Sinkbound witness/fugitive couldn't increase volume, pending electrocution's wet-handed threat. Demitrios's shift-ended proceedings better proceed uninterrupted.

"Sexball sidepocket," echo startles. Somewhere I've heard like-cadenced teutonics.

Tingly recollective itchiness raises goosepimples. Cigars' blueish smokescreen surforms head-level, bright-lit cloud obscuring facial identifiers. Post-shot shooters're decapitated inside smokiness's glacially slow rise. Amidshot, aimers squint, battling parallax, vogueing loose-lipped stogies, cool calculation's stagey frown. Miserly spoken remarks dribble few vocal identification hints.

Half-past weathercast, Demitrious Rex abdicates stovetop's unsittable throne. Dishes've exonerably degrimed, unslimed; steady work terminus approaches. Departing, chief cook bestows snack-scale food prep authorization (garnishing, microwaving, baguette slicing, boiling), hereby prospectively overburdening platter latherer's chore-packed catalog.

Poolshark apprentices eschew feeding's distraction. Minnesota Babyfats stickmen self-mythologize impossibly romantic alternative careerism. Archly reenacted shot-mechanized Englishes, needlessly showy blast-flourished powerplays distinguish distinguished gentlemen masquerading loutishly. Must-see/can't-watch tensions enliven Corningware penitentiary's rockpiled workhours. Excruciatingly viewable manquees' miscued flubs entertain.

Smoked-in images solidify, shape recognizable individuals: predominantly, paunch drunk slumming yuppie palookas. Fringily representing somesuch social classmates, square-headed Nazi blond zootsuiter posture's goose-stepped formality rekindles recognizer's weak spark. It's Trollenwhosis! Brown-nosing blacklister redlined ex-temp Raymond's redlining banker course, purged citywide temporary employ databases, alerting hiring agencies: achtung! dishonorable discharge!

Bending lightward, gold-rimmed monacle's positive eyedentification reconfirms accented suspicion.

Concurrently, Sheba's whispers slander "Hubermeyer's Ubermensch," owner-favored pals accorded supercustomer status. Nevertheless, off-clock staying's triply tipped, she says.

Extra moneyless compensation's offered whence Chuck's friends tank-up multiple liquors, untap frothy laments. High-class viewpoints revisualize workplaces' gloomy toning, proclaim self-serving victimhood. Dues payer testimonials commence.

27

Eightballing lawyer holds court, recollects Baby-breaking Boa Case. Dateline: moving day, Anytown, USA. Six-foot pet's disappearance commandeered otherwise-preoccupied movers. Hirelings' herpetophobia, packbubbled underbrush, time-pressured itinerary mitigated against searched thoroughness. Rushed exiters haphazardly canvassed crannies, attic, cellar, closets, snake-friendly nooks. Cage-slipping reptile unfound, decampers relocated. Newlyweds arrived. Dreamhoused copulations eventually impregnated wife, engineered nightmarish litigations outgrowing embrangled sequence ensuing classic catastrophe: hugely pregnant woman putters happily stirring soup, whereupon fumely resuscitated appetites release ceiling light's encircler. Kerplop! Divebombing serpent causes miscarriage.

Dentist antes laughing-gas chippie. Erotic entrepreneur hygienist nocturnally assignated patients desiring kinky dental care. Latexed fingertips, tightfit nurse's microskirt, sterile aromatics, pain-inducing instruments' latently sexualized perversions teased uptight jisms regular humping wouldn't unleash. Semi-actual dentifriciality buffed enamels, flossed molar pockets (S/Mers requested unnovocained drillwork, tartar pick-axing). Oral healthcare foreplay fulfilled hyperimaginers; unfulfilled, groin-oriented ejaculators craved hygienist's labial stimulation. Full-service dentistry enscrewed, sucked-off nitrous oxide, fellated wangs gone limp (drugged ennui taking evermore deeply breathed inspirations). Sucks overtook sniffs. Voracities sapped anesthetic's supply, hooker's vigor.

Inevitably, once-tidy arrangements slopped well-into unhideable obviousness. DEA's NO2 monitors routinely checking pharmaceutical depletions implicating notorious pleasure-enhancement substances saw poolroom DDS's joy-gas tanklevel discrepancies linking gas expenditure/nonexistent surgeries. Hypothetical root-canalwork tickled g-men issuing summons, 5-figure penalty. Busted root canalworker, unhypothetically, tackled g-spot assistant. Gastank's only co-operator (dismissing janitors, building's maintenancemen) admitted, repented; mouth-to-cock resuscitation solicited restitution.

"Didja?" cuestickers cajole.

Storyteller embraces Fifth Amendment's non-incriminatory protection.

"Zumtimes," slurs cyclopean sharpshooter, "vun sonofabitch sappers die schturdiest schpan."

Dentalman's sexploits recede so tipsy tempmeister may wail woes. Discharmingly slobvious, bilingual slangs beg comprehenders' indulgence.

"Diesem bullgesheisser mit diese resumpahpah spielt werkbildungsroman ingekommens," reinvents yours truly. Incredibly accepting faux resume's truculent, harmless joke, reteller retails far-fetched notion: he'd assigned liar subjecting reform's cruelest intention. Silly reasoning figured fantasizer'd adjust, confronted task; bank'd, coevally, reapply lackadaisical, disrespectful jobholder's grip. "Aber naturlich, immer kaput."

Short full-day's billing period, T-berg answered flaming phonecall. TransBank personnel's departmenthead gave thirdhand incident reports which've transmogrified simplistic insubordinational pranks. Intermediately, temps've acquired Mansonesque reputation fabricating sodomies, killings, ickily spewed smearings. Security system's bottom-level "mauve" alert unaccountably disengaged, upgrading fearful heliometer flashing cyans; lunching guards belatedly responded (guns drawn, cops summoned), proving urgency's need. Temps' insubordination punishment already undertaken, overdone, booted outdoors, still-terrified banksters wanted tastier revenge. Reason damned, they cancelled Temp-u-Serve's contractual understandings.

Rumors insidiously infiltrated downtown officecore. Human resource depots uncannily heeded signals insinuating Temp-u-Serve provided psychotic workplaced aides, whereby company-level blacklist thwarting Trollenberg's enterprise roughly paralleled irons branding renegade sheep.

"Ich bin gefiched," blubbers, head-in-hands.

Ostrich posture inviting lam, traceskipper tip-toes doorward.

"Fellows, hearye," Huber blows, horning-in poolhall's latest scandals intermixing asshole headbangers. Precis recounting local-sited Peloponnesian wars exalts dishwasher/hero.

One-arm pedestal pillories eluder, introducing chap contemplating ruined livelihood.

"Scheiss!" throatward leaps.

MUNIFICENT CASH-PAID SEVERANCE assuages guilts restauranteur might've experienced discharging newest potwasher. Patronizing's imperial ukase overruled commoner concerns. Kaiser-for-a-day insisted: dismissal (fusilier squad execution existing over-and-above favors even exceptionally granted bosom buddies).

Remembering midday, shootist's putative accomplice rethinks homeward toddling. Stake-out fear overcrowds lonely nocturne's reverie, justifies cafe-crawled itinerance. Foul caffeine, hammed eggs, greased caked sponges agglomerate accoutremental elements emblematically necessitating nightlong dawdle.

OPE TWE T F UR HO RS E N VER CLOS , gaply neons greasyspoon oasis. Cartoon dog embellishments flounce traditionalized kitsch omniscience, interchanging canines-for-humans partaking illustrations. Urinal murals expose hindleg-standing dogface pissers (waist-up/frontal). Barroom proper's mural showboats cardsharps, purebreds' differentiations reestablishing anthropomorphic traits: bulldogging bulldog, ace-pinching Doberman, happy-go-lucky mutt, hair-sequestered sheepherder, spitzfire Akita clench paws-to-vest, unmindfully noticing spaniel chanteuse's sad-eyed chienneson foregrounding painting-within-a-painting's oblong leggy Afghan bitch nude. A L R AD EAD T TH DOGHO SE, wags tail.

Nonsleepers munch toast, imbibe swillish blackluster beanjuice, wiggle egg-yolked humors. Offstaged lounge headliners (rockgroups, piano-bartenders, comedians, geeks, stripteasers) intersperse post-lateshow attending audiences, crimeplotting conmen, ramp-straying freewayfarers. Track-rat recognizances glimmer: stiff gesticulations finesse unwanted hellos.

By-and-large, doghousers negatively perceive smokecutting swoosh coinciding execuclassmates' postpool sprawl. Trollenbergless, slummers're celebrationally lighthearted, unaware—socio-impactwise—rerunning depression-era movies flaunting grotesquely witty rich shitheads' repartee. Bantamweight banter reiterates midlife weariness mercilessly overheard.

Highfive/lowsix-figure salarymakers poeticize impoverishment. Colloquy's gisting shadowboxes my shady upbrought downfall, quicksilvering left-for-right imaged deportments. Middle-rich musers' classdrop favorably considers Simplification Ideology sacrificialities: nongourmet coffeegrinds, grease-injected dietary esthetics, lumpy motorlodged lays (full-sized wetsuits, triplewrap condoms, oxygen-masked inhalations healthily repelling whore-bought sex-transmitted fluids). Electively skipping seedier courses, school-of-hard-knocks enrollees (nesteggs paying tuition) naturally'll miss true-life maladies others'd suffer.

Unmoneyed majority's gravity-defiant upperthrust hardscrabbling contrasts golden parachutist's soft fall.

Autobiographic self-associations irritatingly affix fanatasy-prone poolaholics. We reasonably educated white guys pathologically hatch what-if daydreams divorcing nice wives, quitting well-paid career niches, detouring straight, narrow, victory-aimed vectors, veering hellward (providing hell's only-borderline unendurable).

Coffee-refilled timekeeping's sunless creep caffeinly varnishes homebound wobblers. Sobriety's veneer superimposing, attorney feintly suckerpunches oral-surgeon's hippocritic check extraction. Exiting straightmen doubletake pool parlor dishwasher's apparent presence, ignore.

Many cities tenaciously recycle citizens, inhibit low-flying escapers flitting persistently job-to-job, home-to-bar. Re-encountering acquaintances, strangers, ex-workmates, playmates, otherwiseguys Moebius stripsearches inevitability's infinite-but-bound universe. Bloodsite's semiseen bystander seeks anonymity's nonconsecuity; re-meeting same folks makes coincidence treacherously nonmysterious.

Closure-rigged systematics, parenthetically, bind infinity imaginability paradigm (you-go-where-you-know). Backtrackward explorers blaze pre-burnt trails; forward-oriented explorers're rare.

Breakfasted dawnlit countenance self-inspects, compliments proud autodealer floor's emerald Cadillac showroom's tatterdemalion glassman. Unslept madness fuzzes unshavably. Apartment-returning's trap, motel-going's expensiveness, alley-roving's degeneration tri-pose problematical jobstacles. Fugitive brinks civic quicksand's engulfing scums.

"BERSERK GUNMAN SLAUGHTERS EX-BOSS," macro-
heads *Post-Intelligencer*. Subheadward dribbling shorthands ghoulish gists
repainting photo-illustrated hemoglobin overpouring desktops, pcs,
bodybags, watercooler watercolors' pointilistic gray pastels. Patched re-
membrances picture cubist testimonial alignments controverting similar-
sited reference frames. Pointilized fuzziness allowed, drawn-by-numbers
accuracy re-engraves avenging "angel's" preamblic ramble. Antebellum
bluster antiposes police-blottered factoids. Paltry deathtoll (three, coma-
tose outcome-depending) deflates newsworth. In-city nearness, weirdo
factor's perverted attractiveness, execucide's taboo appeal heliumate top-
story's zeppelin.

Kiosk's hawker confides, "Motherfuck 'adit commin'," commonheaded
wisdom brooking nonsense's nasty conventionality. Nicotined mouth-
parts, navyblue apron logoing yellow journal brandname, gnarly eyesock-
ets draw newsie caricature. Crackpot gospel jibberish informs foreor-
dained ministries.

Newsstand vendor's appearance resembling customer's, compatible
worldviews're superassumed amongrel furry stubbled chins having mis-
laid shaving kits. Whatever transactional superiority accrues he-who-
pays, kiosker arguably represents bumming around's future. Corre-
lational appearance-degrading habits fraternalize oldster, youngster.
Smelly fart-cutting, diningroom nose-picking, impolite vomiting provise
shared ideals? Really, substantial inferiority acclaims skin-deep presump-
tion flaying poor elder newstanding coot. Lowest commonest denomina-
tor two-bit suppositions delude presumer deeming scummy, unshaven,
stinky personal sloppiness won't count counteremploymentwise.

Anyways, manpower dynamos demotically sift-out slobs, selecting neat
facemen, prim maidens.

Moreover, newspaper version's descriptions set forth heavy-duty
grooming priorities. Coagulating A-section's minutiae, alleged sidekick's

qualities entail dirty modifiers. Uncleanliness's overdue bath exfoliates frontpage stench. Steamroom destination, thereforce, lodestones bathing's north arrow.

Sidewalker reads enroute, extrasensorially apprehending STOP/GO directives. Refrained "friend's whereabouts sought" pre-sentences detentional entrapment. Sketchy descriptors scribble ht/wt estimates circumscribing half-foot/fifty-pound leeways, facially chainsawing horrendous gashes. Sooty disfiguring daubs beyond-the-pale integuments (Turk/Kurd? Mextizo? Albinomulatto?) definitely blackening white-maled oatmeal complexion.

Mortally wounded receptionist's vouchering languishes undeposed; coroner navigators deadreckon flesh-dark holes. Meanwhile, "gunman's accomplice's" accessories provide extraneous markers: 2-wheel legpowered transportation (tidily hidden), ballplayer cap (mid-40s Rainiers, regretfully unusable), Larry stooge hairstyle (bushy bumpers), dumpster-quality loungewear (disheveled ascot's untying royalty), cigarbox banjo (inaccurately recalled), garlic halitosis (voiceprint's unalterability).

Composite clue's model error disavers identifications which'll eradicate soaply.

Hot-tubs' suburban relocation concedes urban public's bathing facilities, exclusively leaving Spago's Steambath. Singular-form depluralizes mini-cubicled semiprivacies, esslessly confers unruly gangshower voyeurisms stimulating energetic accostings fogly lubed? Sharded signlights, pissy basement doorway, skidroad locale (incorrectly neologized "skidrow," postetymologically) co-introduce attendant ogre's seen-it-all smirkscreen. Sparkless narrow-beamed eyeballer scans enterer's intentions. X-rayed judgment predetermines nonvagrancy, nonmalignancy, snappily distributes towel, dollars-per-hour.

Entering locker roomed catacombs, filthiness incarnate nears ungodly cleanliness. Brazen mannequins solicit statuerial rapes. Adonis posecards express-male urgencies zipcoding addresses' digital routing. Benched disrober unlegs scabrous pants, scurved skivvies; unfoots days-old socks. Modesty's tinder flammability incendiates flamethrown stares.

Terrycloth microskirt's surrendering whiteness befits neophyte ingressing air-thickened dews, whisped multivalent strata, heatwavy supersaturated ether. Quickened breathers formulate unsighted perimeter, disseminating lipsmacked ordures. Hissed infusions irregulate steam-layered visibilities, occasioning stark-naked coital mirages' hair follicle clarities. Dyed scalps bob. Mucosally sibilant vapor rewhitens outlooks underscoring steampiper sextets. Aged sphincters spew vascular lubricities, sneeze involitional compliances—conducted laval sputa shunning insulation's prophylactic vynaline. Bare-walled reverberative schlupps accompany frenetic maestrobations: wandly membered conductors extemporize beat-the-band fortissimos fuguing homogenous themes.

Wallflower daybeds unearth residue: semen-filled rubbers engorging mixed-breed colorations (pinkywink, whackblack, orangetang, redcap, bluenger), cockrings, buttplugs, amyl-nitrate packets, ballpoint inkblots (blurry phone numbers?) daubing matchbooks promoting gay nightclubs. Smoldering tobaccos corrupt steaminess's chlorinated freshener, waftily incensing private-leased rooms. Entrances cracked ajar beckon roguing wolves.

"Ahrooooh," hallowly howling prayer preys.

Ambient cloudnine heavenly/graveyard sinister fogs interchange clerics/werewolves. Thus-fabled fact exaggerates heterosexual bathgoer's paranoia. Steamed-out pores openly tremble. Orifices' heat-dilated hypervulnerability shakes earthbound ptolemaniac egotist subversing Alphacentaur constellations twinkling firmament.

Declouding, alienated novice re-immigrates lockerland. Putrid rags teaoff musky steepings pinching nose's unlaundered bundle. Rejected habilations disempower outgoing perseverance.

Lockless lockers avail perloincloths? Musical chairman circumambulates unoccupied spaces, hearing mulberry bush's sirensong, popping easily weaseled loots. Pantaloons, muscle-shirts, jumpsuits appose conservative regalia's three-piece tweeds, worsted wools. Airhole peeks, unhappily, disclose padlocked Brooks Brothers threads; unpadlocked tartwear garishly dares grabs. Morehover, sharp-eyed attendant's post oversees underwear.

Toiletry vendomatic dispenses fifty-cent plastic-handled shaver; towel-kilted laird jigs mirrorward. Hypernatural humidity sanctions barbershop hot toweling, handsoap sudses lather, blade shaves.

Flipflops herald arriving observer—hand-to-chin intraspection empathizing.

"Hereyago," relays razor baton-style.

"Pour moi?" accepts throwaway gesture's unintended hint.

Sharply nicked blood-brothers negotiate fragile truce. Parasexual vulgarizations imprecate confessional airing toward engaging bipartisan satisfying pacts. Dirtier outfitted, clean-shaved brother poses perversely nonintergenderal crossdressing idea, id est, shavers'd swap clothes, underpants-to-outerwear.

Scantily pausing, similar-sized dudes don each other's skivvied personality, armpitted empathy, colorscheme patchworked quilty pleasures. Sweaty redolence exudes pheromones laundered cloth lacks? Eager vigorousness animates otherwise-civilized habitual bathgoer. Antistriptease caricatures lusty quavering rapture. Piece-by-piece, sleaze enslimes goosepimpled ecstasy; snappy dresser's latent cologne subsumes slob's trenchant odors, rendering glueplant aroma cultivations free-associating carcass blooming peeyootunias.

Stolid, sterile-fibered businesswear's cotton Oxford shirt, drycleaned slacks, snakeleather belt, cowskin wingtips, off-white boxer shorts, off-black hose tingle alienating agitations. Crablice, allergic reactions, homophobic cooties interweave finer threaded fashions? Larceny's incipient accomplishment unnerves.

Surreptitious breakneck zippering outpaces clothespin-pal's languidly delectable one-leg-at-a-time pantlegging.

Tantalizingly moldy triple-E Thom McCan "winos" foot-fetishize wallower's degradational completeness; freshly shined D-width straitlace streetshoes imperil stealer's transdressional heist. Quadruplecrossed toeholds impact podlike feet. Walking's impractical; nonwalking's unacceptable.

Still-writhing ecstasizer doesn't notice pickpocket strolling awaywardly, wallet enclosed.

SHINSPLINTS ARCHING MUSCLEBOUND tendons rein-
vent perambulation. Painful footing devaluates sartorial spiff's $10-cigar
smile, crashes unmarketably sour grimaces. Foot travel's impediment
overriding stylishness, traveler maps-out retail reconnaissance. Western
saddlers, safari outfitters, tennispro golfspike basketbrawl cleateries,
handmedown consigners (rapaciously rediscovered stuff winging 800%
mark-up) open 10am nearabouts; outlying Goodwills, Costcos opened
earlier plat bus-covered grids. Florsheim, Nordstrom, Eddie Bauer estab-
lish downtown's conveniently surcharged high-rent location.

Financially dickering, limper unpockets just-exchanged walleted ca-
chet. What! Genuine cowhide's practically stripped! By-now worthless
AmEx, Mastercard, Visas taunt rigid, plastic-righteous taunts. Library
cards, driver's license, SSN card supplicate fake-IDs christening GR, TLR:
Terrance Langhorn Rafferty. Misfortunately, green negotiables equal
scant $3.

Using no-pay bus zone's innertown core, tenderfoot yo-yos uptown/
downthrown. Fareless parametric boundaries constrict 4–5 principle
storefront-lined corridors, facade posters advertising close-outs, cut-
rates, foreclosures, liquidations. Windowshopper's bustour concentra-
tion eschews shoeless advertisements. Pediterra islands delve crashing
mercantilistic seas. Displayful $250 power-leathers shod mannequin
studs conterpaning skimpily straplinged heel-teetering clotheswhores.
Ensuingly deglamorized windows depart department stores' influence.
Accentuated sexuality fetishizes footward (variously heeled boots, domi-
nantly), work-oriented speciality particularizes protections (steeled toes,
hammerhead shanks), costumed frivolity mesmerizes, nominating sug-
gested identities (clownshoes, finally?).

Unlaced rider, relaxing, notices late-morning commuters tacitly sug-
gest store clerking openings. Tight footwear disfavorably foretells future-
as-shoeseller, altogether wastes wearer's size-sensed acuity, crippling
aisle standing's endurance. Neatness's fundamentals, rebuttingly, exem-

plify clerkhood's ultraservile precepts lipservicing abnegational mercantile grovels. Self-tortured style-crazed bliss bumps function's accommodating importance, forwarding pliancy's tractability. Cross-bearer personality's cooperativeness attracts slavedrivers.

Bathhoused sleep deprivation mellowly anesthetizes corns. Expansive drowsiness transfixes lackluster scene: shimmering aura spangles teardrop dew's newfangled sights approximating freshness. Vilest, ugliest, despair-cased commercialities reintegrate, sembling colorfully facinatable working areas. Correlatively, belches retaste pancaked eggyolky bacon-greased caffeinistic acridity, heartburn's feasted recall transforming corrosive breakfast.

Anti-burglar storecase light deterrents revert, rheostats chronicling ten's daylit recognizance; gates clank asideways, open-signed greetings flip streetward, awnings unflap.

Metro bus's freeloaders, job-bound retailers, errand runners, truant juniors, daytripping seniors impactedly co-exist. Stoop-shouldered, slackjawed commiserators grumpily interalienate, practice close-quartered dissonance, inhale neighbors' germy breathing. Overcrowded misery exacerbates innercrowded footings.

Knifelike, turkeynecked jostler wedges truculently, without self-pardoning ingratiation. Umbraged codger yips. Emphatic yowls sirenize canine sympathies venerate age, villifying fowl-throated, blade-thin, well-dressed go-getter. Somewhat removed experiencers resent overloud insurrection. Shhhing scolders conformulate scowling majority, outnumbering howlers, unknowingly upholding aggressive fop's rudeness.

Hyperbolic brouhaha demarcates communal riding's free-zoned tolerance. Sympathetically suckered factions blush, withdrawing. Sociopolemical detented restrainers disallow fisticuff resolutions. Spaceless arm clearances thwart haymakers. Uppercut knock-out punches outlawed, squabblers bicker everso noisily; reshod wobbler ripcords brakemaker, bails.

Stop's outgush flushes zoftig longstockings, rumpled dumplings, stubbling rabble, scrabbling scribblers, newspapered nibblers. Square-tiled minimall vistas artificially upfunnel wastepaper tornadoes forming odd-angled wind-blasted dervishes whereover unflowing fountains decorate placidly sculpted gust, exaggerate plazaly expressed void. Spiring store-bought microtowers evince skyscrapers' castle-raped bastard spawn. Malformed architectures package swankish boutiques, especially franchise-backed tenants. Arby's Wendily Burger-Kinged eateries banished Manny's Redmill, Bruno's Mexican-Italian Restaurant, Turf. Temporarily, transavenue's Waldenbooks spared Q'raz, Mr.T's Hi-Tone (tarty haberdashers "respectable" clothiers dis). Recordmart's recordless shelves stocking CDs, Pipedream's cigarette-packed cigarstore, Sammy J's Booklet Sachets complete mallover renovation.

Glass-paneled, steel-girdered turrets guard conventionality's consumerarchy. Garish hypernormal happyface attitudes suburbly repopulate madeover promenades. Chainstore presences control quality.

Controlling extends: circle-drawn, line-slashed NO-sign ousts plazaland's fittingest activity, skateboarding. Newly masoned interlinked scallopian bricks enthrob clicketyclat wetdream railroad strums, ball-bearing ball-tingling emission temptations. Fresh curbcut ramps vamp; sexually frustrated rolling woodmen break rule, petitioning confiscations.

Beat-walker constables, incidentally, spot goldmine prestidigitations stowing fey Moroccan hash. Underhanded exchange's blatancy bestirs slothfooted crackdown. Discretion's nonchalance respects shoppers' sensibilities; street-level legislations underwrite decorums suburbanites (suburb-minded urbanizers) crave. Beep-beepers roadrun, confidently unpursued. Posh spending's conduciveness diswarrants bludgeoning, bloodying, gaudy arresting drug-dealt furtive hand-offs that've occurred more-or-less unnoticed.

Aforementioned transavenue storefronts exhibit pimpwear, strumpetries, rapper discs, discounted stinkweed cartons, Waller-to-Waller bestsmellers. Intrusively quoined phallic 7-foot rocket signage upthrusts Army-Navy Commissary, MSSgt. Stanley Sinkiewitz, propt.

Discontinued unstylishness dangles bargain footwear's gumsoled hiking muckstompers, off-color gymnast uppers inexplicably mismatching wrestling matsoles, polkadot golfshoes mostly odd-sized sixes/twelves. Whatever's remaining, surplus-stocked generous splendors downtown're appreciated.

Limper's bell-announced entrance foils fleeing shoplifter truants. Ratfaced scurriers spill clattered booty (penknife deerskinners, compass-inlaid daggerhead pitons, neatly compactable screwdriver coctailbars). Dominoed aback, scuttling rascals feign disablements, gulling hamhanded apprehender's clumsy clutches.

"Git'em," tackles dustbunny cottontailbacks.

Wiry eluders run clear.

Anticrime alliance joins patron sent sprawling, businessman kept standing. Woe stories debriefing shopman's travails waylay boot buy guy's sorely indispensable replacement shoes. Marauding gypsy conartists, slicktalking shortchangers, upsliding rents, everspreading taxations polarize annoyances blackmarket-to-redtape. Distracted complainer tardily realizes ally's fallen condition.

"Fer petesake, champ. Y'ain't harmed?"

"Naaah."

Storekeeping's liability peaks listed terrors; injured gimp shoplift collider's apparently crash-caused hobbling elicits litigaphobic gratitude's distinct advantage, leveragewise, shoehorning employability. Complimentary rubberized, web-width/waterproof Duckfooters (was-$80/is-$19.95/yours-gratis!) surplace bonecruncher dresspumps. Instantaneous perspirant puddles enlayer reddishly chafed insteps, bunions. Dressy attire's mallardly slick neoprening displays surplus's deficit: conceptually extreme outlandish styles outlast ravenously marked-down prices. Placards converse salable namebrand blems; stockroom retains wacky quack-wear.

Slipshod booby prize slippers pry job-opened apertures. Recovered benefactee flatout asks.

Benefactor assents, enlisting petty theft foiler (imparting pettier mini-wage).

Simpleton orientation indoctrinates procedures. Operating cash register (tax-evasive skimming unmentioned), S.S. puritanically pleads accounting's methodism requires keeping tapeless totals. "Free-sovereign" declarations secede; cutting nationalistic fiduciary IRS-tied "indentured servitudes" inform retired NCO's commentary co-explicating unusual bookkept practices. Allegedly "robbery-preventive" strongbox receives unrecorded receipts.

Duty commences. Two smallbacked perches enroost catbird sitters focally centered withall convex corner-posed looking glasses refracted floor-to-ceiling-to-counter.

Retrovated infantry's fieldpack crank radio buzzes rightwing propaganda. Unpatentable falsehoods incite insights: survivalist manifestos, pro-life crybabying, fluoridation re-condemnations, Revelations-affirming apocalyptic apocrypha improvising post-Soviet nuke-happy madmen triggering unbonded IanFlemmations. Gunshops, goldsellers, religiomaniacal rallyers, pyramid pseudosavings bankless moneymakers sponsor shitheaded rants.

Stanley's conceivable tendentiousness tars nutty programming's feathereheaded fun. Surplusser adds, militia-toned patter pushes ordnance, paramilitary gear; mongering's commercial inducement excuses hate-mongering's unimpeachable presidency.

Peacefelt togetherness, anesthetically cynical, accretes layer-by-layer. Noncommittal skepticisms blunt opinionating, socially paving communication's dullest access roads. Loony tunered neo-Nazi screeds riotously bi-

43

furcate: hilarity, sincerity. Irony's built-in disavowal preserves dignified aloofness allowing each's private prejudices.

Duckfooted subordinate re-experiences clerking's peeves. Idleness bores nondaydreamers. Radioacrid natterings, accompanyment's mandatory socializations scrape nether-level attentiveness. Overhanged weaponry (replicas, sarge sez), overharangued belligerent talkshow degenerates, sergeant's advance-planned taxpayer robbery counterattacks conspire counterclerkwise.

Fatalistically, camo-clad paramilitarist yields sincere notions exalting violence's recent manifestation.

"Retributive action's operationally instigated, provoked, mandated, supplying causus belli," ex-soldier delivers. Layoffs constituted incursive skirmishing; uncompensated maiming instituted hostilities declaring all-out war. Firefights, howsoever egregious, weren't surprising, given untakeable circumstances.

Soldier-of-fortunately, Sinkwits segues, presuming I'll've thoroughly known what's reported. Steelmilled grist details're ignored. Instead, action-taking fantasies overthrow stable reality. Cardboard-cutout villains sporting jerseys lettered BATF, FBI, etc., attract automatic target practice's witlessly blank rounds. Conversational poverty's blood-starved cravings increasingly marginalize surplus job's unquestioned neediness.

Armory show-quality inventory's dummy gunnery Zippos, defused grenades, megacaliber shell ashtrays, firingpinless Tommyguns, stens, Mausers, Manlichers, M-series riflery artistically state war's thematic continuity. Loosely war-related items (bivouac equipment, mainly) assault senses: snakebite suctioncups, sewer purifier tablets, icefishing tackle, bedrolls, tarpaulins, trampolines, roundball slammajammas (8-foot hoops), ABA-style (patriotically colored) basketballs, Uecker-endorsed softball bats, tetherball maypoles, odd-ended 2-wheeler componetry (28″ spokes, non-metric spindles, freewheel cogpullers, odometers), X-C ski-skates, C-rations, porta-shovels, portosans, female-adaptable urinary appendages, tent-size trousers, trouser-pack tents, amber insect tomb keyrings, quartz ID-kits, novelty micecubes, Groucho-style x-ray specs, vacupack spam-carved maggot farms, Armour Star Cookbooks Vols. XIII–XIX, claymore mindreading palmleaf teacups, Sherman tankards, saltpeter, WWII-era pin-ups . . .

   . . . CO2 CARTRIDGES, DOGFIGHTER modelsets, waterproofing aerosols, elephant glues, squid-flavored inkstain gums, ping pong netclamps (sans nets, pertinent necessary accouterments); well, sufficiently summing inventory'd exceed counting's novel interest. Processing workdays' necessity, list-making digests multi-houred glut raising Sorrentino's "postmodern convention" wisecrack (Imag.Qual.Actu. Thin.). Subsequent recounts reveal treasures undiscovered yesterday.

   Carousel-held postcards depict Northwest landmarks orienting tourbus proclivities, provisioning shoddy geegaws. Mts. Rainier, Baker, pre-erupted St.Helens, cookiecut Olympic peninsula rainmakers surround skylines nocturnal, wintry, gloaming (preday/postsun), gleaming (noonbrite/starlite), iconically Space Needled. Tastefully photographed jackalopes, whale-sized steelhead trouts capsizing brash canoes, gooeyduck genitalia begging licks, conquered native cultures enacting quaint rites round-out carousel.

   Loitering busloads grabbing cheapest possible merchandise rile Stan. Disregarding traveling's lightness requirement, shopman reviles "skinflint thieves." Unfairly resented patronizers trigger badly aimed salvos. Indiscriminate (hyperdiscriminate?) blasts ultimatumly flay Sinkiewitz's creed, cheer intolerance's freedom.

   "Dere wuz disguy . . ."

   Words thicken, hate drips. Expected boogeymen, whomever, survive unpummeled. Liberals, pantywaists, red-tapers, lightfingers, slicktalkers, browsers hereabout elude condemnation. Contrapuntally, reprisal's sung employee-from-hell theme (c.f. dilettante poolshooters, Hollywooden scripts).

   Jimmy "Hawkeyes" McGonigle oversaw wartoys' playpen yesterautumn. Initially, JMcG embodied city-savvy clerk perfection, deverminting rats/petting mice. Vigilance par excellance enabled SS's requisitioning forays, encouraged furlough scheduling. Leant reliable assistance, trade boomed (relatively correlating scum-sucked bottom lines). Hawkeyes'd surpassed surplussing's basal criteria, squinting through 6-point font opticalcourses cataloguing wholesaler's bargains, slaving overtime, missing lunch, reporting early.

Hyperefficiency, could've indicated embezzlement; actually, shrinkage attained all-time lows. Profits increased.

Misgivings shelved, S. went camping, (Army's mustered factory seconds quartermastery equipped). 72-hour pass's R&R reconnoitered rainforest's miraculously rainless panoply. Hotspring waters, fir-filtered breezes boosted survivalistic self-deceptions envisioning woodsmanesque hallucinations: society-free existability! automobileless auto-reliance! old-growth tree harvest's perpetuated bounty!

Thoreauly addled camper returned. Refreshed perspective salvaged squalor's pulchritude. Eyesores previously overlooked—utility-poled reticulations stringing telecomwires—represented lurid decay's flourishing reasons why anyone'd reject civilization. Supreme ugliness thereby rationalized purging's good, foregoing beauty's uglier purifications. Anticivilizationist's logically genocidal tendencies sterilize city's slimes.

Shopfronted belt-level yellowtape welcomed Sinky home; POLICE-LINEDONOTCROSS fouled pure musing, barred lawful shopkeeping. Retoned macadam's enigmatic splotch foreshadowed entrance's door-tacked invitation sinisterly advising SPD precinct housecall posthaste.

Scofflaw skateboarders clattering plazawide glissades shouted freeform commentaries scorning "Gung-ho Gunga Din."

Wheelers narrated Hawkeyed pessimist's kill-fated swoop. Bursting outdoor, redhanded thief juggled unsacked swag, trigger-taloned Hawk chasing, gape-jawed plaza folk witnessing. Hollering standardized testpattern Halts, Stop-Thiefs, Freezes, TV-trained marksman pointed bodyward, squeezed five quick shots clustered in-and-about suspect's clavical.

Watery justifiers rinsed blood-thick indictabilities. Manslaughterer surrendered. Cadet demeanor curried approbation; shooting's cold-bloodedness prevailed, sentencing asylum's evaluative open-ended committal.

Jittery warstoryteller foreshortens upshots: fundamental distrust infects tempermental health, contaminating every underling's repute. Unavertably, anyman becomes psychoclerk, symbolically: herefore unemployable.

4-days' wages, regrets muster out substituted duckfooter.

UNDER-THE-TABLE STIPEND, redone billfold's steam-cleaned name, old-news killing's detente lure ex-George (now-Terrance) from culvert hiding. Unwittingly requisitioned (stolen) GI sleeping bagged impromptu bivouac's contrived field test exonerated inventory exploitation, endorsing equipment's worthiness. Unavoidably, Terrance's sub-viaduct basecamp's suffered plundering. Useful things're taken, including Schwinn, makeshift hut.

Rubber-clad feet've festered ornery fungi. Apartment-housed footworn comforts, personalized mementos tempt risky retrieval's brass-balled daytime panty raid.

Terry Rafferty's keys'll ineffectively pick G.R.'s locks—forgetting T.R.'s untappable accounts'd nicely settle George's debts—placing loiterer herewith entryway's doorswung range. Mid-scaled edifice's renters total high-thirties, discounting managerial family's half-dozen TV-glued tubeheads. Sitcoms, quiz prizewinners, soap-op arts hypnotize watchmen, facilitating lurker's sneaky game.

UPS vans, pizza racecars, postal carriers, repair technician missionaries swarm hillsides; neighboring flats admit service-called prostitute sing-songing "Stripogram!" audition unto intercom microphone. Tenantlife exits everybody else's goddamn roach motel.

Unbelievably, somebody's unlocking Tubehead Arms: apartment-stuck crone #1A2. Old-age nearsightedness prompting mistrust well-founded, she'll surely remark slinker's infiltration. TV-doctored managers'll procrastinate follow-up check-ups, diagnosing benign eventualities.

"H'lo," cordially bypasses suspicious glare.

"G'dafternoon, young man," cruelly recognizes deadbeat tenant.

Sweat-footed squeaks squish, wetly encased tarsal meats project horror flick sound f/x tracing creature's plod. Threadbare carpet ripples soundwaves rebounding tanklike walls. Utmost stealth resonately obliterated, slinky tip-toer quickens stepping; squooshed repetitions mimic copulated

49

frenzy. Hallway faretheewell full-body kisses? Indecency's salacious attractions coax door-cracked peek, keyhole viewmaster patience: anybody looks.

Adjacent studio's peekers observe neighborly apparition studying sheriff-signed eviction edict, padlock doubly stopping keyless ingress. Lightly shamed silent eyers Jerome Chestlink, Sylvie Chantrell self-introduce, beckoning hallway's loud-footed flopper. Eat-in take-out dining's suggestion vicariously visiting Siam, Cuba, Mongolia coordinates feast. Jer restaurant-hops, Syl escorts studio-wide sitdown tour.

Sheets drape carefully chose thingamajigs comprising recently diplomaed college graduate fiances' trousseau. Funding future's massive purchases conditions present-day thrift. Cultured TV-fed budget diet (disallowing theatrical stagings, films, concerts) starves minds; someday's series-ticketed shows'll purportedly rescind former cultural negligence, staging veritable renaissance. Leanwhile, ghostly draped China hutch, armoire, CD-less CD-player stereo, kingsize bedposts, uncouchable tailback endtables, unmatchable heirloom Flemmish provincial loveseats anticipate storage's termination. Sylvie's tour-guided depictions suffice, fashioning show-and-tell completely verbal, mercifully (guest's noninterest assumed?) curt.

Tediously protracted vaguely nasal aristocratic tones oddly comfort listener picturing hostess's endless legs, garter-belted; naked, pussy-tufted, bent-over fanny. Soulful violet irises hardeningly transformulate gem-cold amythests prefiguring calculable fortunes. Guesthood's ungratefully opportunistic hostess humpin' hard cock abates, becoming presentable.

Materialism's May-Day parading gently lapses. Betrothed accumulators self-deprecate, jokes commenting, "Jer-ryyy, dahling, suppose Buddha calls. Gurus'll teach refusing materialistical accumulations."

"It'll particularly've tantamounted 'n excellently misspent unspent youth."

50

Couple-coded cuteness sugarcoats speech, dusting powdered wit's jelly-injected soul. Hiding's privileged evasions endure preppies' raillery, world-clash dinners, fakerobrews (faux-micro, major brewer product-lines: Whorewester, Pissed Alleycat). Moreovertop, discussion stops, television resumes.

Update bulletin reopens investigative parajournalism exploiting now-ancient forgeblaster bullet-riddling. Whodoneit's whoseenit mystery haltingly revives coma-ending expiration. Thumbnail-sketched "slaughterer's apprentice" munches Mongolian meatballs undetected, facing screened reproduction.

Fittingly, identity's topic arises. Sketched likenesses inhabit city-bound universalities. Jerry, Sylvie've reckoned they'd met me-like phantoms roundabout marketplaces, crosswalks, busstops; this's hall neighborhood's unprecedented socialization. Months've transpired—coexisting proximately, unintroduced. Eviction's imminence stimulates questions, good-byes. Dicey, wildside walker savoir faire enthralls matrimaniacal shut-ins?

Acquisitively inclined couple, underhandedly, knows dinnerguest's culprithood, plans entrapment's bountiful reward? Questionable motivations seem unlikely, assessing curiosity's glamorousness.

Evermoreso curiously, hosted interrogations cease/self-told sagas advance full-bore. Chestlink's prepschool farrago bi-dimensionally mixed soccer stardom, academics (ho-hum); fatefully (thankfully), straightness's arrowheaded sobriety dove inunder addiction's scourge vat. Coked-out kickers' undefeated season's Waterloo crashed championship's finale, losing 23-0, revealing druggies' problems. Afterwards, mass-counseling restored college-bound tooter booters, reinstating "high" standings.

Chantrell's similarly uplifted upbringing kicked viler habit: Catholic school's dildo-wielding nun. Tallest prettiest thirteen-year-old gabbily annoyed Sister Fuckhead (demurely nicknamed sadist's monicker). Sassslinging blonde often incurred extra-thick ruler's remonstrations. Menstruation anxiety's exceptional peaking composited one-time self-defense, later pled "periodical insanity," thereas clobbered student smacked physical punisher, spoiling rod: spare chair childishly flung upside Fuckhead's noggin. Evertheless, corrupted holiness's righteousness damnnear railroaded victimized schoolgirl along reformatory tracks.

Patterned outgrowths wearily replicate teenage triumphs, like-minded amoralizations, overweening foot-landed falls. Self-confident boors discourage negative comment, contrary anecdotes. Quasi-religious cupidity impels soonlyweds' continued exemplifications. Soporific sermons minister off-nodded daze nightly, I'd guess, slumberneath turned-on mute TV.

DRIVE-TIME DJS' CRASS DUET awakens floor sleeper. Obnoxious immediacy lengthens, till untended alarm-clocked jabbering leaks another drive-time's double wailed song. Fuckly grunted climax outshouts birdbrained crowing announcing Whitney Houston's postcoital drivel.

Snapper youngsters' sexual calisthenics, deejaybirds, mainstreamed unctuousness, current shower-sung falsettos aping radio-played muzak shatter calm surface's dignity. Hideous disco-era nostalgia emanates soapy shower-steamed colognes scenting singalongs. Overwhelmed, freeloader pens thank-you, dashes.

Morning's third-floor corridor'll take dominant work-bound traffic 7–9:00, postponing reclamation plot's secondary phase. Fire-escaped nook clandestinely abets evicted fellow. Self-absorbed uncoupled neighbor sidewalkers pass undernoticed, bent heads avoiding misted skies.

Sequentially, commuting outgoers, dawdling stay-at-homes induct television's deadened quietude. Stairwells' magnificent amplifications mangle mingled audios floor-to-floor, distracting nitpickers who'll incorrigibly summon lawmen perturbing minuscule overblown infractions.

Hall's trespasser re-rates transgressions heretofore accluded, comparing trespassing's pettiness, accomplicehood's unproved allegation, breaking in's incontrovertible misdemeanor. Furthermooring barger's inbound slam, remembered possessions tepidly instigate recovery. Vouchsafed Yale's Moslerlike bolt, old-style door's oaken bulk, unbelted karate parodist previewably ransacks abandonable treasure.

Reno matches honoring casinos, Exactagauge, Temptation's greatest, Roy Orbison's gems, Wm.Morrow's compleat horseplayer stud bibliography (Ainsley, Quirin, Quinn), elsewhere-published Davidowitz, Beyer, Pittsburgh Phil, Dowst, Maul, Sarton, Brouhammer, Erickson, rundown handheld Contrascan-programmed computer, ft/sec conversions untracking variants coast-to-coast, b/w videoscreen, AM/FM tuner, turntable, de-stereoed one-channel amp, cablespool dinette, Oporto crate chairs, futon davenport, torn linens, unhung closeted wire clangers' wardrobe desolation, underpants-packed duffelbags, effete menswear remnants (hankies, ascots, suspenders), DRF's backtracking twelve consecutive west Washington racemeets, jokerless deck, dice, jax, unrecycled cans, unattended postered dramas/exhibitions unviewed, Filth Film Festival placard spoofing SIFF's promo, martini glassware, untapped Vermouth, 6–7 gin empties, 5–6 Antonio Cleopatra dessicated petrified grenadiers, dust-encrusted grenadine syrup, castiron skillet, platters commemorating Georgia, Florida, Missouri, Arizona, ashtray Utahs, Nevadas, Kentucky Derby julep tumblers, Bend Bucks visor, Fantagraphics comic anthologies, ReSearch studies, Hardball zines, Mazerowski preseason guidebooks ('86–'92, inclusive), Miskowski midseason playscripts (Duende-Camille Claudel elusive) Tacoma Tigers polyurethane stein, Everett Giants decal, Bellingham M's prayerbeads, Spokane Indians warbonnet, Portland's Beaver dentaldam, Wenatchee Chiefs daguerreotype, unpawnable literature, defunct addressbook, disconnected phoneline, unpatched innertubes, soapcake shampoo, toothbrush, towels, seventeen pizzaless carton coffins, childhood's photograph mausoleum, and hole-soled, lopsided, raunchily stenched wearable clodhoppers.

Reasoned objections equivocate; anarchy kungs fu.

Splintered smithereens unjamb doorway's plywooded hasp. Workmanlike single-blown crunch reaffirms hindsight's conjectured cough? Rubbernecking #3A2 pensioner instantaneously deserts high-volume boob box's Dialing-for-Dollars preliminary matinee (*Beloved Infidel? Abbott & Costello Meet Frankenstein? Spartacus?*), ascertains break-in, dials-for-collar.

Sirens'll converge—oh-ohhh—nothing's left!

Delaminating hardwoods mirror skylit vacuity. Wall-to-wall emptiness stresses emptied nest's eggless neutered worth. Evictee's possessions've flown coop.

Self-inflicted burglar defenestrates (undercuts 3A2's view), downslides firestaircase's banister. Dumpster-cushioned landing's cat litter softens insulted injuries. Mashed turds, piss-soaked sawdust dapple once-dapper swiped clothing's elegance.

Alongside, well-ravaged cardboarded hoard remainders ex-tenant's dispossessed estate: books're untaken. Strewn itemizations, anywherever, yield discombobulated order, homemaking alley's renovative bedroom.

Subverting garbage's unmade bed, coveted shoes're resting.

ADDRESS'S DIVESTITURE SHIRKS INVOICES, frustrates

pursuers, prolongs anotherwiseguy criminality precursively unwritten: unpaid IRS-called "windfall tax" dunning exactas, trifectas, etcet'ras. 1040-form filing lacunae red-flagged T-men; computerized compositions pretentiously garnished unfounded earnings. Equally pretentious bravado circularly filed matrix-lettered missives.

Impecunious estates couldn't've tempted federal audit, insomuchas succeeding paymasters' W-4s inevitably'll entrap deadbeats. Failing's erosiveness, morever, snares scofflaws, vagrants, petty-theft operators manipulating small-time con-games.

Downhill wisdom's momentum propels litterbox fugitive's catalogical jobscan highlighting gigs donating room/board (boardroom positionings presumably filled). Lake-rimmed drydocks glitter luridly. Hulls scraped, paints reapplied stripe bright reds, abyssian ultramarines, hanging upstrung trawlers, skows, gillnetters: vehicles bearing sealife's "carefree" romance. Fishing's cash-based economy suits vagabond jumpiness; residing on-ship fits livelihood's tightest requirements.

Lakefront properties cluster condominiums, seafood bistros, chandler-themed shoppees re-issuing antique replica harborware (rusted winches predominate); rezoned upscaling nudges chandlers carrying workable shipboard fixtures northward (off-premises waterfront's lucrative shores). Insouciant arsons char piers, razing unsightly, unprofitable warehouses bulkheading just-dredged yacht basins. Fisherman's Wharf™ conscientiously reinvented fishermen's wharves, franchising comptrollers succeeded craftsmen's line-caught trollers.

Past Fort Lox Smokers, colacorp-owned "Francaise Bakerie," naughtily nautical clothing boutique (dummies modeling gob garb marked-up 200%, relating Navy's surplus-tagged price), pleasureboat marinas, industrial docks refit riggings, engines. Autumnal chills Octobrify September's penultimate week; silvery sun's squinted brilliance coldly invigorates initiatives. Winter weather futilities vindicating inaction encroach, dooming vain hope.

Tiny boats're readied, headed northwesterly, overcoming Aleutian trench swells, blackest gales, subzero windblown Farenheits. Hazardously fractured fleets risking survival gather crab, trading succulently meated crustaceans' competitively abased worths, packing Pacific coast's media events death quotas' requisite sinkings, drownings, disappearances. Crabbing's death-dealing lifestyle, reconsiderably, disqualifies untaught aspirant.

Reluctant fisherman superimposes anti-nostalgic pelagic memories regurgitating ocean-going sprees. Jersey offshore partyboats pitched/yawed tranquilly, urging bilious egg-yolk sticky dry heaves—squid aromas inspirationally overstepping diesel's salt-tinged emetic. Boyish manhood customs swallowed puke, stonewalling discomforts wiser fools forswore.

Landlubber quayside institutions doubtfully lend dayjobbers housing; nightshifters (guardsmen, custodians, graveyard's machinists) alike nap off-duty, off-site. Drastically curtailed opportunities're arranging impossibility's gauntlet. Seasickness counterbalances seaboard cruises' delectations? Puget Sound's moderately stilled expanse supports inland waterwayfaring's seafaring fantasy. Riverboat gamboling piracy trumping lowlit salmon poaching (penny-ante heists) bluffs minimally gainful vandalizations (cf. 1890 Hudson/East River-runners).

Pantywaist badass wannabe's excessively unfeasible demiworld extrudes tangible signs outstretching sailboard rental stands, Alaska canning basecamps: nineteenth century-era masts rig skylined ropes, bundled sails.

Eighteenth/seventeenth centuries' influences affect schooner's structure; overall, grunged-out chic fashionably disguises mushy design, expressing disuse's perpetually renovated (unfinished) palimpsestic aesthetic. Amalgamation's tack-on forecastle, mizzen, crowsnest, bosomy

57

bowsprit grinning sabertooth tigress, wheelhoused electronics, deck-housed V-8-powered twin-screw shafts, peeling ever-darker shellac un-shell tri-master's sloppy complexity. Loopy goldleaf script festoons mud-colored stern: Wanderlust.

Wanderlust's crew furthers incongruity's splaying, unashamedly echo-ing Anycrew, USA's wartime propagandized melting-plot filmcast. Bitterly sniffling redheaded frecklefaced stork kid personifies temerity, full-arm poorly drafted tattoos diagramming cunniligual marsupials? unbearable agonies? butterflies? Yellow-eyed, fat-lipped loquacious non-specific (Samoa? Guam?) islander joker's corpulent mirth contradicts teenage-old pessimism. Taciturn Saharan mulatto (delicately lineated face parts, black/olive integument) sands barehanded, non-strop. Silvermaned an-glican lion roaringly supervises. Stubby "panethnic" Brooklynite (Irish-Italian/Bahian-Pole) completes diversity's hoary quorum.

Defensive arrogance puffs accosted lion's civility; humblest salutations' proffered assistances annoy, intrigue, beguile foreman's weirdly con-flicted intents. Crewmen's heavy sweat, stacked unlabeled provisions, anxious roundward glancing collaborate, besetting sailboat's castoff deadline. Something's disturbingly familiar: arrested fascinations iden-tify newcomer's physiognomy.

Sharklike circling tightens.

"Blimey, wouldja looka thar?"

"Spittin' imagers couldna come cleaner."

"Avast!" roars.

Chin-held nodding's confirmation smiles, claps backslapped manly re-assurance's stabbing doubts. Duely impressed, recruit boards vagabon-daged voyager, encounters introductions.

Captain Ebeneezer Malone presents freckly tattooed redtop Whitey Sherrard, fishpuss Lucius Zamboango, Afro-Arabian Nair, Brooklyn's im-itable Gilbert Dordio. Wolfishly slobbering courtliness attends debutante cabin denizen's installment. Assigning choice porthole hammock, thermal blankets, sou'wester slickers, anti-hypothermia floatation suit prepare "Terry's" place, hereupon urgent portside sanding resumptions indicate anti-procrastination's uppermost goal.

Emorycloth, kneepads, gauze masking, protective eyewear appoint newliest sailor lowliest shitwork: administering head ultra-thorough scouring. Urine vermilion mariner plywood pinkly disinfected, alcoholic diarrhea, multitextual barfs orchestrate symphonically melodic aromatic strains. Abovedeck tarring operations filter porthole's freshening. Hypnotic woozy natural fumes spellbind toilet toiler, attenuate unendurability's reach.

Tarp-wrapped cargo likening ex-neighbor fiancees' phantasmic furniture, unexplained purpose riles spooky apprehensions. Piratical contingencies eerily outgrow musings; livable dreamlike contrivances evidently hold generative powers.

Elbow-greased goo remover uncontrollably meditates skullduggery, rechecks portholed worldview.

Lakescape grayish whitecap coruscations glint tinny overcast platinum tungstens. Tugboats tow field-sized oildrum dumps, seaplanes overfly day-sailers, alight aloud, sailboarding daredevils interglide hardline vectored commercializing coursers. Debatably fortuitous accident-avoidance sustains forward motion transecting nonmolten, unfrozen chilly silver liquid's rink. Rust-encrusted expired gasworks' lovely museum-quality wasteland menaces lakeshore businesslife, polluting groundwater waterfront clambars' tonier eatery establishments tap.

Medium-height condo/office complexes base shedded anchorage prickling masted shortwave antennae, stern-mounted flagpoles flapping cocktail pennons.

Yachtsom's lordly pierage, piledriver rafts, post-arson predevelopment worksites, glassy multi-story reflectors, rusty monocultural pollutors array ostentatious shabbiness, elegant elan, brute riches.

Scenic panner notes siren honker harborcop prettily frothing wake-lined picturesque bisection. Mothergoose wrathful indignance wings unswung bow's headway; abovedecks, dread rumbles. Mistakably, magazine ammoclips interject weapons! Kick-started 4-cycle burbles thunderous anticipations muffling shout's command, particularly while scenery shifts.

Disembarkation? Moorings, fueldocks, chandleries grow smaller; waterway expansion enlarges malignant possibility untrained diagnosis imputes, encountering locked-from-outside WC latch.

DAYS'VE PASSED. Icy salt fluid intermediating gaseous vaporous states solidly crusts glassed port-lids; mere polishing smears, unstoppering hole induces shivers. Shutting port-lid re-intensifies brig confinement's shithouse putridity.

Thrice quotidian porridge allotments gruelly force-feed captive puker frumenty, cinnamon-flavored apricots' dried-up batch, which's circumstantially repulsive. Gradually roughening whitecapped choppiness's swollen swell overwhelming, pre-oceanic sea sickened prisoner. Trepidation's queasy headtrip watched receeding coastlines' unreturnable distances. Existence's nauseatingly reductive bunk fetally positioned nonsleeper osmotically drank leaky plumbing. Present-timed backwards slippage bodes ill; tenseness, strangely, unwinds.

Vacating Seattle's manmade channels, armycorp-engineered shiplocks, headlocked preemie seaman estimated shakedown cruise's practical joke'd expire miles foreshadowing Pt.No-Point. Turdseye viewer bizarrely enjoyed touring locales usually unobserved: suicide bridge's underbelly, rail trestle's haiku graffiti, cataclysmically eventual mudslides underpinning viewpoint mansions, Discovery Park's landsend, sewage treatment facility. Portsider's westward orientation's eastwardly scudding dusk squall adumbrated squalid Bremerton, darkening Bainbridge, overpassed Pt.No-Point's perceptibly unlimited juncture, tarnishing Wanderluster's since-hoisted sailcloth. Sopped lufted flopping aloft, gusted rains drowned hold-held thumping, screamed "lemme-outta-heres." Worstcase frankly informed dogwatch's neurotic logic's abundance: nonrunning pistons' conserving unburned fuel windicated sail-powered preference's long haul capacity.

"Oakland? Okinawa?" queried shanghaied dyspeptic, receiving stonefaced jailer's lukewarm oats.

Impassive noncommital blankness characterized whoever'd delivered nutrition's bowl. Executioners sharpening guillotines, oiling gallowed platforms springlatch trapdoors, preparing electrications maybe share similar determinations. Incommunicado shiphands withheld planned mischief. Perforce obstinacy, inefficiently, prickled imprisoned fellow's predicament. Escaping's unlikeliest feasibilities, whatevertheless, crept inward.

Seasickened weakling's options monotonized: overpower feisty thug undoing barricade, evade cronies, dive overboard, swim ashore. Ashore's reachability varied, headlands squeezing occasional straits threading thickly knotted currents. Non-fatal hypothermia slimly excepted non-survivable miscellanea (principally, gunfire, watergunned deepsix whirl-pools). Holding brig's occupant alive imparted hopeful trapped animal foolhardy encouragement. Somatic debilitation undermined matter-of-course flighty stratagems.

Repictured geography acknowledged Whidbey Island's landfallaway, Juan Fuca's Straitaway. Southern Vancouver Island/Northern Washington's widely outlined shoot-the-chute mitigated oceanic turbulence; in-bounding freighter, oiltanker churned gargantuan wakes. Twilit shore-lines twinkled farewells paradoxically welcoming dawn's liberation.

Re-polishing salt-smeared glass, shivering stinking unfed jailbird idly ponders morning feed's elision. Routine's disruption heinously forebodes cyclonic proportioned changes. Overnight's freakly unexpected gusting blew hands off-deck? Continual motorless propulsion's sophisticated tacking 'round Cape Flattery disproves ghostship phantom piloting. Multi-whichway adjustments coping sub-smallcraft warning windspeeds creak timbers, luft unflappable sailcloths.

Dry-heaved confidence bolstering sea-legged expertise, free-standing hostage careens headlong breaching unlocked secure gate. Deepened pitches yaw steepest—Flattery's inlet? Hull-walled rubber ball bounces loudly throughout steerage; orlop declarative bopping continues uninter-rogated. Flimsily slung hammocks furnish bumper rebounders deadening free-fallen impacts. Maststep crutches implement compromised biped locomotion; practicing, stumbler perfects striding. Dimly lit cabin's obstacles familiarize dilated pupils' scene-sucker inquisitiveness. Seabags, steamer trunks mundanely occupy emptiness's unbearably undefined purport. Dizzy reeler's conclusions cobbling shitheel piracies concealing smuggled illegal powders uninformatively fix fitful stomping underfoot. Kidnapping's pathology foots bill payback normally associated.

Ladder rungs leading topside offer dumb responses. Thriller conventions, James Bondly, instruct villainous paranoids regale heroes, who've befallen "inescapable" capture, fate's calamitous result.

Unhatching fetid confinement, refreshening breather incorporates wind-resistance wobbly stance. Slicker-clad shipmates regulate complexly roped spinnakers, topgallants, spankers, topsails, mainsails fore-to-mizzen. Upgathering expertise's painstakingly learned. Chess engrossment, fearless nerve, tedium's withstandability assist high-wind, deepsea navigation. Landside, suchlike mouth-breather idiots'd frequent peepshows, videogame arcades, taverns exclusionably tapping national-branded brews; asea, genius-level supercessional feats're theirs.

Astern, radar scantenna post-industrial electrical gadgets upsiding wheel-housed dais spin; pre-century conning apparatus traditionally equips wood-spoked steering wheel, sidereal celestimeters, lodestone compass. Manning helm, Malone's watchful attentions diffract. Sightlines scrutinize seaborne geometries bounding main's horizon, wavelength azimuths, minding wind-shifted subtleties. Descrying unhatched hold's seawash susceptibility, skipper upbraids supernumerary landsman.

"Batten'nit, ya'turd!"

Northbound wind thwarts southbound voyage's bee-line? Larboard coastlined temporal variances distantly flatten; tacks zig-zag, zigs relinquish sighted landfall/zags sight breakers' formative curl. Overtimed

63

heading's ssw bias shadows shipping-laned N/S highway. Constant companionship's freighters, unavoidable uscg helicopters, plentiful fishercraft frustrate nefarious commitments.

"You're pretty bizarre, shipwise. An'yet, nobody's seeing," stowaway prisoner's ice-breaking observation coaxes captain's mercy.

"Bleedin' poofters! Tharn't curiosities stronger'n cowardice."

Arrogance's soliloquy curses mealy-mouthed officialdom, law-abiding traders, stand-offish proprieties permitting free-run corsairs. Wanderlusting's xebec superstructure's outlandishness undoes accusation. Face-valued devaluations disingenuously recognize pirates sailing hyperactual pirate vessel: costume-dramatized assumptions protect criminals.

Gruffly confiding defenses, Cap'n quasi-apologizes. Warlike situations offset combatant smuggling consortiums. Estuarial tributaries enclose low-grade freebooters, looters, salvaging geniuses raggedly agglomerating gangs. Restrictively miniscaled thefts provoke intergang skirmishes policemen condone, supposing mayhem's unnoticeable, thefts're insignificant. Undercover "Kon-Tiki An-Tiki" shipfitters adorably please tourist-hungry merchants, enforcement minions ruling seaside hamlets; scathingly anger uncovered gangmen pillaging overlapped territory.

Kidnapped passenger's entered hostile tiff entangling Maloners, downstate marauders. Gray's Harbor-based hoodlums filched Wanderlusted bosun, aftermathing hazy affronts involuting missed meth. Retaliatory snatch took Aberdeen speedlab's chemist (since-snuffed). We'refore rendezvousing midway, producing bogus switch, George/Terry being chemist's replacer.

Superficial bodytypes, balding scalplines, racial colorings, heights link liquidated scientist, incompetently described factory's crimescene refugee. Unreassured, duplicitous doppelganger dreads enraged downstaters'll exact reprisals, post-exchange.

"Malarky. You'll threatn'us mor'an dem."

Guessed likelihood: outrage's letdown, inchoately conceived upshot, flailed vengeful machinations, hostage's consequent freeing. Surehanded slickered deckmen deal sheetlines, skill countering prevalently winded energies; correspondingly, Maloney baloney counteracts prevalent expectancy.

Underpanned drippings sizzle superheated oils, overcooking roasted rationalizations. Shipmate imprisoning's explanation imprecates smoke-inhaled gullibility.

"Aye. T'wasn't 'tentional. Dordio'd scuppered ye, shoot'nis maw."

Dordio's dockside compromisable blabbing ponderably penetrated belowdecks, initiating quarantine.

DINNER'S GALLEYED: GIL D, Nair're simmering leeks, pears, fishbones. Topside's 2-man abbreviated sail tenders widen off-coast drifting. Wardroom admiral's quarters sequesters bowl-slurping, chart-reading master aft; folksy fo'c'lers indulge now-sprung brighead, dinnertime yarns replaying poopdeck leeward shitting. They'all confess enjoying scandalously scrofulous daylight mooning population's inland-seas' shore; moreoverboard, appreciating ocean-going's bathroom non-deprivation. Gil's exorbitantly regretful.

"Dat's d'shits. D'ain't no-howse way'ta dangle yer heine ovah dat gunnel when's pitch'n-rollin'."

Rueful Gilbert's overhearable foghorn Brooklynese indirectly incarcerated present company's messmate, instigating commiserable affectation.

Nair's ungenerous coolness off-balances equanimitous voluntary. Tight-lipped, self-containment depersonalizes African-Arabian sphinx.

Shipboarders' anti-romantic alliances prefer frowns, suspect smiling. Trustworthiness reintegrates, positively interpreting negativity's hopeless outlook. Skullduggery's loquaciously open-face chatting insinuates secrets're safe (tabbing hostage's predestined demise); close-mouthed carefulness, indubitably, grants hostage'll re-enter society's guardianship.

Fishy gruel creaming floury milk-powdered thickener coagulates midthroat, effecting projectile vomiting's futile blockage. Cannonade fodder eructs. One-shot food-service criticism wryly clears immovable feaster's shoulder, inspirits Brooklynite's Bronx jeer. Seasickness's fickle glottal fingering embarrasses, hand-wiping messed mess disgusts.

Seagoer's vertiginous stomach unrest agitates pity. Jailer sailors pervert antipathies anti-fraternization disassociation required. Appointed impostor jeopardizing undercover's deadly ruse incurs fatalist consolations' commiserations. "Anything's preferable" crappy-go-lucky ethos liberalizes puker's anticipatory acceptabilities. Seasick swabbie mops.

Swabbie's assiduously self-effacing neatness coddles messmates.

Watch-changing dinnerbells bring Luke, Whitey's suppertime hitch. Swabbing's supplicant galls awestricken feedbacks.

"Fercrissakes, matey, b'lay't," Sherrard's skipper-aping diction prehensilely clambers limber syllable, contractionally tenuous limbs.

Shorebound dispositions invert: kid's scowls've brightened mirthfully; Zamboango's wharfside cordiality crab-walks snideways, mumblingly scuttles congenial floats. Underbreathing wheezed, gruel-muffled mucous, phlegmatic albatross hawks globular mouthfuls, expectorates spittoonward. Freckled analyzer claims bronchial infection's caused Lucius's bad mood.

Peppy counterpatter intensively rankling, scrawny teenager vexes cabinmates. Weakened upchucker mixes peppered slang, salted stolidity.

Whorled viewings overtake consciousness. Food-deprived, dehydrated, fever-fed illusions supplant rationally appreciative understanding.

Hackneyed LSD-quality surrealisms propound blacklight posterboy inclusions, sticking pinheaded imagery anywhichway. Gratefully dedicated Fillmore Auditorium showbills, maneater scorpions, easy-pieced 60s-movie promotion striders, ultracool Egyptian and/or Zen tomb-looted iconography swirl. Kaleidoscopic revision schematically "conquers" predictability.

Unmerciful cliched inspiration juxtaposes disparately quirky "random" doodads, answering imagination's cacophony. Compugraph transmigrations' subconscious wilds resemble civilization's apotheosis: televised commercials. Orcas turning sailboats reverse mirrored lagoons, resulting lagoonlike glasstop geologic's instantly upthrust cliffs spell logos pulsing nature's phenomena (rainbows, hyperdominantly).

Recurrent individualized nightmares divert antiseptic, aboveboard visuals. Boyhood's pet sodomy services ever-compliant Boston terrier (why's sex always concludingly funneled?), snapping unconsciousness's undesired hiatus.

Deep-sea cold's showering spray wakens sick fucker. Concerned hud-

67

dling seamen manhandle noodly limber muscles, slap slackened jowls. Spitless gurgling bile obeys gag-reflexed expulsions, exhibiting superb relative fitness. Dunce-capped pupil bobblings postpone instruction; capstan perch balances precariously pawled rope-a-dope. Lifelines tethering stupefied percher benignly protrude unconnected anchorchain, sensible recoverer's understood, cherishing little courtesies.

Midwhile, incessant rollers show irregular blinkering third-to-half mile distant? Distance addles, apparitions found hallucination.

"MATEY! LOOK LIVELIER. Jesus Keerist, y'seem deader'n frigate guano. Gilly! Oars, m'man."

"Ayeyaii, hereyouse gottem. Lotsa luck, babe."

"Zambo! Boat's alower!"

"Lowered aways! Aloha, haoli."

"Lookouts?"

"Signaling's okayed. Lifeboat's launched," redhead replies, adding, "Ridem, cowboy."

Gathered shouting send-offs quietly contrast Nair-faced stone-eyed terror. Powerfully gentle bicepts deposit weakling alee, bestow oarlocked rowers, tacit advice: row like hell, thataway. Hull's wind-blocked convenience ephemeral, oarblade chopper entroughs hill-sized waves coursing, athwart guestimated reckoning. Backshoulder peeking ducks frigid brine spume, descries intermittent cresting vessel's outline diminishably varying, stroke-by-missed-stroke. Drift incrementally segregates oafish stroker, steadfast westly oriented staller, parallel-coursed mothership, hyperactive approaching dinghy.

Weaker oarsman sidetracks; one-track minder chugs, evading sure collision. Gruesome seepages purulate yellowing lesions marking progressively worsening abscess abominations. Bloodshot socket vacuoles wrench painfully gained, blindingly self-centered awarenesses; yelled warnings debunk parsimonious blindness.

"Jump! Save yourself!"

"Save's" meanings tighten. Jumping's hypothermic self-murder creates solutions unresolvable quandaries "invent."

Receding dinghy's oar-sped wake bubbleates, tracking rain-pelted disintegrations. Rain's irrelevance drenches redundantly. Coruscated pocks beautifully bleaken rower's plight. Numbed aches. freeze-framed pains're subjugated. Subject's objectiveness prioritizes rowing (attainment's presumed, insofaras south-based gangsters're necessarily previewed).

Untimeable periods desert incompetent mariner's seascapes. Pogostick crest-topped 360-degree perspectives now discover desolated shiplessness, undetectable barren lands.

Bailing's proto-emergency disabuses stupidity. Unwarranted balast depth creeps upwardly, commingling leakage, rain, transgunneled slopping. Uncanny double-palmed dogstyle digging'd provisionally bail, relinquishing control's hyperprecarious countercapsize portentiousness. Gradual sinking's inevitability swamps getaway's plan-x (indefinitely unrevealed wave-rider flowing landward).

Waterlogged tobogganing dory slides everless steerable; steepening slopes outdo arm-powered speed. Bow straying off-course, whirl-prone motion's danger distracts motion-sickened boater's gut. Adrenaline lifesaver rush's brinkly fatal: clearheaded, sickfree boatman freaks; panicky oarwork co-opts headway's miserable achievement. Whirlpooling overpowers retroactivity.

Amidswirl, screwing's clockwise twist constricts verbose flapdoodle, articulately spinpointing drowning's vital medium. Seaward argot funnels downward. Billowed lungs're exploded, resituating legendary dolor whereunder fish're copacetic corpsephages. Attaching legends twirl, tentacles intertangling Moby Dicks, Jonah swallowers, salvage voracity's gaped leviathans mandatorially interposing drowner/mortal victimization's storykiller.

"Shur'nuff, gotcha!" godly lifters pull spun-out sinker aboard fortune's Octopus, Humptulips, Wn, fisher-rigged Q-boat.

Netting cloaks mini-armory alluding (apocryphally?) backward, whereinto war-storied comicbooks concocted diabolical Nazis camouflaging gun-bristled raiders. Q-boats (etymorphically abbreviating "Question," rhyming Germany's U-boats) literally antedate WWII (Geoffry Firmin's Q-ship sordidity inflaming German stokers: Unde.Volc;ch1). Illiterately, adolescent imaginings free-associate adventured gain.

"Fergie, holy shittin' hamsters, you've withered." .

"It'ain't Ferguson."

"G'wan, lookit'm."

Sickness's ravaged visage concretely crumbles statutory physiognomal laws; speedlab cook's mugshot is/isn't recognized, plastered beside rescued doryman's lifelikeness. Arguing Argonauts' goldrush desires fleece methmaker's particular skills (cross-referenced goose laying ovoid ingots, indexed: killing, pro/con).

Fergus Hempleman's reincarnation debate Solomonly resolves: successful production'll validate identification's bona fide facsimile.

Downwind-driven Wanderlusters northwardly vanished, sham fishermen return upwind. Unbroken sand extenuates flatline, anti-scenic, gray-headland deadliness previewing fogged-in foothills' rainforested greenery. Diesel atmospheric transfusions encloud manifold destiny's clean air repellent, whereinby domelike hermeticity excludes briny purity. Resickened passenger gurgles respectfully, expelling spewables tobacco-chaw style, clutching dixie cup portable spittoon. Camaraderiely, snuff-sucker chawbreakers accept subtle vomiter's vice, mistaking it-for-theirs, submitting milder, unspiced, broadleaf curings.

Kalaloch-to-Copalis (overnights/underdays), winetaster refinements-'re offshorely applied; snoose connoisseurs differentiate flavor profiles, textures, afterbites, spittle viscosities categorizing mildness, wildness, contentiously prizing specious brands: Coonhound Rawbone, Hick-a-lick, Goatmount's Ballplay Tic. Dissectably disgusting intricacies charm arguers. Harbormouth buoys welcomingly suspend coastline boredom, prevent mouthful endorsements I'd've anxiously refereed.

Nonintroductions, anomencultural hailing, unquestioning acceptances demarcate Chehalis watershedders. Queenless drones busily comb honeyless waxwork bayfront's faded blooms: demi-abandoned docksites, downstream logging boomtowns hopelessly bust, de-licensed fisheries

71

unburden themshelves: plunderable dross collections recline stockpiled nowhere people'd scope thiefs. Marginally indictable garbagemen glean discarded scrapmetals, servicing community's infrastructural requisites (pleonastic self-help gastank refillings're unspokenably pardoned).

Supervening 9–10 pick-ups, lunchpail extortionists downthrottle. Ruddering atrociously amiss, unchanneled prow staves alderwooded shorelined groves. Unfazed deckhands upend felled, pre-severed branches, utilizing showily unviewable tackle-blocked rigs strung trunk-to-trunk.

Aheadways divulge multidirectional sloughs.

BACKWATER'S RACKETEERS MAINTAIN half-sunken ex-fish canner barges euphemistically called "houseboats" outlining plankless quayed pile-driven dockeological ruins. Flatbottom skiffs slovenly festoon makeshiftless harborage? Devastatable underwater deadhead logs rebuke unguided entries—haphazard mooring poles're incidental slalom gatemouths directing incomers anti-hazardously. Subaquarian rivulets alter readable eddies, behooving complicated helm-tuned adjustment spinning dual propellers' oppositional thrusting torques. Painstaking 300/400-foot passage's piloted husbandry babies mothership's precious hull. Grimly congregated spectators portray foregone century rogues' gallery daguerreotypical collective stare. Softish bonked resonations tickling skeg syncopate low-rpmed putt-putts, sly reggae sidestepping ska eruptive breakthroughs.

Environmental breakdown hillslides, counterpotentially, demonstrate stumps bristling clear-cut floodplain backdrop. Salt-eaten pontoons bolster houseboat flotilla's highwater adaptability; bushwacked salal, kinick-inick instill woodsy pretensions aiding unemployed loggers' rugged individualist solipsism. Mongrel-patrolled junkyard folklore clinches toughness's automythological conception.

Chainsawyer involvements asnide, impoverished woodcutters spryly recalibrated econometric measures. Resourcefully political, they'ven't banned criminal moneymaking policies nor overtaxed timber landowners' permissiveness. Live-and-let-take libertarian "populism" popularizes scavenging's glamour; unglamorously, scavenging "libertarians" behave apolitically, pilfering salvageable crap, gulping homebrewed hooch, devouring rancid unrefrigerated leftover stews, spiritually nurturing rage.

Prescience creating faithful rendition, exchanged inmate confronts newer jail's parameters. Territorial Rovers sentrify neighborhood dividing encampment/road. Barking, snarling, yowling fangsters challenge intruders, hassel extruders, locally govern. Treelimbs' overland route cos-

73

mologically falters (starcrossed firs nowadays doing nurse-log shift). Aforewarned waterway's treacherousness quashes Alcatraz breakouts requiring coincidentally flawless tidal cooperation.

Probationary diplomacy chaperones frail relational affairs. Gainsaying briny-eyed boaters, land-based cadreheads discern retrieved "pharmacist's" distinctly different. They're duped!? Duping associates captivators, captivated. Deferring narcotic bonanza's motherlode riskiness imperiling profiteered acquisition, leaders gauge unknown captive's able-bodied utility.

Utopic settlements (inconceivably, there're utopian-minded idealist narcissists rife), covet aptitudinal diversity. Scientists're narco pharmers; humanists're . . . lawyers? teachers? jesters? Pantheistic competence worshipping liberally blesses talents' omnipresent bestowing.

Incompetence's value, moreunder, outcrops rockpile chipping's everlasting usefulness. Unskilled labor's ditch diggers've founded societies.

Slave auction mores oversee felt-up appraisals apprising handlers inspecting seasick-weakened groaner's muscle tone. Emaciation's flab flaps sheetlike, tremoring slackly. Unremarkable height weighed, judgments downgrade optimisms exaggerating strength's promise. Obtuse unresponsiveness predisposes witless capacitance (manual drudge's asset?), restricting officer-schooled candidacy.

"Throw'm back," feelers, prodders conclude.

Freedom's briefly entertained, rebuffed. Juicier diversions're proposed: assign doubtful he-man's apprenticehood Pygmalion-style. Enthrallment-planned servitude's playfully arranged.

Hannahbelle Traxler's nominated, seconded, acclaimed (unvolunteering disallowed). She'sn't Amazonian, precisely; leaner sinuosity, whitening blondness ages her edges, shedding voluptuous bulk's hardened babyfat. Endurability outlasted peak fitness's hormonian convergence. 35–50-year-old estimations expand compact flesh's possibilities.

74

Sexuality's inherent attendance stalks communally imposed unions. Male/female intersections're immaculate concepts idolizing fetishes, prioritizing magnificently metaphorical groins. Fucking's epiphanies bore post-adolescents, bedevil everybody's purest altruisms, legislate moralities, populate worlds.

Peckerhead leers hotwithstanding, dismal termagant uptakes charged counterpart. Uselessly promising bile-splattered refugee's sleaziness plainly irritates Hannabelle's letter-perfect regimental disciplinarianism. Undercutting Bogart's drunkard boatmaster Ornutt (AFR. QN. 1951, D: J. Huston), ex-racetracker wants resourcefulness's crudest rudiments.

Intangible choker chain leashes rednecks' 2-legged bowser encroaching 4-leg off-leash bowsers' rightful terrain. Interbred huskitas, dobradores, bullterrors, scotwhilers teethe once-recognizable chew toys corresponding dug-up humanoid bones. Dominator mistress's disdain psychically yanking chain-forced heeling assures awful alpha pets: neophyte's ranked omega.

Casually parked road-warrior junkers reconstitute Detroit's assembled lineages. Fords Dodge customized Olds-mobilizations. V-12s mount bare chassis, fat-tired trikes souped-up fuel-injected double-intake manifolds extrude flame-decaled gasoline tankful anti-ambulance amulets. Unrunnable heaps outnumber active cars? None're visibly decommissioned (dysaxelic, unmotorvated, unwheeledly).

Negotiating watchdogs' yard-sprung traps (rakish autoparts), towed visitor defers questioning. Osmotic teacher-pupil interchange's prudentially insured: observances, unquestionably, fabricate self-explanatory idiosyncratic oaths ignorant outsiders swear.

Outsider-viewed insides, peripatetically, unveil inscrutable seances prefacing orgies. Cubicular partitions' saggy fabrics invite voyeuristic peeping. Intimate smells' noises transude disintegrated tasteful soundproofing. Real-life mattressing locations copy fantastic fourgasms devised about ex-bankmates? Slumbering ex-lumbermen laid off'n'on mustn't disappoint randy spouses. Contagious horniness spreads, mandates uphold womanizers intersecting wangster molls. Consenting adulteries vaccinate, staunching transgenerational incest's epidemic.

Hannah's barbaric accommodations dankly install horseplayed huncher's cornered aspirations. Molded bedding's artless mucosal recitative colonies augment fossilized sperms?

Exhaustedly emasculate, uncomplaining daydreamer collapses ungratified, relieved.

MOTORCYCLE MEMBERSHIP'S gangly polemical scaffolding stays executions: substitutions're dog-piled melees pummeling dogie offenders. Trounced beatings' antisexually passionate wails prevail, obliterating fantasized sexualities' unrapacious, desirous consents. All-for-one musketeers justly punish niggling offenses, exercise professionally bludgeoned aplomb.

"Anything'll provoke'm," H instructed sea-scraped flotsam aurally punched awake. "Rat-tail mustaches, queer sneers, too-smoky campfires, uncleaned latrines. One'll yammer, 'Geronimo!' Others'll leap, shitkickers afly."

Goodly conduct's meddlesome cautions superseded good-mornings, outcrowded burgeoning hunger's venturesome sentiments. Inchoate yardape free-for-alls emboldened astute timidity. Ignorance's inexcusability applies pandemically, H'Belle tells now-alerted heeder, felicitously "legalizes" post-partum abortions gutting fetal-posed grown men. Quasi-courteously, women're exempt.

Primitive tribal divisions respect sexes: penises maraud, vaginas housekeep. Instruction's liason-status diplomatically immunizes HT, sanctioning excursive trial-run tests measuring student's testicular gumption.

"Deep-down, they'rall weenies," divulges experience's voice.

Nonspecific whimperings isolate lately pummeled goat bleedily bleating obeisance. Sniffled growls signify jealously tongued dogged ministrations. A-wolves salivate, treat licking's wound.

Unofficial hands-off protection'll defend learner's permitted gauchness; learning's honeymoon sets apace.

"Coupla days'n . . . pffft, showtime's rockin'," roughnecks collude initiation entertainment.

Fate befalling drop-outs, wash-outs, haplessly reprobated incorrigibles? Renegades' renegades're butchered, mongrels dine happy.

Orientational prerequisites layer onionskin dicta. Religions're started comparably! Dogpack-modeled leadership hierarchy rituals've elevated strongest, debased weakest, according fist-fought (streetfighter codes enforced) challenger system. Finely reticulated prelim joustings heckle hackled superiors: wimpy incipiencies temeriously bait bullies, stronger assertions obviate brutish put-downs. Difficulties abounding, leader laddering rerungs night-by-night. Shrouded bushwackers suckerpunch unsuspecting strollers. Roman-style cornholing disreputedly ices cakewalking tall, voiding taboos disrecognizing sodomistic conduct. Rank-advanced necessity's fundament distaste repulses underling codpiecemiel smallfry; smallfry're unmercifully fried. Rectification's rectal preoccupation, rearingly, unpacks canines' nobler assortings: penitentiary "edile idylls" reform advancement's moral code.

"How're y'able t—"

"Shhh," stifles anti-authoritarian chatter someone'd overhear; strained restraint silently sings unvocalizable yearnings.

Domesticities inaugurate trainee's communalization. Firewood chopping/kindling tindering comprise village idiot's stupidest rudiment. Intermediate-level complexities (swampy dankness, drizzled humidification, tinder's scarcity) bluntly perplex. Keynote groper fumbles hatchet, mishandles sledge, gets shavings wet, fizzles match-lit beginnings. Instructress's pitiable sighing equalizes wheezer's rasping; pitilessly, sigher demonstrates fireside chattel's easiest obligation.

Ineptitude's exposure palls. Horseplaying's abilities're absolutely untransferable, (except roundtripping some-200 miles/day qualifies Portland Meadows commuting's community-minded contributor, who'd confidentially "pledge" sure-won disbursements). Crude plumbing's circumventive conduits, paralleling wood-fired cookstoves, daunt untrainable maintainer. Hand-pumped hydraulics necessitate tricky priming; dopey pumper handles settlement's second primary operation abysmally.

Heating-to-plumbing-to-composting, jobs're overpoweringly involuted, involunteer substantiates.

Ineptitude abnormally endears dunce—haplessness fascinates school-marm endowed teaching's thankless grant. Know-it-all dickheads horn-swoggle instructors; average students disenchant blandly. Innocence's tabula rasa avatar, highhandedly, bewitches.

"Gravy Train, woo-woooo," tombstone epitaphs allusively tease dog-food boy. Survivor dearth concocts doggone ignominy: watchdogs're meted live meaty runaways (squandered slugs'd chip dainty fangs; hunting's selfish delights reinforce dog-eared loyalties).

Condemned mandibular exercise's 160-pound chewstick disbelieves coached exhortations. Pee-wee football's likewiseguy verisimilar dime-store motivational speeches ridicule shagging's lethal fetch. Teasing's re-pudiator, invitingly, re-targets sharpened darts.

"Yee-haw, Purina, getamoveon!"

Wheelbarrowing compost crystalizes slave-labored comeuppance's downfallen splat: unwell, feeble, functionally disabled, problematically useless, restrainee does lummox's lot, insufficiently. Noodle-modal quad-riceps vibrate untuned. Bass-drummed pulsation backbeats oscillate ventricles, auricles, arteries, veins. Unsung shrieks transubstantiate heaved exhales. Undependable disharmonies disband meager brawn coordination's wheezing racket.

"Whoa, kibbles. Horsemeat, ho-thar."

90-minute diagnostics've relegated apprenticed colonialist: ejection's foretold. Fanged earthmovers, air-hung nooses, waterways, firearms pluralize elementary execution's selectivity.

Altruistic reprieving contortion dignifies worthy jester appointment's station? Tricks entertainers competently display're lacking. Ventrilo-quism, prestidigitating, 3-ball juggling, unicycling, ad-libbing, singing eluded myself-styled predevelopments. Untalented/untutored; untrainably incurious, estranged, bedraggled, doomed: dogboy sulks.

"S'okay, milkbone, tonight'll determine what'll happen," consoles composter.

Harder subcultural drills (tirejacking, deerskinning, possumplucking, vinegar piebaking, jerky jerking, clamgunning, burl sculpting, moonshine distilling) fulfill sulking loser's failure-packed afternoon. Sadistically perky cheerleading counterpoises ridiculous, inept struggles—optimism retoning lugubrious consequences. Tonight's tribunal counsel assembly'll reprocess Trax's collected data, activate (deactivate?) channeled mediations conducting dissonantly accidental-prone member's orchestral integration.

Clubheaded (Shriners? Rotarians? Oddfellows? Buffalos?) males amuse empowered dame. Goofball straight-faced incantations dismiss seriousness's brutalities, softening rigidities, lightening burdensome weights.

KLANSMAN-STYLE SATIN SATANIC BEDSHEETS enrobe

thronged acolytes. Headmen wear plaid sashes betokening port-author-ized subways? Subordinations lower-ranked chieftains respect're plaidly color-coded; gold chintz signifies upper-ranked supremacies. Demonic demotics accord everyman akinship, junk insignia crowning poohbah wannabes. Rhinestone medals aluminumly luminous reflicker candle-lit wicks ascending floor-mounted urns. Seraglio intaglio urn pictures mythologizing erzatz Vikings sacking Anysultanate, Arabia, consolidate cement-headed smugness bedsheeters obtrude. Nordic rapists dispatch scimitared eunuchs, debauch awfully willing harem courtesans, torment-ing racistly chiseled potentates' dying consciousnesses. Enfabling head-shrunken planets viewably divagate solipsistical orbits, circumflexing in-wardly, enshrining worshipped Valhallas.

Hunt lodge mystics encant ululations robbing cinematically verified graves. Rumored masonic elk-dropped fraternity secret ceremonies con-fabulate wacko persiflage mirthless believers recirculate fountainlike (perpetuity's machine-assisted turbodynamics electrically re-impelling flow).

"Don't laugh," attorned counseling's sage whisper imparts.

Trax dons overcoat lining, inside-out, British solicitor's wiggy head-dress. Docketed subject models custom-tailored tinsel loincloth.

Ululating ceases. Throats unclog, scepters salute grand muckamuck's stoned Rhinegold shower-curtained splendor. Incongruous clove incense emanating hashish pipes fuses redolences smoldered cannabis sativa con-tributes, vented armpits spice, unstopped flatulence broadens. Redneck hippies demographize monstrosities uniting evangelist Christian's ob-sessive loins, biker's post-crash cranium, Ralph Kramden's affiliative propensity, meany-first destinasty's pioneer spirit, Woodstock national-ism's constitutional anarchism, Dead Garcia's Merle Haggard-imperson-ation forbearance.

"Ellow-fay embers-may, iends-fray, ountrymen-cay, isitor-vay," shifted argot's announcer astounds uninitiated participant, "uh-thay ost-may igh-hay ommodore-Cay arshal-May acCallister-May."

E-way ise-ray—unlaughing. Savage mauling premonitions preclusively gag laughter. Courthouse protocol's pig Latin niceties protract. Ferally scruffed flatlander hillbillies manfully grapple extrapolated tongue.

"Ast-hay ou-thay ame-nay?" MacCallister inquires.

Rib-driven defender representation's nudged cuing re-applies identifier's quandry: which shopworn name's apropos? Virginal appellations're supercessively unexceedable.

"Asper-cay illingsly-way," I-say, "our-yay, onor-hay."

"Ources-say ay-say, e-yay ave-hay een-bay anted-play y-bay emy-enay orces-fay. ow-hay o-day ou-yay ead-play?"

"Eg-bay ardon-pay?"

"Ot-nay uilty-gay!" awyer-lay ispers-whay, half-second's late.

"Ear-hay ter-enay, etition-pay or-fay ull-fay ardon's-pay elease-ray," gavels upmumbled consternation. Anslation-tray? Willingsley's petitioned full-pardoned unfettered emancipation. Guilt's/insanity's; non-guilt, non compos mentis, nolo contendre pleas're attainably faciler. Unreiterable pleading interlocks protocols eviscerating compromise.

"Ice-nay oing-gay," defenseless defender's bleakest convictions're validated. Lingua porka oinks idiosyncratically ornate passages. Salem witch hunters dispensed humaner justice; aboriginal nubile aging rites're firmer fraught rigors; fratboy elephant-walked daisychains objectify cannier corollative linkages (pre-graduates studiously intaking coprophagia's lessons).

Adjournment's pro-tem uling-ray devises miniature golfcourse mazes testing ranger. Fir-crazy loggers're wooden, idea-wise: trees embrace gauntlet's framework, outbranching lumberjackass jamboree stunts. Highly practiced ability's prerequired; minimalistically accoutered shinnying (stubble-trunked bared pole, haphazardously limbed), deerhunter hatcheting, nailfile-scale axe felling 300-year-old Douglas, logroll flume dancing, chokerchain whiplash acrobatics variegate obstacle's cursive amusement. Sequential death-defied skits'll infallably tickle numbskulls craving demolition derby's soapbox operas.

Stunted stuntman doom's sheer verity postpones weekend wargamers' festivity.

DAY'S ERRANT KNIGHTS SALLY, conquering dumpster-ized tribute. Surviving's grimiest grit ennobling brackish waterwheel tilt-a-mill Quixotes, ceremonial rigamaroles quasi-dignify indigent peoples. Preappointed woodlore jouster's jest awaits crusaders' postpillage home-coming.

Woodsmanship introductory seminars intermediate practicer's im-perfect techniques. Forestry's circus expertises re-emphasize rustic do-mestic's campsite ineptitudes; diverging domesticity's boner joshing, Hannabellicose drill-instructored yelling disconcerts. Omnipresently, succeeding's grandiose conceits subsidize b-plan annexing shunted off-shoots: realistic pessimisms accent cheating, discount beating fairly rigged bloodsports.

"Chances're, axing deer's th'easiest outlet," sympathetic apostate si-dles, de-euphemizing deerhunting's terminologistics. Hatchet-armed "hunter" chases unseeable cervines, serving fox-impersonated role's doggy bagatelle.

Orienteering unexplored wetlands, wading stumbler'll swiftly forgo quarter-hour headstart. Duckblind sheds fringing sedgefields instilt view-ing pavillions sanguine latter-day Romans attend. Eventful excitements pack boxlunched tailgate picnic anticipation feastily drooling; overprized contests sloppily replay mismatches pairing unarmed humans, lions. Recapture's crushing outcome's inconspicuously gainsaid: whisperable loopholes perforate dragnet inescapability. Submariner periscoping reeded oxygenation, landlocked happenstanced intersections (intercept-ing strayed truckers, BATF-deputized posses, maneuvering commando battalions), aerial plucks involving copster whirlybirds, alien spacecraft, nuclear waste-hatched mutant pterodactyl hexameter American eagles po-tentiates reprieves.

Christlike superaqueous ambulatory skills'd nimbly skim murky quick-sands; sinner's footfallen plodding'll irredeemably enmuck scared run-ner. Interventional low-hurdled woods amaze puzzled orienter, rerouting straightest byways. Unsunned east/westlessness overcasts unreadable direction. Lapping waterlines lakewise encircle islanded strandee's locus sensus.

"Th'island's trapezoidally diamonded," chalk talker diagrams afterwoods.

Bayside lengthiness deceitfully pledges safety ("crosstide rips'll cripple ya'til patrols arrive"); bayside's vertex-forming counterside-A leads northeastward ("fens, bogs, rivery runnels, puddled ponding lakes"); ditto counterside-B's southwestward avenue ("'nother peninsular morass, 'smore bay"); side-C's lonestar southeast hope's, obviously, anticipated ("guards'll probly seal th'leaks").

Bedside strategies dispassionately counterploy variable delusions daydreaming Houdinian disentanglements. Buster Keaton cinematics' unedited real-time stunts're unrepeatable; quintessential.

Abed? Slumber-partied intimacy accompanies doleful tactical workshop blueprinting. Sharing dark-voiced ungiggled breathy evocations correspond confessionally pleasured admissions satisfied lovers rollick. Hermetically co-instenched, smellers in/exhale autobiographical whiffs.

"Gracie Toledo was Ma's afterthought; Daddy didn't 'cern hisself. 'Names're toadstools,' Daddy'd bray, jackass kickin' shitfaced blotto."

Protonamed GT, HanTrax withstood steadfastly artificed incestuous undertoned overtures (Mozart's Giovanni-scored tuba-registered farts); matriarchal zephyrs condensing ammoniated antibacterial perfumes. Radon motherlodes propitiously claimed Toledos' homestead; broken homemaker abdicated home's queendom—contaminated forevermore—joined Zealand-bound pilgrims emigrating pantoxic exposures. Houseless household header (IRS-certified) carried then-fourteen siblingless daughter awayward, magnanimously interproposing Tijuana matrimonial holiness, residential squat blighting unspecifiable jurisdictions (Tangiers? Interzone?).

Alcoholism's advance-staged impotence, Daddio's corruptly sentimentalcase romanticistic fibrosis paralyzed unfantasized swordsmanship. Amidslumber night's vomit aspirating orphanized then-fifteen-year-old.

Gracie's canny orphanage aversion crowbarred dastardly ruses. Isolating Phoenix suburb highway-gridded self-containments prevented nosey solicitousness; backyard's ornamental grapefruit orchard gravesite, howeverlasting, baited coyote disinterment's inquest-ordered autopsy. Unplanned flights appealing, housing's elemental stucco shelter homesite induced shrewder movement: unfamiliarized Toledo-paired family "moved," "Hannah Tracey," single clerical staffperson, self-installed. Friendless Father mouldered unmissed (buzzards exempted), remade fatherless Grace-Hannah matured overnight. Newgrown loquatiously assertive personality-profiled rakeover hauled ash.

"Stockings, spikes, make-up'll metempsychosize."

Prostitutional dating's conscientious flirtations prospected favorable, charitable, sweet swains. Weekly Toms recompensed monthly bills; dickered harried liaisons shuttled cocks. Steadier boyfriends replacing cokeheaded mansters consequently settled sheltering's roundelay.

"'Fonly I'dn't married Ernie Witherspoon."

Ernie's ideal mateability factors summed cunnilinguistics, bedspring gymnastics, unpresupposed negotiable bondaged presentiments, semirich liberal-minded parents (donationally able; dictatorially disinclined), poetic leanings, materialistic sense. Flip-side detractions? Hypersexualized self-image's bedridden manliness, standoffish cold fish parent frauds (committably unstrapped; assertively disempowered), e'ermore poeticized prioritizations dislodging materially sensate touchstones nonpoets haven't trouble touching (paychecks).

"Breeding outfoxed divorce."

"Aborting would've shel- . . ."

"Who'da predicted? Ern, me're pretty-well hitched, content. Why-nots outscored whys."

Triplets outdid prophesies, enslaved child rearers. Motherless mothering (mother-in-law's marginal disinterest compounded) burdened 21-year-old. Poet breadwinner attended parking lots, clerked night desks, waited countertops, carhopped. Rollerskating carhop seduced abandoner.

Scandalized, ancestral Witherspoons privately forked overmuch dough (Ernest's loafing riseably humiliating familial honor). Alimonial child-supported remunerations persisted faithfully hell-into teens.

Brandishing G.E.D.s, triumvirate sisters straddled lifestyles reconciling riot grrrl thrash band rehearsals, fastfood trainee managerships; understandably, Mom booked.

Disconnectable companions arear, Northwestward looker discovered Astoria, Oregon.

"Columbia riverrunners, riverrun," droningly chanted falling unawake.

CROSS-POLLENATED INTIMATIONS drowsily mesmerize involuntary manhunt's featured participants. Biographical mundanities translate hereinto profundities, post-midnight, predawn. Paraconsciously voiced divulgences becalm unsuppressed confessions; spellbound absorbers forgive boring sins.

Minutely attuned closeness interlocking telepathic wavelengths, brains synchronously jangle alarms. Moonlight clearance eclipses sales tamer salesmen'd advertise: must-go circumvents circumspect prerogatives.

Rapidly dressing, single-minded lammers survey slumberland kennel's boneyard. Rancorous curs snore viciously yowled snarls; theresnore, sudden waked umbrage's perceivably irrelevant.

Languorous cars're something meaner. What're dependable, unsmoking, enthusiastically gunned? Sawed-off hoods, jacked-up suspensions, clotheshanger tailpipe rewirings equip vehicular homicidal maniacs' machines. WWI-era motley monoprop aerosquadrons classily prototypified highwaymen's quadrowheel groundhog days. Merry sorties debouch barracks compound's roofless hangar; aces engage enemies, skirmish, regress—harrowing tales apotheosizing self-slimed heroics. Haphazardous automobiles embellish escapings' narrowness; quasi-crucial engine chunks littering blackened ringthrown vaportrails jauntily imitate shot-down airplanes' smash landings.

Any'll start; continuous running's doubtable. Ignitions daringly droop keychains flagging key insertions (highjacking's unthinkable moxie potentiating slam-bang car-chased apocalypses thugs expect). Tiptoe tapper napping dogcatchers circumambulate mongrel horde, commandeer 80s-vintage Chevrolet Caprice (fading trooper escutcheon rampant), turnover unmuffled implosion.

Fishtailed sluice waggles sayonara; insultingly injurious collateral damages maim wakened yipping chasers. Sputtering exhaust's ratatatat shoots blankly, wasting smoggy wisps followers'll sniff.

Roadwise, Caprice's flagrantly illegitimate. 4-color bumperstickered Gatorfarms, Parrot Circuses, silkscreen Rushmores trumpeting roadslide afflictions decorably highlight 4-year-lapsed license's plates. Unregistered, uninsured, unlicensed motorists, quite pardonably, seek stealable sedate conveyance. Frustrating hounds lawfully badged/lawless badgerers means committing gradiently fouler unlawful deeds.

"Let'em eat nailcakes," speeding driver indicates anti-pursuit caches enabling deviances.

Wide-headed roofer's brads strew, righting point-ends tireward. Ensnarlment's arsenaled roadway fuckeruppers boast low-tech simplicity's failsafe science (oil's indisputable slickness, spined endings' anti-synthetic penetrability, M-80s' dynamiting dimunitions).

Pursuit, extraordinarily, atrophies. Macadam rubbish tackily forfeits coolheaded sportsmanship's cardinal parkway containment. Momentarily, internal decombustions wheeze arguments defending non-pursuit, ridiculing speed's histrionic freneticism. Autonomic trashmission unilaterally severs drivetrain relation pinioning transmission's shift-pointed adaptations: therefarce, downshifts jam unalterably. First-geared shudders whinily keen upwards forty mph.

Reblackened smoke flagellates slowing's wavy undulations, brazenly announces trashmobile's odious compulsion. Trailerpark millionaires, clearcutter landed gentry, seedy gentleman treefarmers, service-sectored industrialists (FIRE-eaters: Foreclosure, Insurance claimjumping, united Real-Estate's denationalized rent-a-park concessions) unrack shotguns—wagons circled—possess bank-owned property. Testosterone heartens lying's self-reliant pride.

Autotheft's revolutionary politics aspect (depriving drooler class timberhead apologists car-transported franchise) weakly adheres. Amorality adequately deglamorizes radical chic's flairs.

Logistical scramblers expel sophomoric rationalization, relearn unteachable reflexed resiliences. Carlots, tautologically, contain sedans. Used buggy shysters, factory-dealt provenders'll predictably oppugn stinkpot ride's presentation; resident carport harbormasters presuppose drifters're crooks. Papermills, accessibly, assort coupes, half-tons, 4-by-4s workers've stationed. Estrangers always're lurking aroundabout papermill vocational fortuity windowsills. Diligence's masquerade exculpates loitering's joint casing.

Two-score four-wheel driveables insituate unlined slots outside Aberdeen's downstreaming effluvic sludgery. Featherbedding sentryboxed guardsman sneezes amidsnooze, awakes, rejoins hungover misery's vicious companionability. Groused begrudgements acknowledge nonthreatening incursion. Overheated radiator's hood-lifted capitulation lavishly explicates trashy visitors' deliberate acting: jug handling comely womanfolk divining waterspout/craggy manfolk beseeching charity.

Frozen hirings frostbite hand-to-mouth appliers; formful mannerliness automates skittish reenactments. Painstaken resumetic regurgitation delays, abetting felonious monkeywrench hotwire trick. Resurrected steelmill corpses revisionarily prance pulpmill anteroom's stageset, interrupting dawdler's unutterable soliloquies. Interchangeable decors officiate unsettling matchpoints.

"Applications're catalogued first-come, first-serve," hypocritically lubricates friction-free mesh gearing preferences.

"Much obliged," hee-haws glibness caricaturizing straw-sucking hayseed demeanor's bovine complaisance.

Tieless shirtsleeved minion's reserved moderations peripherally prompt undebatable non-interview, showing forced regret meditating unemployment's toughness. Lignocellulose acid dips, chlorination bleaches overwhelm politely muttered remorse blockheads profess.

Sentryman's perusing girlie mags; Chevrolet's unhooded innards're shamefully exposed.

"Two-toned Skylark," confederate's murmuring guidances nod, "hide-a-key nook's magnetically stuck underside dashboard's glovebox."

Huddled briefing's plot pits diversionary distressed damsel enticing masterbatory obsessed ogler. Fetching Jill's Jack-offer pail gambit'll replenish leaked coolant, removing lot's watchman. Unwatched Skylark'll flutter off-lot, roost clandestine kilometers downroad, re-encounter discardable Chevvy.

"Understand? Move."

SKYLARKING TRAVELERS METICULOUSLY ransack compartments separating title, insurance's certificate, operator handbook, gascard carbons, tollbooth coins, crumpled folding ones, fives. Intently penetrable personalizing rummage deepens auto-heisted violation: diary/ wallet breeds offsprung revelishments (refreshment-oriented revelry ravishings relished, revealed). Credit-carded undersigned proofs trace naughty blames.

Kenneth Corning, Squim-based quim chaser Grade-F cunthound moonlighting Deforestry Expert, Packaging Division, SAPCO, recreated drugstore-wide condom selectability padding bucketseats. Modest porn library's collection, dildos, sani-wrapped undergarment restraints subsist betwixt optimistically half-full liquor bottles appointing rear seat's false-backed trunked cabinate. Factory-installed audiodeck woofers bassly reverberate retrodisco anthems Tarantino movies've recirculated: coy appropriations "ironically" milking Barry White's, Al Green's red-blooded, organ-grinded throbbing.

Lewd music athump, throbbers interpret skimpy tissues libeling Northwest's slimiest roadhouses (hereinclusion defines slime). Woodpecker Inn, Skamokawa; Windy's Blowtel, Bonneville; Bob's Bigfoot Mouthbreeder, Packwood; Veronica's Trucker Massage Hotlinks Barbegrill, Pe Ell, configurate slippery itineraries Kenneth'd skated. JROTC school syllabi, daycare ride-scheduled algorithms, beefy florist voucher toasting "Annie" (oversized vases' orchids, petunias, roses, lobelia) stretch homely togetherness's elastic mask, countersketch filial revolter's peccadillos, rapprochements.

Two-tone two-timer's Buick's mid-compact adultery confirmations possibly'll intimidate Kenny, forestalling undelayed help's summoning? Nonsense. Trusting thieves've approximated pre-lunch interval mediating heist's notification. Outlandishly, full-shifted working'll outrun capturers, constituting distance's lead-timed obstruction. Indelibly, dual-colored lavender/chartreuse'll de-necessitate tagging's confirming enumeration, assure apprehension whenever patrolmen stop laughing.

Subsequential plotting's presentimented anxieties spur evaders. Hyperefficient police're conceptualized, transmitting informants' incipiently shrugged languages clueing clincher APB radiowaves. Rodentine, cheesy authoritarians're cooperatively postulated: vox rattus populace's suspected tattling keeps officers up-to-the-minute. TV's "true-crime" criminologistics, rationalistically, lay foundationalized pomposity supporting police-stated precincts.

Canada's international amnesty's preposterously misconceivable, interstate flight's unappealingly mundane. Intrastate constriction's weird enticements forfeited, highwayward robbers peregrinate closest state's nearest border: Astoria's bridge.

Broaching state-lined boundary invites expungible indictments outpouring near-forgotten obligations (undisclosed eye-witnessed massacre's recapitulation, primarily); Hannie's broach's stickier.

Mobland's ubiquity frays, unravels, erratically reconnects. Strikeminded poisonous moccasin gangs're poised estuarially, legendarily anticipating malevolent striking's lended motive. Ubiquity's brainwashed irrational tangents annex landlocked counties, zones far-removed. Inland's jerkwater militias, coastland's drydocked anti-deserter legionnaires drag Internet seines.

Han's overdeveloped persecution complex's downright idiotic.

"Horsefeathers! Nobody'll bother."

"Bothering's easy. Ignoring's difficult."

Unmanned patrolcars gracing rinkydink town's purlieus remonstrate careless deflections. Corning's itinerant undertakings (unscheduled arrival/departure stints) may've prematurely unearthed plundering's slapdash burial, notified authorities. "Paranoid delusiveness" phraseology misconstrues persecution's actuality; paranoiac's rubbernecked furtivities, maddeningly, disconcert populations affecting normality's insouciance.

Contrarian logic appeals. Journeying unpredicted routes fleetingly soothes; hereinafter backtracked strategies're approved.

"Stead'a scramming, let's hole-up," initiates Bizarro planetary orbit, jumping Traxer's steel-railed resolve.

Misdirected sleights prestidigitate added adventitious counter-logical movements. Guileful motorists'll "dump" car thusly: crooked pit-stop garage'll receive Buick, proverbially run-up supercharged exorbitance performing unneeded maximal overhaul, unimpeded minimal fluid-changed maintenance. Renaming ourselves Matthew Peretz/Margarite Youngblood, we'll pseudonymously cipher Mr./Mrs. Smith, registering motel's no-tell travelodge logbook. Henceforth, lamming planners'll reconnoiter purloinable discreet discretions.

LOINABILITY INTERVENES. Willapa Hills' Whippoorwill Will'Inn deskclerk ceremoniously marries honeymoon-posing "Smiths." Restrained leer umpiring luggageless check-in, centercourt doublebed monopiece furnishing stark roomette, motheaten coverlet's invitational seediness serve love's smashing overhead followthrough ace.

Intervention rallying dallies; tennis metaphors disintegrate, prolonged cunnilingual, fellative, copulative reposes more-resembling languidity's uncompetitive concupiscences. Physicality's ultimate legality consummates courtshipped messages. Interlocked, sated heartened lovers're gooily glued.

Famished gutted stomachs're droolily cued. Post-orgasmic energy recession's hungering relief umbilicates Mom's Hormel Cookin,' Gooseneck, Wash.'s 5-star truckstop cafe. Gooseneck's sole eatery's excludingly Spammed: menu entrees're unthemely variations flubbing tin-potted hamlike meatness's porky motif. C-rational fleshbacks irrationalize loathsome surplus-quality meals. Meatpacker tie-ins ameliorate budgetary ligatures strapping rural economies. Pepsico signposts, Millertime clockfaces, Maxwell Coffee-housed "Expresso" sodafountainlike syrupy pumpers bountifully pre-infiltrate Spam's magna carta declaration relegating nonSpam edibles expensively ala-carta (oyster stew, $9.00; Spamhattan clam chowder inimitable Surimi-inspired sidedish Spam-based crabmeat imitations, $1.99).

KC's tollfund changebox, seated crevices yielded some-$7, financing board. Ex-Hannabelle's prolapsed debitcard secured roomy provisionality lasting 2-days, tops; spameaters hungrily inspect bankrolling diners. Rolling's implications confront difficulty: these're big-ass, no-nonsense truckstoppers; unfortified muggers're feebly underpowered.

101's off-highway consignment vanners trafficking moderate freightloads, fresh-cut evergreens, consumable replenishments, maritime shipfittings congregate; Goosenecker's townie contingent (wall-hung javamugs rollcalling Bubbas, Albies, Becky-Sues, Noreens) grumbles com-

95

fortably, lard-armed school-aged waitstaffers refill see-through caffein-ated liquids. Ultrafamiliarity conspires greasemonkeys, bowling alley-cats, beautyshop queenmakers: merchant-classed ranklings. Locals/teamsters alikewise ostracize flagrant vagrancy shabby-assed eloping interlopers personify. Appearance-wise, deskclerk-married newlyweds're amphetamine injectors gate-crashing Mormon church ceremony—needles, tourniquets handy.

Antipersonal biases thickeningly insulate hotwirers attempting interpersonal highjackings. Fumble-fingered pickpockets, stuttering double-talkers, deaf safecrackers bear cognate handicaps.

Agreeably renamed, Matt/Margie digest lunchmeatloaf viands. Happy-faced Spamfest begins fitting-in's arduous strain. Unsophistication's imitation bumpkin glee pries incredible saccharine smirks fighting ironicism's true comical gravitation. Mini-dimensional gargoyles haunt Hormel's wholesomely re-institutionalized dinner. Creepy homogenation attempts hyperbolize alienation's weirdness.

Nervous servers, roadies, yokels ogle odd couple's antics. Margarite's softboiled eggshell sensitivity quavers. Chicken Little's fable hovers ominous, foully flavoring by-producted porcine succulence.

"Dessert?" entombed yellow-beaded cream toppings're mentioned, rotting withinside plexiglass coolers walling counterbacked recesses.

"Spam?" Maggie unhumorously previews pies' gelatinous sheens.

Overreacted giggling irradiates contagiously. Meatheaded cartoon-drawn visualizations romp, defacing plainness's prosaic physiognomies. Lunchmeat treatments reproduce Mom-style cooking's venue: oblong-legged aluminum can-cans' keystyle peeltops kick highroad gastronomies, espouse you-are-what-you-eat proverb's hallucinated exactitude.

"Mealticket, 'fyaplease; dessert'll wait," neutrally negotiates extrication.

"Yeah, raincheck," sarcastically neutralizes rudimentary signal ploying antennaed goodwill.

Sarcasm's bare-assed embarrassment, reversely, dispossesses truculence's baggage. Nastiness ventilates niceness's constipated intestines. Farting's safety-valved mechanism diverts head-butted intersection. Tipping vanquishes ignorance-based resentments, reinstates subservience's mightier hatreds enthroning royal patrons overlording serfly underclasses.

Roadside America's Goosenecked outpost resonates melting-potted piety's slapstickly hurled rebuff. Inhabitants/itinerants unifiably detest non-allied antagonistic stragglers, ethnicity's aberrants, politically accusable red-ants. Progressive attributed differences conserve innermost friendliness. Minimized toleration balefully swears democracy's hypocritic oath, witch-doctoring voodoo's dolled-up economical adulation.

Countrified isolation's quiet peace hereaway transmigrates: geese honk, crowbar martial art fledglings caution, mockingbirds Carusofy C&W-tweetered Twitties, blackbirds underplay blues riffs' bass-thumped countercultural sanctuaries. Nighthawking sedan drugstores swooping lowkeyed circuitous glides enjoy wildlife refuge? Pimpmobiles, flockwise, safeguard chicks.

"Armybase anyplace?" figures Matty.

"Nope. Less'ya reckon th'corps engineers."

Channel dredgers headquartered upriver inspire sugarplum envisionings intercasting intercoastal waterage maintenances, pansexual passageway indulgences. Mudsuckers tirelessly hydrolyzing sludged bottoms, wetlanders daffily ducking self-involved irregulations, soldiers deliriously obeying dominitrixed ordure menagerate unbelievable zoos.

Truer zoography describes plainer species' off-hour rutting. Overused teenyboppers satisfy menstruation-crazed banshees (whore-whooping screamers headdressing bloodstained bedpads), blowjob-prone passivists (laidback dozers reinventing foredone erections), two-fisted batterers (hapless impotentates sublimating sex's sublimation). Whippoorwill's unWillin transactresses glumly persevere.

97

Protoviolent assembly-lined lubricity utterly depresses newlybedded M&M. Invisible atrocities stereophonically agitate tympanic eardrum-thin drywalls. Arm-in-arm, leg-wrapped embracers shiver. Dully slapped fleshy pulp's flattened thuds spank fucking asses, assess toll-taken pleasure, accessorize fetishistically fucked-up playboy playpens.

Microcosmic earthy frights audibly fingerpaint thickening underworld, index smalltown biota's withering, soul-sucking, intoxicant Americana pandemania. Vices're joylessly expended. Crimes're uncommittally punished, amoral decisive counterpunch retributions outslugging/correcting law-forced correction squads' corruptable predilections. Gunbattles reveling stylishly postmodernized duels use Uzis; sprayful airings pepper hollow-point reminders.

Venetian blind glimpsers recheck outside's commotion. Uniformed deputies cruise soporifically, coming unalarmed, nodding unblinked winks. Respectful panderers, pharmacists tone-down raucous wheelering; unhit marksmen condescendingly lower barrels, superficially hurt duelists pretend wellness. Somnambulant badgemen totter door-to-door, dreamily soliciting bribes. Office-#1-#2, doorway-pilloried tooth fairies submit underpillowed tributes; manifestly toothless sandbaggers collect.

#3's recalcitrant responding innervates antinarcoleptic transformation. Forty-fours withdrawn, wakening deadeyes spring sidewards following seriously repeated portal panel pounding. Unmet gunfires encourage kick-in followthroughs. Blueshirts collaring ringnecked residents mounts Whipperwill Theater's courtyard footlights. Feathery scruffians flop unsatisfactorially, slipping uppercuts, haymaker crosses Gooseneckburg's Finest properly contrives. Uncontributing delinquents're hobnailed, steel-toed, shit-heeled, drop-kicked, outlastly soled.

#4's wanton contributions sycophantically coddle policemen's balls. Teenysloppers butter coppers, spreading heart-stopping lipstuck pouts.

"C'min, sugardaddy," sweetly proposes delay's just desserts.

Lardass badgers' stooped consent buys time. Unfunded retreaters defenestrate bathrooms, plopping atop detrital mulch typically moating man's homeless castle motels. Mushily rubber-padded squishing engulfs ankle-deep landers marvelously bypassing jagged bottlenosed smither-ines, punctiliously side-stepped hypodermics, asbestos dustbins, cereal-box garnets, sapphires, jades ringing disengagement fling outflungs.

Verminous drunken bloat slitherers, human-skinned, rustle leafy un-dergrowths exfoliating septic fen untanking wayfarers' flush aftermaths. Lagoon creatures blackly flounder, hesitating, backwardly eyeballing pin-pricked lightsome orgasmified amplification beaming gumshoes emit.

Head-started leeways're gratifiably sufficient. Billyclub goatish rous-ters resurge percussive roundelays, drumming doors/banging whores. Nondrug dealers by-stand innocently, petaling plenteous overcover vice-squad centurions' paths, endow moolah, cheers, encomious reassur-ances.

Reassuredly, rusticity's openhanded graft sodomly sanctifies rawness's virtuous honesty. Anti-city's unsophisticated nature-stripping bare-ass celebrations aggregate fervid followings.

Illegality's sanction accommodatingly disturbs, prodding movement's impetus. Law exists, understrutting grammatic disorders, unexamined self-indulgences; underpinioning swiveled collusions, alluded pseudo-sciences, physically/syntactically positing effects; overweeningly, nullify-ing lawmakers' bill-passed achievements, zealots' religious superstitions, humanists' worthiest idealizations.

Commonlaw newlywed couplers prowl bumpercars untrailing tincan charivari (alarm-systemed nuisances). Antediluvian Studebakers, stellar relic Jetstars, innumerable Fairlane 500s seep crankcased tar pit miring Gooseburg.

"Volkswagen bug," Marge slightly updates time-machined dial.

Jump-started push reanimates cantankerously anthropomorphized puttering, motorized coughing wheezes. Air-cooled breeze impelling, es-capists're going south.

2

BALMY PALMS, BOUGAINVILLAEA, hummingbirds, lime/cerrano-spiced braziered turtle fillets; slashburnt extrafoliate growths tinging rotten animals, dungs; encantadores bandstanding full-frontal lewdity afore leering mariachis; porchsitter expatriates dabble picturesquely, interiorizing high-noted cantina sonata futilisms soulfully essayed after scrubbing peons worked furiously, earning centavos/hour buffing seats whereon pawnbrokered excellencies preside: Mexico.

Everafter happyhour by-the-sea, derived paradise's third-world dangerbait vivacity, Banco Palenque's mañana pregunta policia exchanging dolares/pesos, Amerotrash filching squatters' shucked snakeskins (Protestant ethic's south-gone conclusion) define narrowly spectrographed charge-carded lightfoot brigade.

Matteo/Margarita emigrated Estados Unidos toting coined moneybags: sacks bundling small-billed big-change conversion totaling $16,574.25. Lowtech coinslot buggering screw-drove wrenched laundromat strongboxes, sodapop dispensers, newspapers' vendomatics, parking's metered plenitude. Intensive caretaking hospitably monitored arrestment authority's side-effectiveness counterindicating pettily self-administered proactive mendications. Proscribed cautionary doses, everlastingly repeatable, counseled moderated (negligible) amount-taking; nickling/diming, immediately perceivable, demurred. Longview's warren beavertowns meagerly outskirted Multnomah's richer tenderloin. Immoderate midcity pry-by-night crowbarring gouged pawns' ransom, multipically. Salem's, Eugene's, Roseburg's Greyhound-stopping destinations handed outgone grabbed smashes presupposing Frisco's golden-stated Fargowellian bonanza.

Southbay metropolises anteed mintfresh pots, folded; unseen bluffers bumped, ran (rambler gambler metaphor sinks: subway turnstile slotsuckers legitimately represent meter-eater ancestors). Densening populaces, overburdened coffers hastened retirement's hasta luego. Disemboweling pilfered meters, piggybanks, etslotera became dangerously high-profile. Lone-car lowlifers "repairing" ripped-off coinmachine cachets spectacularly inhabited suburbanite asphalt-grounded nouveau Hoovervilles. Imminently roustable nomads (borrowing autos less permission, no-less) boarded Ventura-Tijuana express.

Connecting busses, boats deposited unreturnables here.

Expat bottleneck teethers blow one-note ballad rephrasing pastime triumph earning'em paradisiacal rested roosts. Cheap alcohol, metalingualism's floozy exotica (bar-Spanish's incoherently wise communicability), heat's crucible pretention annealing/healing tropical cancers, communalize non-Mexican Americans culturally adapting. Surly enthusiasm participates, employing underbar's tile-lined urination trough.

Yellowy trickles supplement regaled exploitations, "authenticating" grittily vivid autobiographers' legerdemain. Bladder-venting mailfraud tycoon relieves relived scam bamboozling writers: on-line lit.agt.com guaranteeing cyber representation (1500-word sample/outline/query). Saphead creators disbursed $90/pop, praying telecom lit-air connection'd remunerate book contract.

"Dreams're powerful commodities," rattles, tucks, zips.

"Kids're dreamier marks," pyramiding powerbroker unzips, pees disconcertingly browned emissions.

Subadult specializing dangled unmailable irresistables advertised comically (colorful back-cover marvels): cuddly animate pandas, battery-driven subcompact crocodiles, freeze-dried granulated ballfields (displayed backstops, outfield fences), magic beans genetically redirected (stalk's height-attainment considerations paramount), likewide broadside fairy tale appropriating.

"Childsplay," dribbly wangler reminisces.

Ex-embezzlers natter circumspectly. Caution's disciplined practitioners shun publicly pubic-aired drainings' pissing contest. Bookkeeper starchcollar miscreants're typecast: wirerim eyeglasses, pencilneck bone-structured snapable twigishness, bleach-white skins.

Whitesuited Graham Greene's gangrenous rotters' spoiled wastrel intellectualized deteriorations automythologically self-destruct. Eurotrash element colloidally suspends drifted state-asiders; nonwhite unassimilated inert gassers panracially imbue globally atmospherical steady-state unsteadiness's everpresent entropy. Alienly, Mexicans're absent. Portuguese (Brazilian?) barmen Ethiopian (Sudanese?) helpmates operate Emiliano's (Zapata?).

Revolution-wary mannerism intersperses spicy dangers foreigners partake. Comfortingly distanced Chiapas uprisers confer excitement resettling demobilized mercenary sympathizers parasitically suck. Blase know-it-alls gloat conceptions natives repudiate. Easetaken liberty slights hard-working campesinos' constrained lives.

Opportunistically, mestizos mix therewith exiles. Jewel-eyed tradesmen selling sparkly gambits enchant retirement colony grifters. English-spoken pitches're perfectly melodious, serenading crook audience. Recidivist infomercials loop eternity's anteroom; pissed-out boasters relax, bask, soak indoors.

OUTER PASSERS TRUDGE, lade head-topped oxloads/ shoulder-lugged pick-axes, forepacking papooses, trailing recycled fragments. Demipaved dust-mortared cobbles, trodden limitlessly flatter, rumple thoroughfares. Wheelbased bobblers span potholes; walkers, livestock overstep unended rockiness. Free-range cows steer maneuvers Tauruses, Matadors accomplish, dodging collisions. Bouncy hubbub generates panoramic dance, loosening Emilio's cantina-framed viewfinders. Saline zephyr proxies (legend-affirming Chihuahua-sized ships' bubonic plague envoys) reassertively undulate impulses associating persistent rhythms.

Retrograde tourist-traded amenities aslide, Puerta Piedra's naturemade, bouldered seaport facilitates military-industrial complex. Briefcase bustlers ministering aboveground ventures parley, blueprints unfurled. Khaki-clad brigadiers subsidiate militant cadres enforcing castes. Sumptuous papist stained-glass windowdressings bless Cortez descendants; pre-Catholic descendants're impecuniously excommunicated, revitalizing race-based allegiances tourists exploit: indios trabajan abajo blancos/darkers subserve whiters.

Tourist class's superimpositions, counterproductively, fuzz clear-lined interracial comprehensions. Moneybagged slummer scumlords herewithal invalidate mastery's light-skinned indices. Ex-victimizers' renounced potence, slavering decrepitude, ennervated coasting frenzies discredit self-respect. Befuddled go-getters imagining themselves-as-barflies? Whimsical. Potencies' renunciations liably goad loanshark instincts, interesting quick-buck capitalistas, appeasing counterrevolutionary strategistas. Flabby northerners're calf society bilk-fed veal underfed feeders'll assuredly devour.

Laguna beach shanties rented inexpensively instate sprall-to-sprall premature retirees (100-foot cliff overlooms surfside beachfront's nonexistence). Stagnant quarter waterholed mosquito hatchery houses exotically smitten alcoholics. Pole-hung bedding, rattan roofs, air-walled unleaning lean-tos coordinate derangements suggesting pulpy tropicana concentrates: essences mendacious Hollywooded revel-reel grovel planted, rooted, fertilized. Substantially reinterpreted malarial precognitions exonerate morning-after dts.

Roving tame boars swallowing dysentereal cornmeal feces aversively heighten libidinous participations. Nightfallen dark's impenetrability secretes glandestine handiwork; disease's omnipotent bogey unmans cunnilinguist predilection. Foreplayed orgasms verbalize kissing's unspoken terms renegotiating sporadic condom-coated dogstyled spooning. Birth-controlled, voyeur-wary, hepatitis-fearing lovemakers experience Richter-scaled joys.

Colonial sentimentality avails idle whiling. Hobbies refresh drunkards' tapas/tequila fornication regimens: cockfighter winetasting, cockroach polo, liars' knock rummy, contender remembrance conditioning aerobics hyperventilations, rumor edification, esteem demolitions. Lagoonside living's aquarium tank smallness chafes larger fishes. Relentless nonprivacy fosters vehemently guarded isolations. Any tourbus-driven gallivanter who's stopped gallivanting resents nonstop fellowship's undying imposition; unguidable gallivanters individualistically dislike socio-structural regimentation.

Margarita's/Matteo's courtly sojourn adjourns. Indolence recirculates Warhol's cagey sameness; sunbathing's cultivational boon pales, passivity activates dissatisfied schemers. Moreoverhead, slot jackpots prudently safe-deposited erode interest-free. Indefinite finite pesos/mesas equity equation calculates limited obliviousness. Shrewdness'd favor investing multi-thousands efficaciously, bravely executing do-or-die coup.

Acquisition's sneaking emergency motivating alertness, newcomers scan outskirting territories/influxing dealbrokers. Harshly precipitous escarpments restrict nonsea arrivals. Foreshortened maizefield dogleg plateau airport's elway airstrip accommodates mailplanes, single-engine piper cub flyers, gyro-active vertical takeoffs/landingpads. Conventional roads're, comparative reliability-wise, least usable. Numerous slide upheavals, washouts, machotic wheeling challengers' blind-curved pyres, unmodified schoolbus mechanical default routecomes disconnect Puerta's coast-based population/Mexico's transmountain nation.

Just-arrived bussers uniformly avow by-sea departure's (swimming shark-infested bloodbaths!) preference. Meter-eaters ferried downcoast, port-to-Puerta. Interior terrorizations thereforeign magnify. Scrub-forested ravines redefine Amazon jungles, revolting unsupported macheteers're revitalized Viet Cong, free-market shills're feistier new-breed, can-do entrepreneurs, eighteen-year-old soldiers're crack anti-rabble exterminators.

Conversely, familiarities diminish. Tavernous intemperate depths, layabout morningless afternoons, night-for-day negativeland schematics acquiesce ennui's programmed languor. Miscellaneous retirement-bound bunkminsters fully domesticate yesteryear's wilder hellraisings; incorrigible plurality's retroactive fallbacks hustle irredeemable bibelot cons. Schlock heirlooms' pawnshop hawkers buy-and-large recant noncommercial conversant English, authorizing exclusive blowhard tradewind modes where/whenever expats communicate. Benevolent host-country representatives, additively, lubricate high-octane bond performance productivities, well-oiled wildcat strikes.

Seasided tranquility disfavors civilized capital; tranquility's allover worthlessness endorses moneymaking's venal churn. Vulgar denominators allow commonly misconceived idealization entrusting noblest obligible explanations surrounding, e.g., crated armory-shipped freight.

Stenciled lettering quadrilingually prohibits prying child-sized coffinshaped crates carted docks-to-underground warehouse. Mangy illiterate burros asservatively obey Span/Eng/Frn/Esp provisos warding off-limited curiosity surmising harnessed burdens. Glaring teamster riflemen deflect gnats, queries. Nightfall's mysterious freighting obviates Puer.Pied.'s strategic beachhead, poleconomically plotting: covert battlefield tactics're germane, businesswise; counterrevolutionarily, armaments shipments're rational.

Armed sentry mulepullers bringing boxed supplies 0100–0300 hrs? Adventurism's imperatives demand action-packed probabilities.

EMBEZZLING BOOKKEEPERS VANISH. None's encountered Emil's bespectacled lookalike heterosexuals anywheres. Ultracircumspect non-disruptive mildly disposed Tecate sippers exemplified restraint's virtues contrasting loutish bargoers' pee-for-all yellowingly bellowed advices. Uncommonest kidnap disappearance's candidates inactively pursued nonelection. Grudgeless/smudgeless, undisliked squeaky-clean nebbishes peregrinated inoffensively, abided prudence's calibrated aplomb. Wan neutrality goaded bully charging? Officials're unsure.

Spotless vacated adobe bungalow containing left-behinds (unbreakfasted jam-daubed tortillas) drops trifling clues. Untidy place-set crumbs starkly underline immediacy's desertion.

Cautious inquiry courteously accosts travel-classed jetless setters. Caterwauling dipsomaniacs intercontradict, bewildering P.P.'s subfederale lawman investigating misplaced pursers (bank-accounted "purses" mandating searches "person" misplacements uninspire). Last-seen recollections designate matched pair adjoining saloon's sidebar, lagoon's sandbar, preMayan runes' jaguar tableted altar barbarisms glyphing feline gods (Rockportown's "authentic" touristy concession's fed Kodak bearers, codex seekers, hoax accepters). Archeological curiosities've abetted muggers targeting Norteamericanos? Isolatable crimewave surfers're smoothly explained.

Formalities net usual suspects, sparing truthfully dubious thuggery contingents (deathsquad triggerfish, shark-eyed federales, cocaine warlord barracudas, baleen-joweled whalebellied Señor Grandes). Weeklong flamboyant roustings culminate: decrees legalizing liquidational assumption's sidewalk-dumped dispossessing acquit cottage landlord's repossessing.

Recyclic fishiness exhumes shallow-graved yardsale's freeboot condolences: doled inconsequentials raise prized possession nominations. Ensconced nextdoor well-off merchandizing burghers impugn leasers' individual effects're unexpectedly shabby. Flintstones bathsink plastics rinser cups matching Deputy Dawg toothbrushes, uncloseted Howard Johnson, Hilton, Marriot linen, fourteen isomodal britches/shirtsleeves pastel fatigues, fourteen-hundred generic paperback novels diversifying wondrously categorical realms allot 90+% pictorial coverings' unashamed raunch detritus (remaindering sub-10% manifest "literary" fiction Richard Ford-type genrealists somberly campaigned).

Depth-charged submarines jettisoned likesuch expendables, countermoving destroyers surmounting silence's sinking desperation. Oilslicked puzzle pieces gulled airhead commodores, film-historically, faking implosive aftermath's buoyant accretions.

Correlationally, bookkeepers've "inadvertently" bequeathed nonvaluable mattress stuffings. Optimistic viewers hypothesize traditional deceased fakery gambit's scamming insurers; pessimists ascertain blacker industriousness: gringo-farmed harvesting reaps transplanted, vegitatively cultivated green-goers. Failing fiscal convertibility, poorer foreigners're well-marinated burrito fillings.

Wackiest clarifiers oversimplify CIA-tied intelligences coordinating Dows Jones/Chemical, governments DC/DF, bankers Swiss, Columbian, Colombian trilaterally commissioning cabalistic cartels. Howfarever stretched, conspirings' expressive prototypes scream primal alienation. Interfactionalized networking (joining conspiracies) deftly parries mistrust's thrusts.

Conspiracy tailors sew coats Marga tries ontologically; Mate shreds.

Undeclared warbuddy systemic circulation conducts booze-plasmed corpuscles, platelets, hemoglobic hobgoblins cohabiting travel circuit vein. Affinities enlinking westside Euros/northside Ameros integrate effortlessly, English-literate Europeans flourish unsmirking benevolence. Transborder meso-american integrations enlist trickier affinity.

Loyalty's double-edged lacerating proficiency imperils indifferent conversing's noncommittality. Mexicans are infamous, puritans warn: admitting slightest kindnesses indebtedly obliges receiver; exhaustion customarily terminates reciprocity's rally. Puritan bookkeepers're indisposed, nonloyalty's warners overrule.

Irrevelantly coincidental, Christmastime yulery redecorates pueblo storefrontings, circles, squares. Life-sized holyland figurines hovering angelic clay-footed literalities proactively disapprove Catholic-sensitive mass souls conniving devilish enrichments. Deer-eyed wisemen eternally lugging fakeincense goldlike myrrh, dickless Josephs embodying unctuous patience's sublimated goodness, weary Marys' billboarded highways beatifying iconography's swath, swaddled Jesuses implacably winding crucifixion's 33-year clock habituate seasonal installations.

Evergreen boughs, tinsels, multicolored bulbs, glittery garlands, nonreligious ornaments lurk intangibly commemorated, haunting northerners' horrible nostalgic Christmas recalls. Religion overkill cherubically displaces commercialized sprawl's X-mas extravaganza. Displaying creches sell Christlers lot-to-lot. Divertable reassurers consecrate firstcomer's birthday, celebrating seasonably invoked merriness's readymade suave introduction.

"Hosanna amigos," white-suited Panama hatter pronounces H latinate j-style, sprinkling automaton genuflections blessing deals.

"Esplanada Emperador, splendor's doorstep beheld!" condenses pitch. Raoul Lopez Saavedra (call-me-Sal) Salamanca glorifies Jersey's boardwalk aestheticism tempering Arizona's mallstyle sensibility. Messianic trumped-up renovations're blueprinted, succeed Atlantic City Monopoly-boardgame community "salvage's" savaged rite.

Construction projections proliferate, RLSS discloses, asserting self-interested anti-social engineering brainstorm: esplanade's interaction privatizes public-utilized space's eminent domain. Investment-backed streetwalk utilities covenant's unloseable proposition ensures, minuscully, 20%-returned emolument. Civilly bondable splatless netfalls catch highwire investment dancers. Raoul's co-conspirators Jaime, Alberto disemphasize downsides, extrapolate "humble" input quadruplings.

Unflinching nativity yes-men wisely concur: streetway's beautifications outperform civic-improved neatening, attain capital-c Civilizing's Mayan grandeur.

Unimpressed prospective anteers bluff polite amazements. State-supported "bondability's" disasters've retranslated "Mexican stand-off." Pre-Colombian magnificence revering architectural genius, Christiandom's borrowed myths juxtaposing sacrificial compassion, help-yourself ethic, downrighteous ubiquitousness finger pitchmen's screwball deliveries.

Unholy allied agendas underlie noble symbolisms; presigning parties accede investors're entitled absolute personable nonliability. Bodily harm's implicitness nonexplicitly diagrammed, prudent appreciators unerringly note syndication joining's life-insured policy inkling.

Handshake contractors pledging undying's support? Yule regrets're discourteous, ephemeral; commerce ascensions ungroundable.

COCKATOO COCK-A-DOODLE-DOOS prematinally sere-
nade sleepers' erupted slumber. Squawking critters codafy orchestrally
resonant monotonic reverberations radiating overtured explosive boom.
Chattering monkeys, undeafenable vipers, aired-out birds, agitated arach-
nids, angry pumas waver. Copse copers copacetically reassume entropical
nocturnes; townspeople reassuming blast's topical basis reenact animal-
sounded chattered agitation.

"Unanswered. Whew," Marg's guessing reckons effective ambush over-
threw guerilla battle's ongoing embranglement.

"Innocuous propane wagon veered off-trail?" second-guesses mule-
team story covering night-shipped shuttles lading rifle-boxed cargos ship-
to-shore, coast-to-crest: mountain top-secret chalet spa-tacular resort
constructions.

Scuttlebutting kibitzers've decided hilltop's earthmoving entails
bunker emplacement, radar's towers, aircraft carrier-scale flightdeck
airstripping. Double-timed schedule validates leery summations; hearsay
gainsays guerillas aren't blamed whenas order's ruptured.

Heardsaid calculations (government-provided) enlarge foes' rude mul-
titude, inflating forces' farcical proportion. Sandinista-armed (uninten-
tional humor) troops're putatively frenzied. Cocaleaf chaws glazing per-
ceptions (denecessitating food's intake), heartripper heathens stalk
whiter-skinned breasts (unabashed Roger Corman B-movie poster throw-
backs resuscitate "laughable" racist exploitabilities). Concurrent slanders
suspeciously subclassify indigenus indigents: bipedic cacomixtles, capy-
bara-sized pests deserving extermination. Propaganda's backlash uplift-
ing downtrodden rebels, journeying's sophist sophisticates disbelieve ac-
commodators.

Dawning heralds tribulation. Internationalized impacts're ambas-
sadorably factored, superseding localcified Amero/Euro antiheroes: out-
erworld legitimacy's courtship recruits credibility's spokespersons. Day-

light's recon patrol, accordingly, solicits nonadvisory accompanyists, ambulant eyeballs' verifying simpatico linguistics. Opinionating's niceness poises sturdily apedestal bribery, torture.

Presupposed witnesses'll impart lamest governmental crutch upraising insuperable spin-doctored splints. Passably undrunk, nonstupid photogenic attesters're sifted; diplomacy's militants select us.

Heterosexualized quasi-married journeyers disrepresent subtropical bums' mercenarially loose attestations; imagewise, personification's norms asseverate rectitude's rectally wiped godliness. Typifiable Joe/Jane Doe compose well-framed reaction soundbites, eyeblinks (thoughtfully edited) thereupon sighting flamethrower's charcobroiled DOAS.

Curious onlookers'd broaden ingratiation's bases (befriending troopers), advantageously utilize soldier-escorted treescape hike. Non-combat beholder hostages shielding counterinsurrectionists squelch ambushes? Neck-strapped cameras, PRENSA armbands, tape recorders crudely disguise arguable CIA agents.

PR-savvy rebels're vaunted photo opportunists. Dour dispatches preeulogizing postMaya plights've swerved figurehead opinion trendsetters (Unsurprisingly, wire-serviced rewrites forefronting sexy masked subcommandante's sublime manipulative skills've overlaid contentious substance tagging first-world's market-driven economic generators remotely culpable; contemptible destitution's groovy ickiness's harmoniously underplayed). Propagandic propagations soothingly organize designated observers. Obvious correspondent get-ups deter massacres.

"Kidnapping, though's, goddamned imaginable," involuntered unison's realizers declaim.

Loinclothed blowgun sharpshooters cuarefully acupunctural tranquilizations medicate infantrymen's necks, jungle-rotted illogic depicts, saving whore correspondents. Scrubbier terrains uncovering thin-stemmed, frill-leafed scraggly plantlife biotically offsets bushwacking's eventuality.

115

Oddlot sere-suckered fenlands effloresce concentratedly honeymade blossoms, cattails, sealevel ditchwater evaporations. Elevation's initial upswing gains lessen floral vicissitude: right-o-way cleansings've burned measliest weeds. Improvisional dumping grounds've encroached backwoods, prestaging bulldozered internment. Wooded areas've recessed, outwearing schoolyard playfields: sunbaked clays propel rocketing sandlot dirt-colored grounders futuristic shortstops glove astrodynamically.

Oblivious ballplayers disregard outsetting gunners, notwithstaring single-filed singularity: jeans-clad, long-haired gringa walking point. Redyed blonde's gentleman-preferred homage duplicitously flags truce's whitish announcement. Entranced gentlemen's preferencial urges chaperon chastely, war-zoned impendability uprooting erogenous zone-outs.

Humped middles m-form double-laned integrity's differential-tickling byway, stranding lowriders. Treadworn ruttings carve flashflooded flumes? Deepeningly concave demitunnels envelop wide-axeled wheels, encumber narrow-swung footsoldier gaits' toe/heel placement. Hiking's tense casual teeter hereinline congas disconnectedly, dejectedly. Dominant-chorded uncaged birdcall screeches defy musicality's acculturated traditions; adulterated modernistic strains're silenced, unlistenable, unavoided.

Tromped bootfalls disrupt fear's reveries. Divers gravel crunches frightful resonances broadcasting advancer troops' invading residences indians've frantically reconciled. Subplatoon's inadequate number (thirteen-fifteen, counting commentators) bespeaks machismo's deadliest self-delusion: plucky cocksure gunslingers'll shred superior strength (inferior-armed) mulchtitudes, choppers ablaze. Revisioned technologistics postulate Gatling gunner's heyday, ignoring technological warfare's Vietnam.

Hostility unfoldings comprehended, observation's sighters surmise unbanked hairpin turns sport memorials enrolling roadkills. Dismissive guardrails, slippery stones, unilluminated treacheries enable unaided disasters aplenty. Ravines're lousy accident sepulchers decomposing automotive bodies, nonsurvivors' skeletons.

Skidmarks ahead predicate latter ruin. Unboobytrapped placidity surrounds vistapoint's takeoff ramp. Fanning reconnoiterers adroitly investigate talus, overhangs, rock-formed foxholes; depleted cartridges're unevident. Towing livestocks' dead-reckoned mistaken veer puzzles cliffside piecers addressing ostensibly straightforward plunge. Suicidal beasts disprove Camus Sisyphean mythic psychology theories carting happiness's repetitive ponderosity? Blindered oxheaded mules wouldn't've obeyed skywalker dictate.

Snoozing wheelmen, hypothetically, classify countless accidents. Truck-driven overtness obtrudes: skidding denotes motored transport's one-man van.

Canopied brilliant mottling shimmies interglimpsed breeze-gusted guesses reconfabulating chrome fenders, camouclad trailor tarp, tractor-cab outlines. Waterlike warp magnifies, distorts, wiggles envisioned thoughts. Upwafted pungencies windicate ranker opinions exhuming crash's recency: metallish burn-outs barbecuing pork's homine menu-substituted entree, sauced flambe crankcase grappa, radiator muscatel.

"Bueno. Está bien," Capitán Morales benedicts, genuflects, writes-off loss jotting shorthand squiggles. Palm-sized notebook officially chronicles shrugging's yawn. "Accidente," mouths condescending transcultural communique.

"No-wayo," Señora controverts exiting's hastiness. Undiplomatic blurt smothering acceptance's tiniest sliver, apologizer backpedals. Accident's certain; cause's investigable.

Precedented communicational smoothness roughens. Sign-languaged simplicities affront untutorable readers. Reshouldering gunstraps, soldiers'd advocate unforced withdrawal, football pick-up games, rattlesnake rodeos: whatever'd waive instituting rappelling's noosed let-down.

"Hay ropas," gringa's argument confuses ropes/clothes, pointing. Hemp lifeline adorning corpsman's waist lolls.

Chastity besieged, manhandled muchacho unbelts, blushing. Undaunted humanity's right watcher anchors herself-to-boulder, knotting sailor-hitched sheepsheads. Embarrassed spotter caballeros skulk "helpfully," eyeing overage gymnast's unparalleled barnstorming bravery.

Wildlife's creepiest distractions're cold-blooded day-sleepers; centipedes, tarantulas, ornerier insects prod cusswords interjecting one-lined observations. Nonsensical description rephrases jumbled verisimilitude validating military's apathetic decisiveness: basically, chaos prevails.

"Boxes're intact. Confetti's ashes, papered gunk, upholstered foam . . . ," rummages distractedly, ". . . most's grassy strawlike twigs. Hey!"

Frightened shout reroutes monotone's levelheaded cataloguer.

"Ayúdame! Arriba!"

RIVERSIDE ANGLERS COMPREHEND. Bottom-fished irregularities regularly snagging sinkered monofilaments, fishers unvaliantly cut loss-leadered hopelessness. Analogistics cast air-as-water, Margarita-as-bait, crashsite-as-shipwreck; rescue upsets analogical supremacy. Cut-and-run ethics'd eminently appease impatient worm-hookers.

Followthrough's resumption disjoins tangled angleworm lineage: metaphorically unleashed civilian rescuer shinnies hand-under-hand. Clifftop grumblers gripe soldiered protests regimenting picayune misapprehensions, pissant dispossessions, peevish bereavements (utterably commonplace dogfaces' whimpers). Cptn. Morales's begrudged permit feels terribly expirable.

"Diez minutos," synchronizes ten-fingered gesticulation.

Dysentery dieting's lightened weight assists athletic descent; weakness debars climbed return's ascent. Disarmed emusculation, uncoordinated lower-bodied flailing forsakes descender "expecting" top-based pullers' furtherance. Jaggedly obtrusive limb-boughs crackle awakening constrictors; de-nested hornets marshal apian requital. Critical apers shriek jeers reviewing fellow-simian's inelegance. Perspiration slickens rope-burnt armpit, palm.

"Lookout!" reasserts buddy's evenheaded propinquity: directly eyelevel, four-foot nonvenomous snake verminizer gauges fruitless prey's unswallowability.

Conversive realization bedevils rappelled conquistadors: sizable snakes'll congenially feed starved subcanopy wanderers. Slow-mo fleetness, bulked meatiness, unharmful retaliative endowment (biting's tenable tetanus?) provision succulent herpetological banquets.

Fright reintegratedly matures; dread's convoluted adulterations quicken downfall's survivors. Two-hundred-foot drop parting highland/lowland hemispheres, netherworlders acclimate. High-spirited sniggering Capitan's injunction unfastens top's anchored rope, unsnagging ambiguity's diplomatics. Riddanced observers're militarily advised (rapidamente) illusory short-cut's divined underground rivulet trickling ever-seaward. Subterranean-streamed pathways intercarve rocky crags outgushing perilous cascades: amidcliff oversea.

Dead-ended multiplex false escapes deride leisurely venturing (prehenceforth, honestly, gringos believed abandonment's prank halfway frivolous; subsequences shortly deteriorated conjoint disposition, reinstated survival's snake-eating prospect).

Primevally, forest's floorwalkers celebrated noninjurious concurrence, valued uncommon vegitation. Transfoliate lucent green-aired lusters speckled goldening skyward dusts. Smoldering's smelliness waned, humus's putrescent sweetness reclaimed rot's overruling irresistibility. Strewn-about unsalvaged valuables richly spawned fortune pandemoniums.

Match-struck flame's torchlight longevity suffocated aspiration. Strandees precipitously've apprehended apprehensive justifications.

Unimmolated curios dispel oppressive misgiven moods twining armament-potential/abandonment-consequential. Surreality's figure-five-in-gold hangs improbably; no.s 6/7/8 . . . integerate ferns supernumerating hung five's operatically unnatural ostentation. Shimmery colorfield broadcloths palpitate black-lined ordinal definitions; clarity's contextual aberrations dare preconditioned responsiveness misidentifying numerals' original sign.

Blatant cognizance jars reflexive recognizing's flash floodlight illumination. Corroborative clues're unnerveningly openable: deslatted crating peels eyeful fillers intricately demonstrating ferruled phalanges, greasefitted bearings, bolted assemblies ratcheting flywheel-housed mechanisms interconnecting puzzlingly wreck-recrated powerpacks. Piecemeal interrelationships appetize observant feasters. Components'd construct wheeled contraption extending dozen-plus meterwidths?

Munitions're—thank god? explosion? scavengers? preemptive off-loading?—disapparent. Devastation's concentricity combined tanked gas's nearer vicinities, backdrafted trailer foredooming cab's inhabitant. Protoplasm's cataclysmic cosmosis conflagrantly absorbing ID-able tissue, bystanding investigators breathe exquisite corpse carbonic macerations.

Tubercular entertainments repel ashen sifters. Enigmas clouding non-military payloads, indigenous discontentedness, endurance's demands— oxygen-mixed medium's very breathability motivates deserting crash-sited grave.

Outbound vector singlemindedly arrows upward mobility's yen. Reattaining highway's high-ground asylum overshadows dusky spelunkering's downstreamed cavils coiling anacondal threats.

121

FLEETING SUNLIT PASSAGE WANES. Macheteless hackers encounter thorny shrubs, submerging mucks, impassable dreamscapes' stymied retardations whereabout stepping's customary thoughtlessness backtracks, regroups, inches fro. Kibitzing Linnean cousins hurl ridiculed bombast implying advice's plainest exhortation: up.

Diagonally plottable courses're branched, interlinking near treebase crows' cane-woven nest, farthest sightlined objectives. Vines foster Tarzanian propulsion. Edgar Burroughs, precedent-granted, bows; Calvino's Baron incomparably reigns over forest traveling, cosmodynamic grace tearing limb-from-limb.

"S'only fictional," critiques applying allusional acrobat's circumstance autoreferentially.

"Tarzan traveled Africa, Cosimo coursed Italy's long-gone Holm oaks; ours's considerably tidier: simply scramble here-there."

Mite-infested bark enlivening climbers' ascents, knothole footholds boost shaky launching. Arboreal networks surprisingly extenuate, deviate: multi-directional sturdiness pokes planks ever-outward, infinitely nearing calcular rock-solid cliff-rimming limits. Paradoxical parallaxatives purge converged eventuality's impaction. Preconceived attainments're unrealizable, approached close-up. Foliations "unmistakably" overreaching uplands' ledges flirt, teasingly short-skirting uncrossable gaps substantiating self-attained rescue's mirage.

Aerialist rapidity aptitude amuses hopelorn mopers. Open-air freeways expedite canopy headwayfarers. Sloths, too've, repudiated groundhogging slothfulness, consolidating treed clique's convenient infrastructure overpassing floorlevel's counterproductive slogging. Giant cats (pumatic ocelots, zooming jaguars), regrettably, likeways cherish midtrunk branching's wide openness. Security's overhauled, reprovisioned; portability secures evasiveness's haven.

Reptiles've rivaled wagoneering drinkers' optic parades floating scaled, hallucinated, flicker-tongued regiments. May-daylight crispness reveals multiform untreadable marching footfalls. Claw-footed legless dragons shine brilliantly, blending habitat's mottle. Color's imperious vividity overdoes warning's anthropocentric function: reptilian camouflage sparsely acknowledges tree-climbing apemen's compulsions particularizing fang avoidance. Limb-wrapped snakes're evasionally reclined. Languid serpents' postures conceding proximate passways reinvigorate spry hysteria hindering exhausted droop-off.

Hour-by-hour progress's steadily gobbled peanut effectiveness. Satisfaction's unsatable; quenching effort's unstoppable. Crepuscular dimming hastens flightier high-stepped viper baiting. Diminished upland attainability foreshadows melodramatic curtains.

Nightlife's wilderness intimidates. Creeping bugaboos behoove stick walk railbeam balancers locate trainless pullman berths. Brachiocephalic vocabularies reinstill tree-trapped canopy's anticornucopial choosiness. Vocabulary's selectable superintendences, powerever, jumpstart naturalistic stalling: assume treehouse furniture's undeniably extant? Its existence occurs.

Fullthrown hookrugged parquet flooring upholds easychairs, ottomans, nonworking TV-set dialogues (telepathing unhearable teleplayed reruns), nondysfunctional crystal-set radioplays (marvelous filial-fulfilled happiness loops), pristinely re-upholstered davenports, fraily unreliable coffee-tabled wickers, glowworm elec tricklights novelty-shoplifted lamps preternaturally restituting sealed-in wormy deadness's rebirth illuminations.

Unplumbered basin, commode, shower installation, pipedream modern dwelling's amenity conveniences urbane jungle tromper craves.

Sculptural entirety entirely foreboding sculptor's repossession, flabbergasted admirerers uneasily prognosticate meeting mister masterbuilder. Fragmentary lingual tropes latinizing Anglo-Mayan dialects'll

123

semi-translate feckless apology tautologizing shelter's despondency. Uninvited treehouseguests begin "rest."

Zombified glowwormed chemicals' one-way immersions (beamed intramurally) twinkle starlike creepers' blasely blazed gazes, longingly repicturing Henri Rousseau's amiable predators deliberating campsited shepherd's inedibility. Resounding barrier noise layers hoots, screechified growlings, nickers, woot-woots, Martin Denny's phonographic pleasantries savagely eviscerated, boisterously stereotyped, aimlessly onrunning. Unidentified decayings condense sense-drenched humidity's oppressiveness, hinting deathly availability's monaural fume.

Dozing/safeguarding alternates. Deep sleeping's untenability digresses; matinal sunniness uncovers enwebbed slumberers gorgeously cocooned withinstant spider's silk bag. Reptiles coil, impend, saggily drooping circumspeculative hospitality, bordering striking range's assumption.

Interloped awakeners discuss fix's choices.

"Spiderchow? Scaffold framing!" presupposes extricational deployment. Toxin-toting arachnid, emulating snakes (omitting anacondas), shuns indigestible carnage unbutchered humans'd cater.

"Quickness'll startle those bastards," Marg'rita refers perimeter's flathead venoms; "slowness'll piss this-here hairy mother."

Succinctly calculated, tarantula's unpleasant aftermaths're survivable, scareas nerve-poisoned fer-de-lance vipers're fatally numbing. Undergoing poison innoculations alternatively aims: avoidance's obligatory.

Undetectably nonchalant restricted gentleness guides collectively synchronized exhale. Hoverer's ovipositor quivers, egged spidermites deliver slang-bashed "mother's" defacto functionality. Motherhood's protectionistic instinct supercharges nestbusters' electrifyingly troublesome stasis. Cuddling spiderkeeper custody stroking gestures're dubiously serviceable.

124

Panic's absence suggests humans've accepted wild. Imperceptibly freaking, nature-trapped guests withstand ticklish eggings, churlish herpetine tongue-flicked sensings, impetuous monkeyshines. Contrarily, monkeys're irritated. Undislodged immobility stagnates exciting developments. Bugleless reveille buglers rudely mouth-off acappella arpeggios, intruding intimately. Jounced jumps, whipped prehensile paws bounce spidery apprehensiveness? Mothering's attention refocuses.

Divertably undenied, simian liberator snatches, smacks, devours ourself-made website designer.

INTUITED MISSIVE LINKS full-haired/partially haired af-

filiations traversing lower-ordered spheres whereunto bugs administrate, frogs orate, snakeheads adjudicate. Nimble primate lobbyists scamper chatteringly, relish attenders' accompanied dependence. Evolutional pet/ owner relationships've inverted: limbic athlete primacy Olympics priori-tize pre-evolved primates. Cognition's excellent uselessness basely rele-gates abstract reasoners.

"Th' kingdom Kong, theirs'll become," commentator puns, experienc-ing grateful chagrin.

Virtually perceiving cognitive distancers' leaping measurements, gym-nastically overqualified masters scout springboard branchings' durabili-ties. Featherweight test-piloted exertions underestimate masses exceed-ing thirty pounds. Feathertheless, jumpers're forcibly pushed, reconsid-ering hell-established backtrack's undescendable impasses.

Extremity outposting surest arboretum jump-off contingency pos-sesses inarguable crux: motorbike tire-thick constrictor. Five-foot-plus bough's dweller appraises skeletal monkey physiques' frangible limit. Empirical research's calipered skull-torso jawbone extent predictions? Chatterers yank clumsier bipeds' pantlegs.

"Starving?" redirects gutty slit-eyed determinators.

"Chicken-flavored, supposedly," she-wolf concurs.

Mongrelized weapons're childish liabilities: snap-off tool sharpeningly whittled (peeled) rehearses epithelial puncture's sword swallower act's mishap; blunter thoracic plunger prepares strangulation. Orion's star-crossed sequences discombobulate unearthly snakers' premeditated her-petocide. Retaliating defensiveness's struggled bites' encoilings con-templated, poachers fret abrupt lunging'll throw ourselfmade poise off-balance. Weighing considerable kilograms, kill's subjugation obligates promiscuous shortstop juggler's handiness fielding randily tossed ob-jects.

Unanticipated alacrity reacts contra four-handed assaulting. Limbless flexer's sprung judo entwines objectional gentleman's lefthand forearm, contracts tourniquet's aneurystic clamp.

"S'it feel?"

"Th'opposite. S'numb."

Heaviness deadens swing; smacking whole-armed attacker upside-into barked trunk's retardedly ineffectual. Stoic resignation unblinkingly restrains nonocular orifice vulnerabilities firmly shut.

Acutely poking lidless vitreous humor's lensed retina foreseeably forcing maw's lockjaw, snakecrackers cram suffocators gutward. Hyperextendable gullet capably skips feedings weeks-months; henceforce feeders transfer goatloads. Detachable vegitation's clumped fistfuls, expendable vacant purse, catchable multipede crawlers (venomously potent?) distend stomach's incapacity, internally reconstricting constrictor's chokeholded vise.

Slaughtering's humdrum brutality dejects luncheoneering game-hunters. Disgust overcomes life-threatened anxiety, autonomically twitching offal's mealtime temptation; gaggers finish nauseating ordeal. Disengaging disengorged appendage, winners shuck spoils.

Bush buffet's appetite-suppressant grisliness rededicates arbor evacuators' flying squirrel skydive attempt. Battle-fatigued branch leans enticingly tor-ward. Twentysome leglengths separated, cream-colored underbark exposes fracture endangering crotch's propped soundness. Two-for-one giveway fells supersessional karma? Keatonesque physics again're invokable, faulty branch's swinging defect doubling phenomenal landing jeopardy's culmination.

Daring duo aerialistically tethers imaginary trapeze. Fraudulent fronds substantiate nonexistential greenery's netless freefall. Bough-broken rockabyes, permishaps; stop-action lignite trunk crotches' cradles're ruthlessly turned babywasters, rupturing fluency's inexorable wordy flux.

Falling's pained interruptions presage delayed dying's gruesomely worsened damage. Helplessly hoping, teeth-gnashed undead carrion'd wish foragers nosh postmortally.

"Anda one-anda two-anda . . ." Welkly enrhythms vineless Tarzans' lilt. Squarely disembarking, weightshifters eliminate returnable gravitations. Unfulfillable formfulness graspily splays hyperventilating homosapient skinny blimps.

Graceful flukes fuse, choreographing midair moonwalk's "indecisive" shuffle enjoining backslid nonheadway's ever-onward glide. Downcast glancing's unpermitted distractions undergo atrophied awareness's deprived rigor: psychic blinders disencumber worry-burdened airborne brutes. Hangtime's parabolic hyperbole arches, aplomb's panegyric self-assurance rises; returning's lured inducements attest land's windfallen, undebatably worthwhile bagatelles.

"YEOW! ANTS!"

Formic acid's emissaries systematize flesh-pressed welcome. Shaled handhold firebiters persuade deadfall's alleviation. Zillions pierce long-stung nocuous feelings. Itchless bites're bee-sting intensity. Wasp, scorpion, demi-venomous lizard stings surpass present-sensed unitary injections; colonized collectivity, appendedly, intensifies beyond past-marked singular owies.

Stingings' stun diffuses, paralytically decommissioning mobilization. Toenails-to-scalp, chem-war infantry entrenches, antagonizes enemy invaders.

Retreat's desirabilities defeat meteoric disablement, motivate cartoonish runnings' wheelspun bongodrummed antigravity verticality. Prestomatically, ten-foot gap shortfalling precipice edge's overcome.

Mid-morning's heated bedrock shadelessly oppresses. Prefabricated stoicism transpires; thirst redoubles, water's cloudbound. Treeline moisture rim traversed, hitchhikers re-experience dried-out distress. Waning ant-bitten sufferings emphasize thirst's discomfort.

"Avalanche victims'd exchange urines," leeringly taints despair.

"Near-death, copulation's pandemic," Mara's rejoinder venerates vene-reality.

Chiclet salivary rivers're floods contraposing ourselfishly urinated tricklets. Gum flavors fade; piss's Wycliff Cellars Sauv. Blanc aftertaste lingers. Uro-oral foretaste foreplaying ora-genital lubriciousness, slurpers address Beatle's copyrighted solicitation disrespecting road's propriety. Preorgasmic juices suckle cocksucker/cuntlapper. Live-on-love newly-wed's motto restores, rehabilitates.

Subsistence's behest decides geni-genital missionary procreative stances're wicked. Breeding's instinctive behaviors resist faministic impotences; genilingual responsible drinking replenishes orgasm plasms. Mounting desire's erection preempts provident sipping.

Cuntsequently, snake-choking antsy spiderweb shredders enlink midroad. Dog-styled bonering reinvigorates autorhythmically. Open-hearted vaginal rubbing enraptures sensationally articulate wang pangs. Pricklish sensations parallel vaguest irritants (kneecaps' pebble grinding, throat's sandpaper raspiness, perspiration's dumbfuck folly), delaying gate-popped promptness calling, "They'rrrroff!"

Suborgasmal tremors rumble. Pussyfarts, pricksongs descant. Chalk-scented oysterbeds sweeten lowland's rotted unvultured deaths. Incongruously, vulture roosters spectate live-acted marathoners' copulatory prolongation. Distractors offsetting titillations, indefinity conjectures theoretical truism: deferred comings defer expiration's omniprevalent goings.

Amidwinterday's ream, approacher's gearbox-mashing truculence voyeuristically groans. Uphill, roadhogs pork noting inevitable passive intruder. Hitchhiking tactics-wise, coitus noninterruptus entreats. Destitution straitjackets, contrastingly, dispute pleasure's gratifications: riders riding bareback impurely embody charity's consummate recipients.

Unprinted highwaymanner codebooks deciphered, mates uncouple. Blushed dishevelments characterize sore wanters, recomposing mendicants. Pilgrim fervor's fanaticism catechismically chants akin overwrought ecstasies. Flesh-mortified excesses're decorously mentionable; flesh-gratified excesses unmentionably preferred. Cathoholic binges, everthebless, shame indoctrinated wannabelievers.

Roadie shams're largely nonessential. Lonesome drivers coveting companionship'll unfailingly aid hitchhiker refugees inhabiting out-of-the-way desolations.

Flatbed 12-wheeler fluttering strapped tawny oilskin cover heaves-to. Overheating's smoked puff wispily updrafts; knocking's grimed valves syncopatedly overrun ignition's shut-off. Mechanically enjoined, steaming engineer decabs. Disgust's compromises've plowed brow-beaten furrows sensibly fallowed.

"Qué pasa?" trucker's cheerful hail obliquely ignores stalling's setback. Greeting comment's impassiveness slackens.

"Somos mortificados," somehow's queerly off-putting: "Hiya Buddy, we'all're self-flagellating sufferers. Howza bouta torturous lift?"

Abandonados elucidation's tangentially suspectable: abandonment labels abandoned humankind "outcasts," untouchables decent citizens'd avoid.

Wisest account convinces. Truth-based improvision flaunts adventuristic stupidity's repercussion cymbalizing gringo initiative's gong: unprepared peregrinators got lost. Cantines, sombreros, ponchos, snacks woefully underfilled/omitted, dipsomaniac hallucinators chased chimerical whimsies.

"Aiyayay, borrachos," vindicates sot factoring's zany excessiveness. "Cervezas?" subtropically transposes Alpine rescue-dogged uncollared brandy kegs: tepid melted slush's fiberglass-walled Igloo bobs buoyantly neutral beercan refreshments.

Rehydration soon inebriates seep-deprived, crotchsucking thirsters. Empty unjettisoned aluminous profusion ecosensitively bloats toastmaster's mastery, numbering 14+ drained pop-topped receptacles. Cordial drinking's agreeability replaces unintelligibility's discursive babel.

Beer's superpremium valuation proscribes suds replenishing combustion's watercooled tubes. Leakiness outdoing water-sparer's apportions, threesome abides. Block cools idlewhile pilot regales intralingually dark-hearted premonition convoluting laded secrets: "caballitos? carrousel como carcel," reinterprets cordillera resort's reputed merry-go-round's hardware disassembled underwraps. Flatbed's trailerload clangings resound calaboose imprisonments, turnkeys' slammered certainties.

Absurdly gossiped figments concoct deviant fabrications secretively overbuilding cloudy plateaus. Dismembering wholly manageable storybook ending codafying builder secrecy's conceited promulgation, truck-hacker dismisses world-class hotelplex accordance, favoring military-in-

131

stalled superjail incarcerating panamerican dopers, hostaged turistas, CIA-planted despots. Globalized expansions recasting marketplaced fluidity evaluates silliest fancies feasible. Incarceration's megabuck expenses (dollars-per-day/inmate outrunning per-guest hotelier's costs) facilitate internationalism's jail schematic (levying solvently bonded bondsman nations). Third-world's nationstates gladly erect elaborate prisons sheltering sadistic jailers confining desirable undesirables.

Restarting, beery compadre implants himselfishly, "selflessly" obtaining thrust-upon guardhoused appointment. Man-handling boys/girls, fantasizing besotted disciplinarian hardens. Openfaced duplicity abhors whoring's irresistible supplication: genuflecting confessor admits jailhouse screwing position's tortuous sex-appeal. Sadean rumination bisexually participating, toothsome upper's masochistic immunity wearies jawed auditory "volunteers."

Hellish circulations stifle passengers. Meanest megalomanias impel commoner's repulsively remedial violent impulse. Unspecified private-suffered vengeances're repaid on general principles. Inebriate phonemes straddling Spanish-English-Mayanesque slanguages slur evil's articulation. Impudent accelerating supplements steering's wheel-played ineffectiveness, sociopath miscalculations. Unamused captives're edging helmward: predictable misanthrope's tirade renounces consciousness's flimsy clasp.

POST-CRISIS MOTORIST understudies surveying inoperative dashboard dials ponder daytime's fly-by-night roadworthy equivalent. Unglassed, dirt-packed, deneedled cup-sized indentations telepathically relay datavistic tidbits (primitively gauged dipsticks sounding water/gas/oil levels) functioning exploits. Unresponsive control-paneled instrumental ornament, lax clutch, slack brakeline uptake, aforecited wheel's lapsing/overheating antifreeze appropriately commensurate central bugaboo: 200-pound unconscious blob oozing corn niblets upchucks defenestrably.

Faultily unlockable door-latched perils obstruct letting reeler abut outwardly liable hinges (fastening Samaritan backside, accompanying skid-mounted shipment, understandably's immoral). Sleepish boldness licensing gropes, zombie wolf nuzzles Ms.M's chest.

"Cute. Why're tu driving, amigo?" rhetorically rehashes unquestionable seating.

"T'was fated," explains frantic firedrill response whereafter nuestro wheelmaestro slumped, hitting 60km/hr.

Unguardrailed curve provoking frenzy's clamber, nondrivers switched places amidshift, shoving fatheaded dominance-prone blubberer, recovering runaway's controls. Unclutched slackening countered upbound momentum's jeopardized acceleration. Herky-jerky rambunctiousness helped stall fatality's extrusion; invigorated belly malady's deliverance successfully targeted window's venting.

Crises averted, trucking resumed.

Autocratic pilot's inconvenient lounge-act upfilling airbag seatmate compartment, waymaking seatmates brook snores' toney bents. Stentorian formulations madly render crooned standards. "Unglove lettuce, dub parrots, see-sawing sallie-maes," SanFran fiscally advises/musically introduces psitacotic bonding.

Cooler-kept enchilada suppers, alcohols punchily mixing tequilas, citrus liquados refuel motorheads' tanks. Steeper incline narrowings tauten stressed-out eyesights; wispy hooded specters reassemble overheater's potency. Caustic stenches acridly actuate unlit alarm.

Passiveness frequently solves cliffhanger impendabilities. Stopping's midroute waits irritate chronic goers; going's impassible. Crooning gurgler burps, snakeless eagle unflaggingly alludes altitude's thinned oxygen, chiller sunsetting counterspins tropic-oriented paradise throes. Indigo gloaming's majestic nightfall interdicts speakers. Reluctantly watchers contemplate rerousing peacefully unmanageable gutteral spewer: intermittently halted pattern's tractable, direction's unvaried.

Darkness's inconspicuous arrival strikingly telecasts crescent moonlight's unmatched luminosity. Galactic smear, pulsating planet sparkle distract pathfinders: lo-beams discernibly're somewatt brighter.

Graduated topdown brightenings intensify. Artificial dissemination superfuses Pandora's box releasing untold jack-sprung mysteries. Oz wizardry, UFO homeport, convention's constructioneering (as-advertised), covertly substratal tinkering, extraordinary concentrated demonstrations camp uproad.

Slope steepness flattening, trekkers achieve first-impressioned panorama's stupefying vista. Fundamentally, everywhere rims pitted excavators stripmining unplumbable declivity. Hitherto trucked, shrink-wrapped skidded pallet materials delegate depot's unloading area. Parkers debark, overhearing bulldozers' mellifluous mufflerless froggy bullhorn 24-hour croak.

Quonset installations're nestled 'tween excavated molehills. Quarry's consomme insipidness digested, forage-minded unimportant arrivers import sotly incapacitated passport ambassador. Compatriot recognizance's legitimacy safeguards safeguardians? Shouldering saggingly overweight slobberer truck-to-hut deserves yeoman-scaled feast's portion acclaiming everyman's hero valets.

Unwarmed potted slops temper appetite. Foregobbled enchiladas eructate effervescent bellyfuls twisting finicky bowel moils. Sustenance's problematic enhancement disenchanting banquet envisionists, uninhabited cots exert haler enticement.

Cocoonish off-work digger pupae deadeningly snooze. Loud entry undisturbs Caterpillar workmen's serenity. Bulldozer humming vacillates scalar drone, chugging interminable irritations sleepers've externalized. Internalized flourescent phosphorescence re-creating hospitals, spaceships, morgues, medicated hibernator's forensic pathologists unload dead-weighted truckdriver.

Bullfight arenascapes, torpedo tits barmaid vamps dispensing namebrand bottle murally program dreamer's subconsciousness. Horny bulldykes gore capering beer-gutted prickadors? Shaken bottlerocket dildo fizzes confuse whoopie-cushioned, hairfair-conditioned nightmare, ala stink eau delaturde.

PUNISHING WAKERS banish cross-dressed bulled impostors' dreamlife insinuations. Gravely tired yard-shifters scrunch corn-chips, smack dominos, slug shotglasses, restructure cicadian rhythm serenades. Circadian recovery's enfeebled upstarts lurch afoot. Restorationally assured, prisonguard fantasizer fraternizes, affectionately heckling subcontractors. Manful laughter's hardy-har-har unsarcastically postdates Jackie Gleason's Kramdenesque gusto: heavyweight derision's salavating grace's unsophisticatedly menacing.

Brusque mestizo redneck-equivalent chortles daunting out-on-a-limb immigrants, chortling repents. Gallant hospitable reparations overdo dubiousness. Halting paralingual efforts're patronizingly agonizing. Mockery's unintention ingenuously masterminds mockery. Overextended homilies placeset savage-witted brunch: Fritohuevos rauncheros (milkless omelet repackaging chunked chips, picantely sloshing undrained remnant hooches).

Soggy tortilla pushers absorb amazingly savory globs. Kaluha-sweetened coffees brighten pessimistic forecast. Obstreperous hombres retire; drug-restored cowboyish yahoo cabmaster notifies unloading's completed.

White-out envelopes clamors. Shadowy soft-edged menacers earthmove, vaporize exhaustible gasses. Precarious pitfall, staking impaler projectiles, discourages exploration. Hefty dew daub clampdowns liquify pneumonial respiration. Lungs clog, revisions tearily merge glaucomic reformings, ex-objects subjectify: reintegrated physicalities overprize radically unmuddled touch. Solidifying dampnesses seat cushy solaces. Doorhandles, seatbelts, steelwork safetyglass, plastic-coated knobs, Baltic seawater-cold clings cinch tangibility's enclosure.

Corresponsive forthrighteous perseverity corrodes doubt's critically important self-restraint. Retaking manipulation's pilotseat, tequilaheaded flyboy revs rpms. Downhill's unnecessarily hammered accelerator outruns visible limitations; accelerated zoom, counteractingly, instills downshiftings' brake-effected (brakepad preserving) retardation. Freewheeling down'd sabotage braking's long-term designs.

Short-term emergencies disillusion grander plan. 1950s-era videotic penny arcade U-drive booths simulating slam-packed roadmastery premodel fogged descent's semicontrolled lunge. Gaunt, deoxygenated oxen's hidebound guardrail potentials stray aroadside, tumbledown boulders reoccur, loll unremoved; mainstreet trolleycar illusively imposing locomotive ghost disperses cloud-formed children hounding Labrador retrievers. Cooptical delusion desolidifies rock? Near-missed formations dramatize papier-mache shadowplayed inconsequence. Huffily doubleclutched braking melodramatizes compulsion's recklessness.

Attenuatingly wide-angled screen careenings induce pacecar's brakeless odyssey. Laurel-wreathed Hardy-jowled Ulysses skirts sirening rocksongs, anthropomythic livestocked big-eyed inconvertible morbid wisdoms; Cyclops peering navigates full-well knowing undermated faithfulness's assailed: flung-by-one, clutch's pedal, handbrake, shifter cables disarticulate. Ungraveling traction eroding unwieldy steers' "surefootedness," headstrong waymakers contrive crash-landed turnabouts.

Upshunting truckstopper rampways wishfully unrequited, downshunted iceless bobsledders self-embrace. Ponderously maudlin swishtailed gazers're battered awayside entraining cowcatcher efficacy. Standard roundtrip expectations're clearly exceeded: ejecting stewmeat repositories verifies despair's inspirational guidelines.

"Ayyyy, Dios," transliterates adios's checkout time's knell.

Wasteful genuflected handjives abdicate antimomentum struggling. Unclasped, whirlaway swerves expertly, abrading outcropped igneous shales.

Scrapings sculpt Rushmore's antithetical abstraction: indecipherable rockfaced chiselings figure stop-signed obedience's explicit gratitude.

Presidential integrities mushmore portrayed: chisel-hearted stone-walleyed ballpeen-busted figureheads omnidentify mankind's highest leaderclass.

Sculpturally accidental appreciation comprehensible, marooned highwayfarers congratulate fortunate routecome. Hyperventing aleatory "self-empowerment," crapshot lucksters mistakenly presume everything's chance-driven, lazily discarding deck-stacked meticulous purposeful trumps. Colliding endurability's topspun daredeviltry counterplays cautioning backspun forethought. Unentirely unrealistic-minded, paper-ass-holed character perceives ubiquitous substructure protecting/condemning actions. Bravery's cheapskates neglect ice's thinness.

"Otra vez?" again's apostatic quest, dysfunctionally, violates preordained "nunca" legalization's overdriving force.

"Andeamos," hermetic answering's sanest volition voices descending walk's untried recourse.

SEACAPTAIN'S UNSINKABLE ABNEGATION influencing
machochistic stubbornness, truckmaster remained, fixing undrivable hulk. Dehitched hikers skittered expeditiously townward. Fortuitously uneventful journey mesmerized. Well-rationed waterbags, deep-fried maize cakes feted Noche Buena's tarde; mountainsides rang carillon resonation updrafting brittle airs, fresh-baked candies spiced mesquite-roasted swine, ethereal fiestas awaited Navidad eve's prodigal slummers.

Sundown's holiest nightclub clobbers sojourners. Diminishing weekspan's miniVan-Winkle absentees admire crassly unprocrastinated creche-landed NAFTAesque takeover's globalization. Disney-trade-marked superstars interlope magi, goofily hobnobbing, mugging, upstaging unneon iconographies. Goggle-eyed Plutos slurp afterbirths, Scrooge McDucks distribute cigar attaboys, slipped Mickeys typify Caananite rubes (promulgating participatory championship entitlements "benefitting" democracy onlookers: Huey's dewy lunacy singly anoints commonweal principalities, divesting supposititious titles—Excellency, Presidente, Highness—reinvesting people with power).

Yuletide decorations detract observance; semi-demolished midtown stores're impressively uninhabitable. Lagoonfront shacks, outbuildings, inhouses, courtyards' cardtabled folding-chaired cafes—everyplace, reserving hotel, anti-insurgents' billet, favored cantinas, cathedral—suffers redevelopment's steamshoveled infliction.

Massing candleholder churchgoers stagger, resignedly forswearing resistance. Meek inherit earthenfloor huts, tent sandcastles, ditches' enrichment. Undertowed hosannas, dirgedly minor-keyed, menace Christian hymn rejoicing. Erstwhile's saloon tuneful carols testifying hopefulness reinstate solemn uncertainty. Compliantly pious colonels, financiers, developers join peasants. Latin's mummified ululation staunchly excommunicates heresy deconstructing ritualistic dogmas. Anyway, deconstruction's autocratically opposed.

139

Pelota Juego Hotel's unclerked registry signpost blazons hoop-hung slashed vacancy's apologistics arithmetically subtracting domiciles, innkeeping Christmas's legendary mangerbound banishment. Charitably unresembling indian ballgame's heart-wrenching pall ousters, Pelota's reversal lets losers leave unmaimed. Unabashing lobby paintings trilaterate guests/winners/mestizos, bash fumbling redskins. Triptychs narrate pre-Columbian hoopsters' tournaments. Revisionally inaccurate Caucasians procuring dominant-indian roles (Scandinavian brows, Roman noses) vanquish stocky misplaying Mongolians.

Baleful representations ramify alcove's reception. Literalized discouragement outlaws lingering: couchfronts, chairbacks, loveseatbottoms orient wallward, spectating gory intramurals.

Dingledong plaintive bell overdubs spaghetti western's audio, cheapeningly improving sedated holyday's unsalable mellow mushiness. Clashed econo-political backgrounds afflict fascinating pressures. Uninteresting pieties mumly mumbled, screaming eyesore abrasions rankly embitter tender sensibility's yawned-out composure.

"Heaven's where nada happens," D.Byrne critique extrapolating Milton P.Lost's, Dante Inferno's superiorities overshadowing Regained Paradisos' ho-humbuggery hereupon's affixed.

Raffish overkill's honky-tonk macroeconomic-generated microcosm sparkles delightfully. Strung-out mangers electrifying Mickey Mouse nativities Reno-vate developmental staging's unsightliness. Panoramically viewed, lit-up gimcrack iconotels correlate Juarez whorehouses; merrily titillating multicolor festivities modestly publicize hubba-hubbas. Distancing's easements pleasingly debar plate-jobbed literalism's analytically fervent interludes.

Religion's followers've preserved creche preciousness, scrounging holier shelters deferencially located (displaced outskirts' purlieu). Sleepy atheists dismantle perpendicular liturgies: upright fenceposts guarding consecrated isolation deficiently impede nonbelievers' trespass. Hay's straw-ticked softness, taciturnly companionable mannequin-Christ, frontlit Anaheim gargoyle ducklings accommodate slumberparty crashers.

Toplight glares persist. Unscrewing white-hot lightbulb's impracticable. Eyelids shade effulgence; semidark redness prickles outkept flickerings. Nonepileptics twitch, apperceiving seizure-induced stimuli.

"Guiltiness searing?" flippant teaser challenging sexpartner provocatively unleashes pervert's mongrelizations combining masque, boudoir farce.

Ladyfriend waylays Joseph's groin, jocularly manhandles woodheaded stiff's shaded allure. Light-aversiveness subcedes depraved bawdiness. Unfrenchable mouth's clenched rigidity adaptably gratifies clitoral grooveling. Purple opaque robes hinder uncraved enlightenments. 69-ing pair's decently obscured.

Mary beckons. Come-hither sultriness exuding blue-robed chastity's coverstory, funky fragrances uniquely subvert premodern maternitywear. Beatifically stunned expression enrapturing multi-orgasmic dithers, Maria iconette willingly topples. Conundrums compound: supple fleshlike substance's enclosing five-foot-two gal; forgiveaway munificence yielding sabrosa subrosa nippled knockers exclaims, "Holy-moly motheragod!"

Orgiastically "compliant" consort masturbating withal Joe's upper-lipped stiffness grunts, "Whaaaa?"

"Una lovedoll!"

Catholicism's topmost distaff personage impersonating skinrag's back-page photograb mendaciously betraying 2-d ideal's 3-d mail-ordered fraud, infidelitous diddlers worry Mary's substituters'll learn creche-crashers've undressed madonna's deception. Anatomically corrected (vaginal sleeve), ex-virgin reposits sleaze-dried icks.

Unctuously debauched desecraters pursue rapture's sleep-inducement?

Hygiene precautions mandate sideschlupping postvirginal scumbagged pussy, availing unrigged anal frottage. Iconic eroticisms reprioritize reliquary articles. Fetish peculiarities assignating peculiarized delectability reformulate unworn Bible-era lingerie: Jerusalem bratichokes, Galilace pantiocs, etslutera. Preposterous anacronistic acrostics prolong stabled intercourse (wordplay equating big-league slugging percentages' memory-exercised detainments prejaculate-prone studs've conventionally drilled). Orgiastic moans counterpointing cathedral's Handel, livery loverboys/galloping girlfriends herd human-contaminated animas.

Concupiscent debauchers, allaying manger's Christ-timed sodomism ban, defile sacred kewpies. Sleepiness's fluent trance slakes unquenchable thirsting lust.

RUBBED HAYROLLERS RECONSIDER begetting offspring

repercussions, embracing saintly heinies. Flagrante delicto sodomizers'd resurrect Inquisition punishments. Dawn risers autodefecate, preconceiving stake-burnt reproofs. Sadism's righteousness'd inspirit cruel ingenuity. Genitalia-targeting comescrews? Softer crimes've received worse spanking.

Prankish surge malingers: selectricians algorithmically rewire characterizational circuitry. Trans-set displacement influence's shiftily manipulated. Mary/Joseph/Jesus principals repossess position, intermingling Disney-dealt cutouts, mangiest mangerbeasts. Minnie mothers Christchild's taxidermal burro—Goofy wiseman presenting frankinsensual gift adminsitration braying baby beholds. Crawling godmother reenacts donkey, Joey tends wisemen/camels, dromedaries expropriate cartooners' upstart affectedness. Tableauxmatically accurate, switches mightn't jar nearsighted farsighters.

Inactive backhoes, cement pourers, carpenters, masons, dumptrucks bequeath holiday peacefulness. Inscudding squalls amplify remodeling's privation. Sheetrock-gray rainclouds fill excavations, co-founding natatoriums. Crapulous flown-in mercenarial roustabouts snipe gripes. Inactivities strand menacingly wearied beer-breathing gillmen. Stiletto toothpicks unstick refried kidneys flicked desultorily dispelling well-mannered nicety.

Ganglike rivalries devise identifiable groupings. Underskilled laborcamp townies despise awning-covered, heartily remunerated displacers; displacing workcrew scorns bumpkins' wretched envy. Investors decry substandardized advances (upgraded advancing standards're unrealizably fast-paced); foremen counterbid change-ordered extenuations upping machinery insufficiencies. Militial glacial impactedness, interventionally, reaches farther afield; uprising revolutionaries pervade farthermore mythward.

143

Unsubjugated tribes stimulate peerless deliberation. Wildness's congenital sexiness, counterauthoritative maverick charisma, invisibility's mysteriousness enshroud native's realm. Rumor-tied mythologistics braid lassoing expeditionary throws: outflung looping troopers're rope-a-doped; coyotes outfox wargame dogs, ever-widening ranges nerve-frayed fetchers chase. Tauntingly, jungle-based ham radiowave drummers impound press-released highground: pithy statements championing antigovernment tenacity blazon airwaves. Contemptibly praetorian officialese-slathered retorts hyperextenuate rebel sympathy.

Quasi-spiritual affections accrue, martyring uncaptured resisters. Sporadically phased detonations restir concern, ineffably assisting downbeaten bushmen? Diversive merit constructively sullies prayers: sympathizing civilizers mourn genocide's transcendent upshoots/undervalue homegrown complicity's roots.

Quiescent submission governs citizenry. Homeowners swapping casas garnered stock-certificated "mallares," mall-implacement dollares certifying primo repossessed right-o-ways. Storekeepers promised newer/bigger/better tillmills eagerly scrapped impoverishingly erosive cash-flowed dribbles, forecasting cash-machined gushers. Mall-in-all, greed stifled anti-builder inertia.

Encampments unfurl transamerican grandstrand playa cabanas, ignorantly declaiming panache's squalor. Rain-washed detainees braise spitted roasters, bake dutch-ovened cookies, refry larded bonbons. Flappy windbreaker broadcloth protects feastmasters; odd-lot droplets permeate canvasses, sizzling piquant brazier plumes. Fiestaday cheerfulness permeates lardasses. Stodgy realists regretting development's covenant recalibrate celebration allowances (habitually, tippling raided booze cabinets incessantly); idealists piledrive badminton netpoles.

Architects, planners, hard-hatted overseers convoke off-wharf. Bismarck-class yachts congest harbor, flaring opulent nest-feathered fantails. Onflowing partiers blur diurnal demarcations; outflowing party-goers requite urinarial nonhesitations sportily, meaningfully urinate shore-ward.

Cocktailers' recurring uric stream-of-consciousness prefigures reno-vation's obsessively turd-world revolution manifesto: dynaflush toilets. Defensively skeptical shopmen insist developers've redesigned infra-structured waterdrive. Global-coded minimums modernized flushing pressure, propitiating thirst-world tourism first-ass comfortability. Re-plumbing's prerequisite penultimately determined Pedroville's makeover (ultimate-swung agreements trustily considered fiduciarily sounder is-sues).

"Pedroville?" shameless nickname switcher discriminates Piedra-dropped, ville-appended, portless nomenclatured uncluttering. "Unac-companied?"

Corporate-sponsored renamings affixing stadiums've handled village's defiling? Naming rights're postdetermined secretly.

Silent-partnered conspirators alleviate slum glumness, tinkling inter-active role-played empowerments. Stockholder confidences hoist sand-bagging assurance. Mercantilism commonwealths surely'll put rainbow's goldpot permanently hereafter. Beachdwellers reinstigate fantail swillers' bloating bladder gladness. Piss-proud penile colonialists seawardly revel toiletless residence's pardonable elimination.

Crossfiring urinaters subsided, creche-fleeing emigrants affiliate shops' dislocated layaway proprietor crowd. Cruiseliner atmosphere overextends degenerative Nativity-scened rearrangements. Adopted car-tooneque mascot boogeyfolk oblige pinata-starved children's destruction necessities.

Disney bashings enigmatically greet disloyal Americanos. Malicious anti-yankee antagonisms're ambiguously entertaining. Omniculturally despised Mickeymice, Donalds, Goofys delineate Americanism: despising Americanism's symbols contaminates sentiment tainting representative Yankees.

POST-HOLIDAY RIGMAROLE consolidates taskmaster enclaves, baskmaster sunslaves, passively reclining viewmasters. Soldiering trenchers, bushwacking infantries, mobilized flatbeds, unmotorized boulderhaulers produce cinemascopically extravagant saga stressing industrialism's blitzkrieg fury. Brutal woundings iterate haste's wastefulness: triturations, manglings, deformations, flattenings resculpt biophysical permanences. Romanesque coliseum skyboxers conjecturably thumb fates, handicapping infirmary's ability. Regurgitated plexus interpretations invoke peacetime workforce's warrior resemblances. Rebelling insurrectionists harm none, countermeasuring uptempo scheduling's sedulous cruelty.

Amphibious invasion's landingcrafts, troopships, pontooned cargoplanes carry modular prefabrications, readylaid brick, E-Z-form joist joiners, piped-in fixings. Pre-assembled Leggo part linkage interforms totally. USA-stamped intermediary refinements recombined Korean, Philippine, Taiwan-made raws; veneerly improved cargos're vigorishly shipped. Miniskilled rustics churning pesos/hora interconnect multiconvoluted prototypical experimental engineerings: exemplarily, saniflush's untested hydraulic sophistications trying antigravitational pumpability.

Wintery monsoonettes grease scaffolds, sustain foundational muds. Solar outbreaks humidify malaria puddle incubators; well-groomed mosquitos' larvae redramatize intermedia metamorphoses. Water-to-air insects' transformations intersect primogenerated amphibians' landscape miracle (off-land LCTs, LSMs, LSTs pervading amphib crossovers associate invasion taskforces, socio-political Darwinism, oncoming ineluctable disease). Assaulted villagers' cruiseship-modeled soiree muddily reconceptualizes internment-camped siege.

Year date progresses. Destructo-constructo progression rampage outdoes gentler build-up's processes. Shallowly reaming World's Fair-strength substructural piledrivers ram expiring diggerfolk beneath pilaster slabbing? Unaccountable attrition depopulates heaviest shoveling in-fighters. Middling highrise skyline weedily grows sunward, feeding-off frightsoil bonemeal fertilizer.

Alabaster ghostmodern minarets entomb profiteering's mildest speculations. Shell-white shells undertaking electrician/plumber modification exorcise poor's devils anteceding rich's habitation. Hermit crabs' licestyle infamously parallelograms parasitic figment squaring nature-legislated succession's concept: takeovers're adaptable.

Piddle-by-little, beachcomber merchants're bestowed latchkey accesses mollifying mall's preconstructive inconvenience. Armed-guarded 7-minute visitations elicit intense gratitudes: remodeled retailer palaces gleam redemptive capacities. Oceanside conversations devolve. Tedious fortune-told crystalizations snowball; anti-profitable scintillatingly sarcastic prophecies melt.

Disney-inspirited merriment fevers infectiously nurture faith. Development commissar donning mouseketeer earset visits camptown; distributed brochures illustrate AFTER's prettified beauty. Bonus certificates suspiciously meliorate: glad-handed backslapping unruffles confederate currencies (debentures maturing futuristically). Papers' receipt vouchsafes acceptability's mantle ambilaterally: recipients're pledged incontestable categorization accruing bondholders; nonrecipients, refusers, rejects dredge besmirched ostracization smearing derelicts.

Papermated millionaire celebrants compliment mouse-eared shyster. Coconut-coal braises marinated skate, sweetening all's suspiration. Intrusive nonmerchant foreigner twosome exemplifies accepting's dependency. Prebanked funds're deferrably unreachable (unserviced tellerstands bear-up rebuilding's obstructions), pocketbook dwindlings drain. Restitution's shopkept promises disapply: unfranchised drifters disowned substantiated property's fallback homebase.

"Laboring's lousier ..." ellipsis implies semicolonial buts rescuing bummers. Cash's decisionmaking plights harass humbly monied micro-economists' examples graphing optimal restivity. Payday readiness's perpetuating dictatorship supremely elects yo-yo populace: penniless spinners'll heed masterful threadworn fingersnaps.

"Starving's lousiest," preregisters subclass enrollment.

Shop-bound beachclubbers snootily expulse nonallied influxers. Immigrated apostates realign excelsior-driven mobilities cliches flaunt. Bottoms-up orientations insult bottom-up's pursuits. Microfortune's macrofortunate originators disturb plutocracy's converts. Tattered anti-style "styling" revulsively irks trendsetter mavens unanticipating grunge-clad barged-in hundreds.

Misfits spend siesta reconnoitering manholes, lade-staged starting terminals, beergarden bureaus occupying thirsty chaingang jerkers; quit sanded gentrification's coastside relaxation.

Demonstrable removal relocating tented holdings, banishees migrate upstream.

CONDUIT ENCAPSULIZATION STINT drafts prevaricating jobbers pretending journeymen's qualification.

Pink-slipped predecessors advertently sabotaged pleasantness stabilizers securing cooled existentialism's capacious extension. Ambivalent hatred (self-directed, tourist-directed) accrued resentment outcoming servitude dupes' allotted saltmines? Intermangled wires, waterpipes, airducts betoken carelessness's contempt.

Frazzled hirer mistook lying "craftsmen," relabeling Mar/Mat Katrina/Stephan, accomplished Sonoran denizens, specialized in doming biospheres. Reconstruction inheres reinstalling kilometrically exaggerated lengths. Dehydration-emaciated Arizonans adapt: ectomorphs slither manywheres fatter crawlers're excluded. Uninsulated itchy crawlspaces compress airless 100-plus Farenheit ovens, baking sodacracker mouth interiors.

Premade cylindrical monads piping dissimilar envirosystems connect end-to-end. Alloy-coded couplings adulterate childlike simplemindedness: aluminum-based copper-sheened metallics darkly interrelate; nonetheless circumference diameters, textural resistances, heats idiosynchronize subtle-patterned distinctions. Braille readers'd decode nuanced usages surehandedly; sight-deprived gropers flail.

Vertigo headways whirl. Precedents' errors're, likeliest, systematized instigations. Sweltering, raling, itching, anybody'd destroy blueprint designations' elegantly limned walled-in conductions.

"Nye cand breed," gypsum wallboard's muffle warps Katrina's breathless complaint.

"Non't talg," rejoinderly admonishes breath-salvaged cooperations.

Upcocked stacking anerobically breech-loads shelled-in pipeliners. Tailgunner Stephan's pedi-bellows influxes hosed recirculation; nosecone extenuator Katrin petitions dischargeable unmuzzling perforated airholes spackling'd retroactively plug.

149

"N'ay tiempo," timelessly refrains productivity's arrogant preeminence. Onrushed Princess steamships're barging packed tourmonger caravans; undone bedrooms dishonor reservations. Preregistered tourists'll appraise finery's gloss, concierge maintains, detecting submattress pea wherevermore stuff's flawed. Spackle patchings advert tacky slapdashed makeshifty slovenliness. Unmarred facings quell bugged nitpicker mindsets. Fault-finding detectors falter, elide banality's gaudiest flaws; hairline rifts, antithetically, titillate complainers' crying jags.

Overstepped deadlines've posted superintending concierges. Finishing toucher-uppers outrace interior-probing linecrews redoing basest underpinnings. Fretting brochure copywriters cringe, lamenting unbackable utility-installed bravados? Trustier fables propose tortoises outracing hares, foxes squiring hens, wolf-faced grandmothers fooling gullible granddaughters.

Quadrupletime bonuses inflate miserably underpaid salaries. Waived paydays imprisoning installers, installment-planned layaways accredit undrainable fundings. Prisoners retabulate nicer splurges. Flashback pans review disastrously crossed role appropriation (battleground abandonments, mid-desert waterless dazes, avalanched cave-ins) resetting buttonholed likings doom-faced suckers stubbornly revere. Hot-fudge sundaes, three-inch-thick Porterhouse steaks, ice-cold Boemia simplistically presubstantiate indulgence's baselines. Baser line item longings convolute ecstasy's sexward twistings. Skinnydippers' linguistic dawdlings sensualize wallflowers' lustiness.

Verbalized pleasurings reheat duct-bound coupler technicians. Vagina lubricant's lovable trickle tickles drop-by-drop, teasing understander's neck. Upcrept resourceful fingertip diligently retraces thigh, downkept tonguer massages freckle connectable dotted anklets. Squirms retrofit ingenuity's gamut: clitoris stimulation's solely gripped singlemindedness hypnotizes orgasmic power's focus.

150

Sighing's exertion demonstrably breathes directive entreaties. Contraptured restrictiveness funneling strengths, strivers forget obligation's monitoring superintendents. Admonishments pound wallboards. Telltale osmotics filtrate juicy organs transuding porously reimagined tryst. Momentous unknowability decidedly defends concealed fingered malingerers. Impotent supers begrudge piscene-scented concupiscence's unverifiable flourishes.

Authority outrage pruriently overextenuates pudenda diddling recess. Vulvic handjobber's up-oriented fascination concomitantly hampers priapic masturbation. Odiferously overpowered squirmer inserts clad penis tubally, raping conduited module's wirewound bunghole.

Postcoitally disgusted, icky fuck-crazed servicers redo pipefittings. Boredom's reinstigation retards wishful timeclock speeds.

Workaday symbolization seizing week's decompression, periodic fatigue mislays time-sensitive acumen. Nitrogen narcosistic bends befall unanticipatedly terminated pipelayer muffdivers. Impairing glazed whitewash amazement disorients insularly stuffed wall-mole squinters. Sun-deprived, movement-restricted, air-rationed sensualists reel. Brilliantined brilliance's rambunctious slickening sickeningly sways ex-humble pueblo's beholders.

Staggering trabajero gringos're monetarily expiated.

PEDROVILLIAN CHRISTENINGS INITIATE. Precocious proclamations annihilate forebodings intimating subcode patches've underlaid wallover workmanship's resplendence (code's lowermost conceptualization provincially materializes free-formed permissions). Fizzy Penedes Cavas replicating Reims Champagnes're tethered, thrown, shattered; bayfront seafare dreadnoughts launch expansiveness justification luncheons. Open-housed cocktailing predominates, roosterish boosters strut boasting bottled glass's smitherine loveliness, rejoice triumphant attainments.

Primly scrubbed exteriors speckling rhinestones scintillate. Reinstalled storekeeper families proselytize neomercantilism's graces. Archways' footbridges encompass peripatetic lanes ushering dawdler Hansels, "demure" Gretels admiring gingerbread houseparty sightseeing allures.

Invasive gangplank debarkers praise Vegas/Miami-influenced poshness. Swanky curvaceous nonfunctional formulaic glitz betokens capital-e Elegante (neon's respelled El-Egante reading immoderately blinked pattern): savvy retrographics' state-of-the-art casinotel. 1920s-era Miami's/1960s-era Vegas's confluential streamlines beautify touring's port-o-call. Festive gamesters gambol undeviatingly wayward. Glamorous trappings stroke stoked-up players. Wild-eyed salivating eagerness snorts excitement's white-lined powder? Cocaine's superfluous, diluting blackjack's kicks.

Preplanned prospering successively actualizes. Puniest lenders obtain initiatory paybacks. Once-homeless laboring underclassmates procure upgrade hovels; nonworker drifter communities undertake upgrades befitting largesse's exigent responsibilities (imbibing higher-toned boozes). Uppercrustiest bigwigs pontificate told-you-so bulls proclaiming globalistic muscle's miraculous omnipotence.

Kiddie amusements're paraded, neglected. Bipederast costume beasties alludely redimensionalizing celluloid domains outlive advertisement's needful characterizations. Mickeyfinned plutocrats scrooging upsie Daisies impersonate unDisneyfied behavior. Underbrushed offstagey shenanigans cannibalizing carnival carnality, delirious besuited savages self-indulge hedonistic masquerades.

P-ville's Americanization, toongoons replete, whimsically reassures depravity's aficionados. Gutterly raving theatrics exhilarate crassness's grasped idealisms. Wildhair speculators outperforming passbook savers correlates liquored Goofies wowing timid muchachos? Slop analogies luxuriate, introspections atrophy, funhouse mirrorscapes redraw lineality.

Childlife, expressly, metastasizes. Pretakeover innocences're unrecognizable contemporarily. Lil' hustler pipsqueaks, harmonizing countrymen's outspoken harangues, barter gimcracks/wheedle alms. Whoring natively supplants undernourishing moneymaker fertilizations. Youth's receptacle sucking overage's spills tidies unkempt debauchees' lustrously messy frustrations.

Immature twentyish female-trained gigolos squire turista dowagers; mature elevenish elves pin Caucasian gent wrestlemaniacs. Heterotically opinionated puerile layfarers relive elders' cocky whorehoused pasts; Anglo make-believe brides spuriously commend swarthy stallion grooms' sleek saddles, wedgy pommels, poignant whips. Homoerotically avid females're availed slurportunities: machismo casualty ennumerations seethe, painstakenly fancying zipless releases. Pansexuality's healthiest balancings supervene off-kilter presuppositions, counterweighing ageist prejudice, preferential sex-preferenced tastes. Sodom's paradigmatic amity trounces Jerusalem's wartorn, Mecca's forlorn, Salty Lake's stillborn antipathy.

Fortunately reimbursed conduit-servicing escapegoats intrude casinoland. Adulthood theme-parked rollercoasters staidly clone roulette, chuck-a-luck, keno's bobbling airballs duplicating carny tilt-a-whirl thrills. Undealt facecards, untossed dicecubes restir unfulfillment's energized portent.

Baccarat contessas redress nines, shaming furs swagger liberal spewings archetype loser neglects. Grouper-jowled croupiers rake losings. Tablehead dealer impassively monopolizes shoe-dispensed pasteboards. Self-dealt eight- nine-point "naturels" parrying contestants, dealer's bankchip lode swellingly daunts.

"M'llamo Supremo, dígame! Soy Supremísimo!" taunter co-opting Berroa's dictator autobiography apologia parody unparodically proclaims supremacy's hyperarrogant "humility" ploys. Nonhispanic ethnicity (Russian?) compounds obnoxiousness, riling rash contestations.

Successive unsuccessful rebuker pretenders deceptively dethrone commissar's reigning dealarchy. Stalwart sevens approachably topple eight-holding prodigy. Propitious extremes chaperoning indecently blessed financier, luck's precipitously delinquent cessation aggravates anti-dealer flinging.

"Motherfucker's overstayed," rubberneckers mumble.

Virtuality's straw-drawn alloters choose next bankbreakers, staring down neophytes. Unnettably insane purse-drained grandstanders enthrall precedingly broke schmucks, enrich ever-bloating winner. Attrition's shake-out deploys kibitzers. Inescapably, ourself winders're unsprung.

Suspense trifles, tying undecided facecard constituencies (king/queen/jacks equaling nil). Sidebetting augments judgement: doped hopers predict worms' turn.

Standoffs fantastically reconfirm. Dueling nils, sixty-sixes, seventy-sevens, fifty-fives prepossess duplex planet's overtaking reverberation. Duplicative experiences're reiterated. Player-friendly houseman regulations unpenalize ties, pushing stakers' obsession foremost.

Mystified pitboss reshuffles multidecks; pairings recur. Mythologistical superbanco jackpot's dimension encircles everyone's outermost bettable constraints. Pocketsocks, moneybelts eviscerate. Uncheckable exchequer biddings're uttered. Honorability's nationalized prerogative directs totalmente trustworthy divestitures.

Supremacist sloganeer hushes. Mobbing's aggravated hullabaloo gathers, recedes. Discretely snapped pasteboard excites banco's riotous outcry, misjudging odds-deemed inclination.

Pooling resources, one-hand-fits-all comers. Jostlers gasp, scoring face-pasted zeros; exult, flipping game's quasi-insurmountable score.

"Ocho!" croupier officiates.

"Nueve," bankmaster wins.

Momentously divested paupers engorge bloodsucking dickhead. Wealthier transients telegraph homeward's angels (sugardads, moms); destitute piper-payers hoof emergency's jobhunter jig.

TARMAC DISSEMINATORS recruited spreaders: insolvent tuxedo, gown-clad wastrels, payment-missing storemen fulminating bankruptcy, out-of-work playpenitent sinners, penitentiaries' tattoo saints. Heavenward turnpike redepicts moralizer masterpiece hellbound roadshow. Sinning typecasters, irreligiously sacrificed, storm firmament's fortress (unadvertised tortop spaplex), plodding obediently.

Bedeviling pitch-blackened stainees fork roadbed permeability analyses, forewalking pungent dumptrucked lavas. Tamping's qualified faculty skillfully tenuring professorial experts, forefronters superintend upwind's untarred vangard.

"Seguro, excelente," ostensible terranean detectives faultlessly divine paveable passwords. "Arre! Ándale!" urgers harmonizingly conform animal-commanding, human-exorting expletives.

Exploitees level bubbling tar's effluence. Untreated dusty surfaces congeal lumpiness; preferentially franchised convoys—prioritized fast-tracked transference authorized—enrut superversive indelible lumps. Idealistically, resurfaced road'll escalate traffic's advancement (multi-ton conveyances entrusted smooth gliding's copious returns). Shuttle vehicle parkway's garden-stated Elysium enables transcendental transportation's effortlessness.

Actualization resurfaces moonlike stubble. Inexperienced rakers underdo, overwork hand-held corrections. Epoxy hardenings approximately assert clay's tarred coatings. Fudged geophysics hereon corresponds upbounding gossip rumbling valvular irregularity. New-fashioned pipes're clogging. Methanes belch pre-explosive exhumations, tremulous prognosticators squeal, certifiably encoding Armageddic reckoning's wreckage.

Gossipy palimpsests interfoliate multibranched leavings. Chain-reactive gangmates fusing wildfire energistics crazily combine uncombinable tenets. Primeramente, rancho deluxe prison cells metamorphose; roach-tels entrapping vacationers pleasurably incarcerate dissolutioned fun-seekers. Escape-proof settlement fattens hogs. Negligent handicraft con-spiratorially implodes bombshelter infrastructuring's Titanic makeovers. Panic-driven shitters (refused cleanliness's first-ordered warranty) fanati-cize crapshooter salvation.

Pedrovilla honorably redoes Pancho Villan cunning. One-armed ban-dits outgun resurrectionists. Boomtown robbery's highway-mannered courting fleeces lamb-brained guest, blathers folderol, reorganizes deb-entured solvencies, disappears. Predecedently "disappeared" Emilitaris-tas, meanwile, slink. E-mail dispatchers, microradio wavecasters, scaled-up government crusades conflate tangibly unprooven contexts fabuliz-ing martyrdom's powered feebleness. Cynics impute revolutionaries're spooks, governmentally "stabilizing" inventions excusing excursion proactivities.

Widespread impending calamity erodes bounty's rhetoric. Sky's un-limitedness, nonironically guaranteed, powerwashes down-to-earth trust, whitewashes backlashing insecurities. Slogans unspecifying veiled lodge's anomalous glamours deepen suspicion's upcast gazing. Dam-nably clever advertisers sensationalize chalet's opacity.

Tarheeled hoers ambidexterously approve enclouded reaping's al-mighty seductiveness. Congame fellowship engages unknocked admira-tion; sunken victim's griping weds unachieved compunctions.

Blacktop petrolium red-carpeted unrolling speedily overscums effec-tiveness's smarter pace. St.Patrick's Kelley-greened striping decadent mu-nicipalities' ancestrally routed paradegrounds antedates herefore's tar-painted slopover. Twenty-strong roadcrew, slathering nonstoppably scheduled trucks' emptying, ascends plenty km/day. Tamping frontmen timekeepers rush unwatchable swath's messiness. Expansively sprayed inklings pointillize coverage's distal effect; proximal inspection strips ve-neers.

157

Leapfrogging caterers, campsite's keisters, avant-lard kettledrummers prefry bean supper. Chuckwagon smog pollusively intercuts tarring's Barolo signature bouquet demoted enophiliacs ally therewithin nebbiolo grape varietal's descriptor. Foodstuff desirability transcends primally palpable intolerance. Noxious hydrocarbons ring delicacy correlations overturning presentimental journeyman food-grouped positioning. Rice-and-beans (meat-and-potatoes) predilection's disarranged. Rerouted tastebuds uncritically assimilate emetically reprobate piquances.

Omnivorous sagacity winely swills kerosene-flavored mescal, gobbles creosote-spiced fatty nuggets. Unrationed gustables ameliorating ravenosity, roadgraders plow roughages.

Postprandial torpor staggers computable siestas. Off-shift resters encamp foresightedly: sleeper's leeway pregauges dumpground's upped procession. Henceforced awaking trailside bedrollees rejoin roadmakers.

"S'incredibly efficient, procedure-wise," ex-pipefitter avows, overlooking routecome's terrible craftsmanship.

"Incredibility's magisterial. Procedures'll pave totality. Pomp beguiles rube critics, impresses glam glommers. Y'gotta b'lieve, y'know?"

"Cynicism's outmoded. Bandwagons're overloaded."

"Speak'na—"

Postorgasmic quickie copulators uncunt. Daybreak's harbinging bandwagon coughs impolitely interruptive fumigations. Stamping tamper reverberates tremorettes projecting upcoming enervated plodders. Tar-splattered spaghetti-strapped overworked gowned casino outcast duchesses refine elegance's definition: unpawned sapphire brooches enbadge lowcut bustiers, tiaras flicker amethysts, emeralds lip necklaced hickeys. Spats distinguishing tux-trousered dukes spruce upstarting royalist sympathizer cavaliers. Polo's mallet calluses manually hardening ungloved handgrips, hardy competitors outwork feebler peasantry.

"Buenos dias," workparty's host genially rewelcomes roused assistants.

Cacao extract's coca-mixed potion revitalizes tarmac's sootsoldiers. Updrafted avis cawing outshrieks subliminal agonistic hurts stoics individually suppress, gripers collectedly weep. Self-pity's equilibrium attaining demimuted volumes, synthesizered tonalities Moogishly subsume drudging's dirge.

Dispatch's superfluent compulsiveness doubletimes: fiesta unveiling apogee rockface magnificence's plotted. Mañana's dawn'll originate duskended cavalcade. Rosy synchronicity supposes roadway's paving'll evaporate serviceably beforehand. Nonstick teflon warranties disclaiming tackiness's residual curing term, messes're destined. Gummy footbound majorettes impair mariachi tempos? Culture-clashed, time-pressed inadvertent sabotages threaten pageant.

STRUTTING MINSTRELS tooting dented horns precede banded marchers: industry-specific harness tetherers, recreation empathizers, et. al. Dixieland funereal build-up (wheezers mope graveward, contriving exhilarated turnaround) presentationally inspiring overemotional tooters, melodramatics glorify cadaver's death-rattled pirouette. Retarded steppers afford pavement makers extraneously elongated seasoning (slackers unconditionally squander). Showstoppers benumb dumbstruck tartars.

Quarterkilometer (.25km, metrically) separates resurfacers, crest. Backsided monolithical parapets cloak functions denying prisoncamp rumormills' corroboration. Crestline skyway cablecars garnish funicular railway embellishment's asinine network. Monkey-sized cabs renderably disqualify ridefarers: perplexing reticulation serves dumbwaitered trays?

Mountainsite problematics generate autoreliant solving. Electricity ordinarily'd borrow upchanneled generations produced hydrodynamically; dust-covered riverbeds tranquilize dynamo rousings. Sealevel's powergrid greeds furthermoor shipping electricity's kilowattage. Sailboat dynamism lightbulbs incandesce: windmills whomp bladed chasm-funneled tunnelings, susurrating windy permanence's affirmation.

Tape-hissed environment disquiet counteracting hypersonic blares, fanfares doubletrack stereophonic ironies. Endemic minor-intervaled harmonics structurally buttress self-deprecation. Absurd humorists admirably attune tar-soled enmiring, sidestepped forgoing (dumpers' toot preemptively reinterrupting), bathetic ribbon-cutting ceremonial's archetypical silliness. Cuervo cantine toters poting cantina's nectars lugubriously introduce followers: high-stepping fishnetted chorines evincing horsehead cowls, unpeekable scowls.

Bangtail rump elaborations espousing mount's zealous unguarded passion, dancehall writhers dedicate desiring's immodestly prominent path. Enigma decencies preconceptually veiling secret-topped protuberances lasciviously strip. Cantering fillies nicker. Jackbooted midget whipper-snappers, silkily clothed, sprout costumes outcoloring florally bloomed dyes. Floatbed trailers carryback Secretariat, Omaha, Nashua, Damascus-ancestored offspun descendant thoroughbreds. Skedaddled slews, mangily gimpy bow-tendoned nonwinning dogfood-fugitive garbagepail lineage'll gallop lengthy oval racecourse begun above 3000' altitude.

Afterthoughts're personified: stubbily waddling stablemen puffing horseturd presidentes, gear-laden valet varlets twirling electrojolt chargers (abolished liverywhere tracks're TRA-sanctioned), veterinarian meatwagon jingling apothecary bottlings, vegetarian oatswagon dangling carrots' sticked allurements logistically follow racehorse caravan. Full-length starter gateways circumscribe parading's barnyard, prognosticating trackside worksite milieus.

Play-grounded flypapered wingers succeedingly perpetrate convertible cruising's topless early-model Pontiac LeMans ostentatiousness. Fins prop photographers immortalizing stewards, mayors, backers, upper-tiered functionary officials. Furtively acquainted physiognomy's referrals queasily curdle: short-lost barstool buds magically reimpersonate highlife exponents. Everyother face's suggestive, magnifying matchmaker's retroscopically indistinct conjecture. Grotesque distortions sprain perspicuously agile namejumping, until embezzlement's idealized ambassadors reappear.

"Subbookkeepers redux!" doubletaken nebbish underlings, abducted/antiquated, now're styled imperialistically. Unrobed, jewelless plainness adorns flak-jacketed, open-collared unisexual pantsuits. Sweatfree trimmings neaten detachees. Cerebral preoccupations entitle thought-to-be absconded pencilpushers? Actuary ascendences're consistent, subsisting programmer respectability's clout.

Nerds gracefully acknowledging celestial rose petals anticlimactically exhaust officialdom's convertibles. Lowly unpedestaled pedestrians adopt vanquished battalion's crusader evacuation treadmill pacemaking. Enthusiasms conflict: serene nosiness subverts qualm-ridden noisiness. Inquisitive acquisitive hopealong Cassady romantics hammerlock counterbalancingly wrestled nihilistic downbeat hesitancies. Nonnatives, nonvisitors, unaffiliated dilettantes, atypical aficionado preemies devotedly sneak enlightenment's implausible attainment encouraging winning's shadowed confident captivation.

Uncountable thousandfold punters, hangers-on, thrillseekers've depopulated flatlands. Queued stick-figured desirers two-dimensionally overcrowd cliff's penthoused dwellings. Post-time opening's predate swarmers petition overnightfall beds, foods, libations. Crowding paradox's paroxysmic uninhabitability forestalls leisure. Mobs infuse sky-high thin-aired elevation; suffocating thickness imposes. Streetwide passages're alleys, windowledges impacting outward-straining gaspers aspire respiratory siezures, healthful mouthfuls're tubercularly unpublicized.

Carnival's prelenten excess fixations overwrite conduct-coded civilities. Exquisitely friable talusine groundworks quiver landslide premonition's flexibility underfeet/hooves, double-axeled tonnages, triple-timed hat dances. Environment's unreported impact-stated nemeses fester. Oblivion's pavilion encloses existential hedonists.

Mountaineering outdoorsmen nevertheless'd endorse rock-sensitive bunkers instating Hopi-reflective habitations. Laddered entryways precommand agility's ambulator capabilities ordaining fitness-minded lodgers ascend roomward. Nonagile pudgy slugs'll cohabit nightcrawler lodgings.

Stables downwindedly localize manures. Eastward prevailing millblade-churning gustiness skims horseflies. Semiunderground dens pamper horseflesh sensitivity's skittishness. Escarpment cubbyholes substratically emplace equine cloister hereunder grandstand catacomb quarry.

162

Quarried dormant volcano hugs bleachers half-surrounding bullring (colloquialism oft summarizing sub-mile podunk racecourse's geometrical circularity), baring geophysically breathtaking panorama. Acrophobia's heightened awareness recirculating asthmatic cliche, choking bettors'll succumb speculating dizzying perchance purchase selections. Unsmellable sulfurs'll contribute light-headed whimsy's influential erupting corruption.

Tar-eyed pavemastered payees hereatop estimate parade's unending swindlings' lucre star-eyed tourist-trapped bettors donate.

163

AGUA FIRMAMENTE nomenclaturely mimics Tijuana's Caliente; mountainous obscurity secreting nefariousness, malleable bordertown ethics're sleazily transmuted. Handicappers beware laxly enforceable narc prohibitives. Jockeys saunter, sixgun-style battery-operated cattleprod pacemakers protruding. Bejeweled trainers paste zircon expressions knowledgeable groomers refract. Paperwork record compiling bygone performances undergoes formatting glitches, e-mailed alignment merging erratic datum gremlins: turfcourse/dirt-based runs blend, amalgamating steeplechases. Midrace saddlemate switchings promiscuously sully hard-earned classlines' dollars/race determinants. Bloodlines rewrite biological reasonings: stallions procreate, impregnating ridgelings; filly/mare reproductively cloning foals reinstalls racing-formed skepticism.

"Forms're senseless," intuition proclaimer gloats, thoroughbredly denouncing datal reliance.

"Statistics miniaturize sense's comprehensiveness. Understanding's hardest; guessing's simplest," biased horsepicker bickers.

"Body language's hypersensitively acute. Toe-danced neck-bowed ear-pricked prancers decimate hangdog flat-eared limpers."

"Decimate'll eradicate 10%, undisturb 90%."

"Wanna bet?"

Marga's forthright persevering uncomfortably settles Math's numerologic structuralisms co-factoring variant-based paces' velocities, class-weighted credits/trip-noted demerits. Convenience's partnership, shoreover, lately's foundered; coitus's exhaustibility overmatching laborious nonrecreative pastimes saps inertial impulsiveness. Malingering doubters outliving ardent practicality envision betting romance's procreativity. Competitive cooperation'd theoretically quash weaknesses, augmenting monomental analytic shortcomings.

Decimations tabled, 10-race programs ideally'll repackage 100-head claimers differently, day-after-day, reconditioning 10-horse fielded categories. Decimal science's economized shuffles conceal 3-Card Monty's hallmarking deceptiveness: equitability. Parametrically enscribed equus profile sketches typical 10-year-old gelding nonwinner-of-2 (10k-or-over) acquiring $10,000/100 races, terrorizing trifecta-pooled flukers Rockingham-Ruidoso, Playfair-Fairgrounds: slowfooted sprinters, shortwinded routers, lasix-dependent bleeders, long-overdue dogmeat oatburners retaining heartbreakingly pleasant mettles.

Dawnhour workouts disseminate seediest ponyrides devisable. Somnambulistic exercise-ridden nags gamely canter, hauling racingdom's top-weighted over-the-hill reinsmen. Quadriplegic anklewraps externally restringing ligaments, dapperly spatted leggings impose faddish stances naive binocular spies misapprehend, appearing stylistically charmed.

"Pitiful," body-signed sightreader winces.

Crowded rooms've improvised plural bivouacs: ours sits hereinside Agfirm's track. Sleepyheaded campers enumerate scores. Dew-saturated woolens emitting vitality's smokescreens multigenerate diminutive fogbanks shrouding ghastly ghosts imitating racehorses.

"This'll reduce transparently," Margari conjures. "Attrition'll decide finishers; finishers'll win."

Transparencies possessing nightmare's daybreak reincarnate distressing conformations. Hobblers' rusty-gaited trots torment empathetic emotion; jockeys're upsidedown puppeteers pulling high-strung (low-energy) marionettes. Bodytalk translators decipher least-wounded strugglers.

"Goats're faster," conclusively broaches heretical cross-breed competitions.

Mountainscape biota interfuses vulpine, caprine, cougar, boar (feral porker), coyote-canine mixture contenders. Merry-go-round rebus kingdoms concocting fabled run-offs shadowbox palookaville sluggers:

Man-o-War's poorest relatives, multiply-removed. Punchdrunk weavers straighten-up, fractionally acquitting contentiousness's lapsed insolence. "Running beats glueing," prorates chance's relevance. Moving's life-affirmed substantiation outflanks speculation's guesswork; rendered carrion doomsday postponement celebrates post-paraded repetition. Handicapper comparers jot downs' participator tics, foibles, markings, musculatures. Noonish sun banishes workout joggers (dashers've antedecedently relaxed), draws buffs/duffers, masterplanner assayers/blaster-panner prospectors, wiseguys/foolhardies. Yesternoon's hornplayer showgirl promenaders rejuvenate hoariness's immemorial dedicating.

Fritzed PA chops orations dignitaries intone. Metalingual utterances syllabically accentuate cacophonic scatting. Relevant notations, blithering encomiums, insurance-mandated disclaimers, invigorating patters jumble; redcoat trumpeter reestablishes counterchaotic postcall organization.

Unobservable paddock discharges hobbled geriatric ponies. Washy latherings, unpricked auricular articulations, procaine eye-popped derivations preselect fittest survivor's stand-out, concurring figuring's prediction. 10-strong field's quasi-unanimous 1-10 favorite ratifies amendable overconfidence, trouncing competition.

MINUS-POOL PAYOUTS dominate premiering fortnight's toteboard tonic melodies. Monaurally straining bifocaled comptroller actuaries're worried. Rulebook minimum remunerates $2.10/$2.00 wagered; parimutuel apportionments strangle payers' struggle contending opposite 90% wagerers winnowing correctly. Desperation's longshooters nonethemore backing 3-legged gimps, chalkplayers overload favorites: $2.10-across compensation-prized consolement disinspires straight-bet hitters, sub-$4 perfecta median expunges exotics hideaways deflecting plunge-minded diversifiers' intensiveness. Sophistication's Pandemonium bankrupts actuarial greediness, smotherwise hampering unrestrained plays.

Bank-returned disinterest's unexciting prospectiveness defunds fun's hopechest stake. Exiguous payoff amounts obligate near-perfect scoring's eclat. Decimatable success's achieved whensoever choicest steed stumbles: 90-1 Pegasuses soar.

All-or-nothing propositions unnerve fairweather sportsmen. Professionals weathering horse-lattituded lifeless wagering pools equate unrushed groundstroke specialists patiently mirroring swapped forehands, backhands. Volleyers attacking net're adeptly lobbed; plungers keying longshots're ineptly "robbed."

Victimization fallacies assuage deteriorating shotplayers; exceptions uncommonly occur, splendidly cancelling hesitancy. Tactics ape anti-tactical swoops. Waiting's gamers study unriskable junctures. Second-best second-guessing rarely distinguishes banal in-the-money placers. Swerving traffic-snarled entanglements emancipate impeded hoofers. Disqualification fouls arbitrate arbitrarily. Sometime chariot-raced opponent whipping's unpunished; uninterventional contact's othertimes fined.

Riots verge. Feeling wronged, sentimental forfeiters overturn benches hereat any/all unfavorable edicts. Toddlers' playpensive tantrums compare sagely, opposing horseplayer's vile moody blue-streaked cursing.

"Thunderheads're dunderheads," cooler appraisers philosophize. Ranted outlashes profit patient opportunist beneficiaries.

Full-serve pump pimps toutly incorporate counselor assistance's benevolently tempered malevolence. Eugenio Bacardi Antero, inquiring reformed tarheels' availability, hypes touting's unbeatable advantageousness: reap payments, sow pointers. Back-assward collection's timetable beautifies scheme; plus, over-66% won/lost percentage indomitably unfalsifies credentials.

Excessive well-spokenness damns best-intentioned inveigler, Eugenio's flawlessly Anglic pitch's intoned. Chauvinistic northamerican subcanadians adventuring Tacoland's colorized sceneries downrighteously beseech blue-eyed guardians deliver'em out-from-under dark-eyed mexamericans. Eugenio'll bamboozle hispanic countrymen, conscript impressive Anglos, empowering seminar lieutenants. Vast deferential membership dependently consuming offhand tossings dissipate sweetmeats/nurse pathetically defensible stratagem.

"Believer personalities infest venture's marble hallways," Eugenic bilinguist deems. "Cucarachas siempre, verdad? Exterminator seraphim purely tend cockroaches' flocks—shearing, pruning—preserve pestilence's essence. Custodios: part-custodian, parta-Dios."

Genetic rooting reformulating societal helix organizing toutmasters' tenderfeet estimation, bookie avatars arrogate E.B.A.'s propounded engagement. Haloes shimmeringly lambent amend priorly lambasted profession. God's servants improvise slated commandments faith-taken catechism studiers memorize concerning dirt-composed partiality, strategically shaped contestability (frontrunners wire-to-wiring, closers inheriting, stalkers pouncing), quantified pace-adjusted class-rated numbingly digitized analizations. Scientific lingos convince unscientific hunchbackers.

Far-flung classmate monomaniacs frequenting prerace talks rebut "randomly" stultifying variety informing cinemascoped disaster castmates. Snottily gifted children're deleted; strikewise nuns, abbeys, rabbis, imams; prostitutes, grandfathers, Jews, Arabs; motherland upholders, fatherland defenders, oases dependers, oilfield tycoons. Dowdy middle-aged tour-busted couples showcasing he'n'she sportswear (unlikably linkable unisex t-shirts) assemble lecture devotees.

Chain-smoker beerless nonpracticing addicts nervously crinkling popcans paraphrase crickets. Anthropoid distinctiveness differentiating bred trait colors, proportions, presumptions subserves superimposed arthropod ovipositions. Bughouse lecturers decline delirium's assimilation. Wilm. Lee's huminsect hallucinations're derivitively trite, patly reapplicable; exterminating's applicablity itches fleabit stimulations.

"Chalk'll choke ya," keynotes prohibitive favorite-played disclaimer; "longshots'll bleed y'dry," counters.

Equivocations stylize lecturing. Counterposed checks balance protrusions, rigging deniability. Choice's either/or interreliant stupefactions petrify wood solid thinkers; fluffy daydreamers sheepishly woolgather. Intermediaries, undauntably, apprehend redemption's coupon clipping: pick-six syndicating.

"We'da gangbang d'bastid," Herman Delveccio, Secaucus meatcutter knife salesrep, dissects incorporatable systematism.

Nonpatronizingly, Jersey-twanged middleman untangles overlaps defraying wager blanket's eiderdown heatability. Loose-packed featherbetting combinatorial 6-race ticket (2-8 syndicators co-hold) possibly outsmarts dumbbell weightlifting's hernially strenuous ham-fisted betloads.

"D'beauty's d'looseness. Mohammed Ali's fluttery beestings."

Guessers painlessly excise overtaxable unlikelihoods. Undertaxed wild-ass unlikelihoods're uncut: coordinated wagering's payment forms overlie multiply permutable readings rationalizing deviance's improbable truths.

Whole-race buy-ins arrange strategizer's constituent tabulations. 3–5 singletons (one/race winner's selected) nominate ticketed permutations inclusively surpassing darkhorses' full-bet fields. Trenchantly, pick-six's winnings standard-bearer toteboarders parlay five-some overbet walkovers + unpredictable oners repaying 100-1. Delveccio's spreadsheet covers +/-six differentiated tickets. Syndicate-financed, $48/$96 outlays × 6 = $500-max, prospecting five/six-digit bonanzas.

"Waita min-," Mrs.D. demurs. "Shotgun shellgames revisited. Dogtrack Ruskie Roulette'll disembrain anyoner."

Factional sidetakers argue stakes blanketing's reasonability. Two-faced discourse plotters berate spendthrift peso/dollar throwing; discreetly rapproach Mr.D., counterposing thrifty four-way spending layout.

AGUAFIRM'S HARDBOILED FINANCIAL DREGS resteep currency's insubstantial teas.

Minus-poolplayers dilute racebank solvency; chit debenture offers're optioned, refunding cash-ins. Subterranean rumblings thunderously revolt, telegraphing dit/dah-patterned brushfires flared afar. Unstable riskers apotheosize abandon.

Syndicationally indemnified calculators, furthermoreover, tramp aloof, unruffled, oddheaded. Oddsmaker suresightedness guiding foursome's fearsome chutzpa, temerity's salient pricklishness brandishes vainglorious quills. Hedgehog offensive posturing (defense attitude's maladjusted rectification) reforms delinquently lazy sloth emulators. Reasserted aggressiveness pulsates subdermal unbruised skin's armor-plated imbecility. Brassy combo railbirds chirp starling silverplated cockiness.

Combination layawager installments vouch surety tresspassing t-bills' safety-netted infallibility; trackside's sporty thrill-reputed ambience drowns outbalanced savings-bonded whispering, vents pit-called elation.

Boxcar fever's multi-digited totelit numberings denumb favorite-stuffed masticators gnawing cuticled stubs. Lotterylike matchbook sulfuric whims enkindle lucky sparks irresponsibly igniting number-based, color-fixed, name-set conflagrations burning debtors' ramshackled hutches. Hunches decompose preconceptualized reviews; collapsing time-framed separation affects prescience's inspirable conjuring. Hocus-pocus focusers incant verbiage illuminating darkhorse flashers.

"Baby's due. o-for-27? Sandbaggers're rebuilding tote."

"Muy despachio? Playin' lame—Notre Dame's injury play, recuerda? Down-and-out passroute ... charleyhorse pull-up ... scrimmage subterfuge, hombre, gamesmanship's oldest trickery. Fake'n'snake, diablo's bluffing recurs eternalisimo."

"Coke'm, stoke'm. Rightly dosed, anyone'll roast. Nostrils dilating? Primed highballing meatball, tenderized/juiced."

Herm, helpmate Shirley, meterthieves-turned-touts effectuate predetermined overlink stakehorse keys, singling outsider quadruped champions aggregatedly chained—segregate motherloads prohibitively uptaking 80% wagerable spots.

Eavesdropping E.B.A. scoffs, "Goldminers! Cibolia conquistadores!" pitiably nudging undertone, "Sabes, Cortez-wise, seminars're incomparable subjugators."

Bloodletting's unhurried depletion outgushes, summationally, heart-ripping's atavistic surgery. Succumbing toutmaster backsliders dishearten Eugen (chieftain insists risk's encouragers mind risk discouragement's pitfalls).

"Rocks crumble, lakewaters dessicate, winds contaminate," Euge litanizes cryptic simpletonian insight's zenish balderdash.

Glacial-paced change's amenable; short-termed upturns're capitalizable. Euge's unsanguine avarice perturbs fourplayers. Afm's glamorized faddishness portends slickened boomtown's backlashed skid. Infringing commandos, counterattacking garrisons, hairtrigger enrageable commoners, kingly past-checkered taxidermist stuffed-shirt reaping gamefarmers empower powderkeg implosions.

Prefatory 5-furlong sprints intercede gloom's cloudbank omen. Bright-clad saddlepads defog daily-doubled uncertainties: paired $2.10-paid victors' parlaying awards chickenshit $2.40-payoff (conflicting authentically valid exotic bet-funded foundations leastly cellaring $10-payoffs/$2-bets). Like-fielded, low-yielded racers dash expectant longshot-hungry grandstanding commodity floggers' cornerings, carreras tres-quatro. 5-10's coordinatively dispirited projection constitutes grandest six-picked prize's undiminished trepidation.

Cinco's sinkers hobble, forsaking paddock's installing enclosures. Martyrs weeping soreness hereupon're reembodied; equinous saintliness disallows doubting apostasies. Someone'll outbid pain's bit, remedying nonfinishing's epidemically pervasive sprawlers.

Precedent expounds conspicuous darling: mightiest supple-muscled unbandaged #9 charger, Whoreadmiral, eleven-year-old roan gelded shrivling, 15-for-123 lifespan (14/15 victories happening presurgically, navigating fourth-rate Irish peatbog turfs), open-line laying'm 1-20. Antecedently (48-hour period's local neostandard respite scrupulously honored) Whoreadmiral'd whomped semi-identical cavalry rivalry. Twenty lengths victory margin, steadying betrickst horrendously out-boring/in-lugging cheaters, branded Whoreadmiral's ultrasuperiority.

"Undefeatable. Fastest durable ticketcasher ahoof. Secretariat's chingaling symphonic reprise," slathers praiseworthy curse.

Contention's fifth-raced charade shambles postward. Swaybacked #3-horse Tazmanian Geranium's jockey considerately dismounts, hand-holding reins upto gate's fateful loading. Equal-odded Riboflavin, 8-year-old maiden (0/77 winless bids), mummifyingly drags peggish foreleg— galloped anapests clunk, repatterning dah-dah-DAH/dah-dah-DAHT henceform which-way-did-he-go moronically dribbled drabs. Unpaired 50-1ers Geraldo Rivera, Cantinflas (Nu.s uno/dos) bewitch name-crazed moneyspenders. Fame's flames fancify fans. Panhispanic chauvinisms overlook farcically inapt aptitudes. 7-year-old Cropduster, 13-year-old Zeke's Jailbait bracket agedness: neither's viably backable, figuring velocity's projectable aspects. Stamina lackers Rudolf, Monticristo, Bandylegs preassure 3-way pacesetting crosstrack blockade collapsibly demolishing back-lagging abiders.

On-track veterinarians helping gatemouth rousts hypodermically elucidate tranquil instillations? Hopped-up speedball syringe inoculations reprove healthier sentimentalities. Flyspecked spongers cosmetically deswath lathering sweatiness; rumpbumpers nudge recalcitrantly budgeable heavyweights. Spring-locked slotted cages shudder, animating starter's mechanistic dragon.

"Y'afuera!" caller decants fifth's inauspicious commencement. Liquitoned unction glibly overlubes rough scrambled tangle. Rapid babbling unintelligibly ostracizes dialectic ignoramuses—indolinguic locutions peppering Mexicanized Castillian idiom hyperconstricts inner-circled comprehension, swirling horserace idioms. Trackish saltiness prerequires seasoned trackers.

Rarefied aerostratal clarification, substandard course's size, plow-motion drayhorse anticerelity foreshorten perceptibility. Hoofprints stickily disengage unstickable loess; clamorous grunting snorters grimace, undersquirming overactive straddlers' horsemanship. Sadomacho whippers repress impulsion, hand-ride asserters reprovingly contend. Saddlehorn finessers undertax exertion's storage, slappers flog.

Amidtrack, three-wide pacers're slowing. Electric outletting guilelessly occurant, buzzering tackers click arclit radiance. Preeminent catastrophes upstage Whoreadmiraled victorious fleetfootedness: pacesetters collapse.

Uncontrolled steeplechase's gracelessly consolidated. Deadweight barricades obstructing straightaway compile additive wrecks. Nearby small-armed gunshots parenthesize menace's recollection; obtrusively deranged barrage bushwacks hazarded equestrians, eyewitnesses. Tripwire westerns' stunt carnages downing unwary beast gallopers predirect 5-race's reenactment.

Money-chosen champion, nowever, dies preclimactically. Non-Kubrick directed crowds're undiverted. Rioting methodically delapidates steward's stonewalled officiation: breakdowns're cosas Diosas, God-acted meddlings above-and-beyond humankind's rejudgment. Limpingly straggled tortoises're win-place showed.

Tazman's Geranium 296.40 97.80 44.40

Riboflav. 104.20 51.80

Geral. Rive. 32.20

Also-rans're unspotted.

BEDLAM INUNDATES AGUAFIRMAMENTAL process. Finalized results're inadmissible.

Loserdom's roaring unanimity lobbies annulment; scarce live-ticketed winners're worthlessly compensated (chit-assed IOUs, unconstrained drink-passed outs), recruiting "haves" thereunto have-nots' army. Cheated gameplayer umbrage incites lavish vehemence interestingly outscreaming mesoindians' wellsprung, well-documented indignities. External commotions, internals coagulate. Unchecked guerilla-armed bands intermix crybaby wailers, jamming rifles cacophonically.

Conductor constabulary surrenders baton controllability. Disorder's allowance enervates fanatic trackbeat percussionists, drastic bell-tolled liberationists. Insurgency flails, barring further-scheduled racecard.

Low-lying syndicator nonagitators eavesdrop subbasemented echo's groundless vouching: grouchy bookkeeping embezzlers (ex-barflies overseeing track's finances) opine pick-sixpack settling's done. Hereafter's quandary posing competition's gunpointed ceasefire, penny-pincher pitchers outpour liquidation's advocacy. Carryover six-bet pools're desirably finished.

"Pay'em whatever'll defuse," calmly sensational voicer sobs. "Chits're reprehensible. Nobody'd risked chit-papered dinero."

Bickering ledger domain's maintainers claim ample cash'll handle complaints. Greenbacked scads've plumped moneybag shipments dispatched coastward. Armored carloads proceeded quotidianly, transferring grubby-handed germs, whiskered whiskey-drunk portraits, enumerated soul-stacked inventories banknote sums denote. Stage-whispered interpretation crystallizes embezzlemental reflex endangerment: absconding middlemen probably've usurped abundant hundred bundles.

Candid Cassandras suggestively photographing scandalous calamities append ransoming glimpse, disparaging six-raced six-figured carryover's accounts payable. Restrictingly, 4-6 tickets're collectable, comptrolling abridgers extol reward's abbreviation eliminating long-lined wranglings. Preservable grand-prized enormity, furthermire, embeds sprawlover weed-grown greed-sown uprisen enrichening wish's invasiveness congesting conscientiousness's enterprising streams.

Sotto voce conspirers elate winecellar wallowers. Sots spurning rioters unurn jiffy-fermented rotgut musts yeastily fizzing. Bubbleheaded mellowbelly flimflam undergrandstand racetrackers' acumens coalesce: we've triumphed. Pooled distributions indispensably backpedal least-resisted pathway.

Official megaphone advisories procrastinating finalization bureaucratically persuades unswayable mob: null're fooled; all're fixated. Obsessiveness's persuadable despondencies snare freestyle Molotov rocktail flingers.

Omniconcessional wordings depersonify politcal campaign promissory rotes. Passive-voiced assurances unman accountability's subjugator, predicating verbosity's irresolute communications.

"Everything'll wind-up fixed," barbarously translates overrefined lubrications.

Migration snowballs: 1 hi tor iced snowy dusted glacier exemplar overtakes avalanchee snowballing impressment's configuration. Onehundred-by-twohundred campesino skidders, declasse stumblebums, swept-up plutocrat impersonators aggregating unharmoniously descend. Facemasked badlanders (nose-down covering's eyefuls beam disingenuity) revolutionize "anonymous," outstandingly suspending colloidal disbelief, flakily refuting blendability's solution. Masks're peacemaker badges, warfare targets.

Unpartable migrators deafly adulate hornblower oratorios; adumbrating scowlers black-out accommodator faction's compliable predisposition. Obstinate sloggers delightedly exasperate automobiling lords.

Pavement's smearers corroborate defective disintegration. Millimetrically slimmed coating crumples processionally, unprofessional road-steaders stipulate; disgraced workmanship pride's reflexes countermeasure weighty crowd's detrimental overtaxing hardship. Decadence shockwaves cascade pebbled landslides. Mobbers' tromp de-oils tarbrushed dirts; stampeding turnpikers restore prepaved rusticity.

Scourging encouragement's forcefulness musters scufflers. Demonstrative massiveness quells twitchy uncertain pricklings. Consolidation metaphysically introverts physicality: numbered bulkiness restates conformity's testily comforting pervasion. Irreconcilable differences're subsumed, farsightedly.

Close-ups disclaim conformity. Unshared perishables, waterbuggering liquefactotums, roadside's pissings, shittings, pukings, airway's concomitant befoulings federate wastelandish cruelties. Additionally, rodent demicommunities suppurate humanistic collective's woundedness.

Ratlike metacreatures socialize bipolar subspecific offshoots. Bulkier, Chihuahua/goat/mole sphinxes lumbering abackside vaunt heft's meat-locker roominess. Bolder meatless shrews insinuate day/night raids. Infestivity replays sprocketable animations recapitulating David-Goliath mismatched underdog dynamics whither mites're triumphantly championed.

Warm-blooded swarmtroopers assail packeted bundlings bunglers transiently misplace. Tanker-treaded fatso ratsos coprophageously grumble arears, munching dingleberries, rumpsteaks, cheeklets, filets dungon.

Hungrier trudgers unconscionably generating salivas simper. Backward-glanced craven ravenosities nauseate picky eaters. Bottom-fed mammalian hepatitis repository vermin carne caters disgustable aversions. Unrecollected socio-spiritual interdictions surely've tabooted gigantic shit-eating ratons' edibility! Heedless starvation-fearing recreants brave viral infectiousness, slaughter slow-footed crapybaras, incinerate spitfire barbecues.

177

Mingle-filed descenders flee roasting eviscerations. Molerat soilers befouling incenses etherize most gustos; anesthetic eating sleepwalkers omnivorously shrink cognizant tasters' permeating objection.

Flamed fecal tripes overlay inversions pressuring downwardly regressive departures. Bonesucker ghouls gnaw contaminant barbecue, lick-starting Texas foodchainsaw massacred epidemics? Foreseeable famine, pestilence, omnipollutant infestations enfold wandering squanderers.

Nipping shrew packrats westwardly drove herded stockyard horse-traders. Sunset luridity wintergrating crisp visibility, splendid pollutants' lambency overthrows governing prognostic doomsayers. Reconstructed, deconstricted freemarket pueblito diminutively nictitates adistant, unvenomously coiled.

TACK-HAMMERED ANUNCIOS PLACATE credulous

dunces. Disruption's administratively abjured. Infernal forces're negligibly deflected. Defaulting likelihoods harmlessly prosper, forewarning depreciated precipitations (piddling squall-scaled downpours countervene financing's tycoon-undoing typhoon). Tourism's combat redliners rezoning vacationland fortifications sandbag lobby-level windowpanes; unrelated fairytale wishing infers bulletproofing anti-shrapnel ramparts merely're precautionary floodplain stopgap levees.

Hunkered, bunkered, zonkered bartenders entreat upcountry's abandoners, sing drunkathonic ballads glorifying passivity's virtuousity. Aquinote tunes croon hearsay's heresies. "C'mere" schmeres luringly waggle silverplate shakers plying liquor's eternal succor.

Ambassadorial cascenic beautifiers inveigling passersby prophesy pointless activity's virtuousness.

Curfew shoos straggler bunches. Guerillas've vamoosed, exercising regiment mob's self-replicating concealment escort. Duplicity's facilitation capacitates sneaked infiltrations. Unbarbecued fastfood's spindle-tailed raiding brigades create craterlike fissures penetrating unsealable fortresses. Witches' catlike familiars prototypecast infiltrators' Sorex insectivores? Disappearing stealthy masqueraders solemnize creepily worrisome carnivals.

Overcrowding nexuses vex sharpie trackmaster estimators. Centralized grouping clusters endanger idlers: crowds clump targetable nodes. Unsafety haunts terrorist wariness, reconfiguring xenogenerative bombers annihilating Haifa synagogues, Trafalgar pubs, Oklahoma welfare administrations. Outgunned terrorist's fighterbomber manual-of-arms earmarks yellowed pages indicating hyperpublic bomb locating partialities almost seconding lifeboat formality's courteous nominatives discriminating spareable worthies.

Secluded isolationists arouse warier surmises. Nongambling, undrinkable tavern sanctuary repudiators singlehandedly magnetize federale iron-heads; unstrung quartets appreciably hypermagnetize detective filings: conspiracies're assumable.

Four-headed winning ticketholders waddle unpopulated nonsingular tracts. Boon's farming harvest season'll pony-up fruit sixteen hour-long daylightless, nightflown eternities away. Suspecting divisibility preclusion, golddigger handicap hunchers usher goldfingered likeminded partners. Eight-legged operatic dragonsuits flout octocular bi-coupled octopede's coordination. Chimerically unfoundable windfalling kitty's boodle binds purblind luck-suited duckfoot quackers.

Daffy insomnial dithering unionizes racecard-carrying torchbearers. Claptrap recap exercises kill dreadful intuitions quelling tote-ticket conversion's imperiled consonance. Hushed giggle, bickered inconsequential abruptness, buttondown decorum's counterformal hysterics curtail low-profiled anonymity.

Delveccian jitter suppression strategy instigates semiprivate portably potable soirees: Herm'n'Shirl swilling unbagged tequila's circulated sooth syrum. Archaically regenerative storytelling elixer loosens inhibiting vigilance's scruples. Ingenious confessors repulse eavesdroppers. Run-on diarrhetic disclosures outflow anus nincompoop diary's voluminousness.

Herman's penile-implanted slabs prove sexily uninvolving. Desensitized lipids fattened libidity's sheath, necessitated hydropump engorgement accessorization. Magnanimous Vasoline lubricious greasings unseated foreplay's panties. Unpopular mechanic dickerings docked painless copulation. Estrogen native-gland effluences dried, intimated desertion's clefting rift. Pre-operative copulating loomed memorably happier, procreating recriminated realizations: implant router wasn't sex-driven; endowment's abstracting protraction outgrew quaking business-weakened presentiment unsentimentally phallically epicentered.

Shirley's respondability adapted. Lingually frank philanderers telegraphed willingness, unsubtly slobbered eye-boggling, lip-licking conge-niality. Laundromats, dressmaker alterations platform venues, fein-schmacker enotecas, round-robin frisbee golf tourneys stocked fishily en-couragable bachelors. Limpid piscene gawks secreted glandular teardrops saltily proposing oiled marriage's discretionary watercolor smudge. Ne-gotiated besmirchments upheld dishonoring's honorable phrases debar-ring phallovaginal intercourse's assent. Multi-tongued trilling farethee-wells delectably equalized turkeyfat baster's tomtomming hydrolicock.

"Infidelities overcompensated," Shirl laughs.

Metafortunately, Hermy's meatcutting blade-traded prowess propor-tionately grew, tabulating fetishism's amulet valorization.

"Stick'nit to'em," Herm's aphrodisiac confidence-building successes confabulated smug, hermaphroditic eroticism, pendulous grossness, sadist inflictability.

Destined discovery's neoclassic masturbator mag sketch come-to-life composed spread-eagled housewife staining slipcovered cushions neath jiggling gigolo's nibbles, door-framed macrophallic unpumped impoten-tate wielding unsatisfied butcher's gap-toothed slicer (caption one-liners irrelevantly subsidiating E-cup bazongas, dugong schlong). Humorous sobbed laughing's humongous honks reacted, cunnilinguically out-manned cuckold recapitulates.

Earshot-range mannerly noticers withdraw. Hermes' cunningest got-terdammerung reprisal repels attentive auditors sneakily sounding-out inexplicable malefic cryptographics' uncoded boldfaced blurts. Melodra-matically methodical madness's insufferable. Crocodile tear phlegmatics disgorge mucousy spumes, undaintily wetting encroachers. Obnoxiously competent, dickheaded monster dominates.

"Counseling'd solve todos, compadres," winking Shirl's shilling coop-erates, instilling supplementary slimy filler.

Discreditable psychoanalyses yammered sledgehammer jargons reworking unoriginal reorganizations—fixatedly, male-organized crankcases. "Cockomania," "phallic-obsessive," "beached whale syndrome" deviantly satirizing, marriage mender's quips purposefully clownplayed boffing's buffoonery. Theraputic jibes deriding husband enraged missus, innervated rebound reuniting.

"Motherhood! You'da concluded Dickie'd sprouted, detached, pupated adultward," half-seriously reassembles that unpaperable adoption.

Motherly lover caresses transformulated whambang brutality's prominence, switching domination rapacities. Dress-up preenings, alphabet tutoring, singalong soothings coddled doll dong; diminutizing supernaturally humanized mondo cane's candycane lickability. Entreatments reared miracleworker fulfillments: pumpless resurrection erection's regularities bespoke Lazarine comebacks.

"Sonofagun," fatherhood's boastful patting fanatically unpants "th'litta fella."

INCONSPICUOUSNESS FLOPS. Inebriated foot-long hotdog wagger bi-culturally offends MPs patrolling curfew's lattitudes, phallocratic barristers abrogating crotchroom airing's vicissitudes. Whistleblower arrests jaunty perpetrator, sluggish "accomplices." Manhandling beggar apologizes; machinegun sovereign rebuffs.

"Déjala!" gunpoint translated, demeans "let'erbe" (feminine article articulating "pinga's" a-ending).

Improvidently pilloried headman leads pubic publicizing's humbling exposition. Doll-sized lacy garters (surreptitiously pre-rigged), lipstick kisses've decorated cakewalk promenader. Freaky chastisement, unappetizing caricatured appeasement slab ludically re-membered, thuggish grenadier astound midnight's childless orphans salmonly rushing, spawning lifelike sacrifices casino-to-bar.

Ventriloquist dummy's skinhead cousin, Slabbo, Globe's Weightiest Retouched Dork, radiates charismatic provocation. Puppy lovability, talisman deification, jarbaby sideshow wonder laud Slabbo's egotistically unsensed conflation. Gawkers sweet-talk sardonic goo-goos, hoot invectives skewing off-target: skewering gutless "pistolero." Gunpoint-held borderline reprobates titter; offended commandeering rifleman unlatches safety's cocker, rips air-shattering roar.

Silencio. Reclaiming clamor's tumult exceeds lethally noisome outburst's putridly pusillanimous manipulation. Birdcalls razz gunplay melodramatist.

"Basta!" mocked guard's spite egregiously flounders. Unhittable psittacine canaille gabbles; on-hand stand-ins whimper.

Nobly unjeering Urogenital Majesty complies. Softspoken bigstick teddybear objectifies unconquerable pretension, vexing guardsman's narcissism.

Jailing carousers unbecomes battle gloryhound's fondest self-seeking praiseworthiness. Jails overflowing overthrowing defendant specimens renounce rowdy journeymen overdrinkers' criminalization admission passes. Fatuously impassioned arrester hasn't deliberated consequential drainage tapped cock's released: watershed outflux sociopathologically eliminates captives gunned-down aspiring escape. Releasing's selection gloomily dims. Bright-eyed triggerman lasers unbreakably intensified beams.

Trophy motivation triggers hunter's instinctiveness? Flabbed mammoth slapping thigh-to-knee dorkily prefabricates fireplace gallery's mountings. Antlered moose, horned buck, staggered fawn, rheumy rhino, maned lionized feraldom's regent accouter well-hung den emphasizing indecipherably contextualized phallus. Seminal killers lop sexing's souvenirs? Apologizing undeters officiating lockstock turnkey. Joshing's unutterably ill-advised.

Bribery's hindrances entwine. Uncashed scrip winnings've assumably inflated beseechings' credence. Looting follows shootings, anyhow. Corpse's pouches unbutton, outfurl, unzip, spilling hid goodies. Strategizing bribers typically'd embroider pillowed frills embedded elsewhere. Guide-serviced swaps (lives-for-treasures) outwhore whoremonger's hoarier hording.

Desexed contextualizations override polymorphous psychosexual inveiglements. Whopping flaccidity desensitizes. Valueless booty's unshakeable swaggering leverage forcefully rubs pubis publicist's humiliation protractability. Face-saving reparational adieus prepared quietly're fancied.

Diversion-wary squadleader crackles statically hearby, saluting penis's kidnapper derisively. Interventionist pyrotechnicalities ignite cross-purposed flares vociferously altercating policeman's estimable foolishness. Crouching terrorists're undermining defended battlements, fusiliering regular's upbraid skein unballs: diversions propitiate infiltrating.

Gunshipped helitroopers whomp-in emphatically, overhang blacked-out hamlet, quashing ambitious vindicators prowling herein. Searchlit forged sunshines rescinding inkiness enlighten mercurial cleansers. Pogromatic streetsweepers shinny downstrung deathlines, invade preselected doorways, machineguns aflame. Purgical strikers' vivisections transpire. Abstracted foreground disputants haggle phallocentrically, unacknowledging full-scale exterminations.

Sobered schlupper repositions schwantz, zipping. Ousted bullet-riddled "revolutionistas" hit streets, dripping. Jurisdictional vyers adjourn lipping.

Curfew-defiant bettors've avoided hangman's noose. Militaristic detention safely escorted well-lighted drunks.

Murder needed darkness.

VULTURING PICKERS, MOURNING DOVES, beaten hawk-ish wimps administer uncooped coup's coup-de-graced croppers. Ski masks've marked convictable mutes; indecent eyefuls're widened, circumforming double-ringed jelled eyeball plasm. Antichrist manginess hoists crash-figured failed dissidents, blood-lettered denouncements draping unconvinceable, irrefutable indictment allegories.

Ejemplo: "Vincente-la-Vibora" toxically herpetologizes slender, down-scaled casualty's memorial. Unrhymed irreasonable poetry characterizes sneakiness, treachery, slime-bellied, quick-fanged krait traitor demonizations rectifying extermination's absolution.

Uncannier circumstantial forensics coronate princely coincidences: pock-marked scrawniness identifies subcommanded radicals to-a-man. Informative intelligence's betrayed infiltrator constituency? Woodlands subsistence ravages brand fungal-splotched symptoms discoloring complexions, pullulating diseases, specifying sapiens' degenerating offshot subspecies. Breedlike discrimination transcending facial-colored racial-featured giveaways uncloaked sickly spy imitators.

Toplessly unshielded armor jeep landrovers coerce ostentation's supercilious pose, taunting snipers. Inconvenienced shopper, shopkeeper grousers resenting protorevolutionary intrusiveness, refocus goals. Pedrovillians connive hatchet-buried ceremony'd rededicate hedonism's thesis. Rollicking liturgical assuagement rubdown lifts downgraded institution, all-but-forgotten race forum. Resumptive strike's smash-hit iteration connects unnerving hazard, rewarding solace. Eleventh-hour announcement'll disperse disbursals. Owed settlements'll rebase pyramid's sturdiest posterity: affirming trackmasters abjure welshing.

Outstanding chit's demographic pandemics heap +/-1000 refunds. Chivalrous cussed accountants nervily riffle satchel's currencial downpour. Double-crossed embezzler predicaments miff belated philanthropists atoning forgettable crimes?

"Ventana 'stabierta," abbreviates window reopening proclamation.

Crabby satchel-faced scuttlers measurably wince. Declared refunded re-imbursements disinclude surprise finale's deep-sixed fiasco. Unreim-bursed sourpusses badmouth irruptive racing's irresolution. Grumbling losers're unreconcilable. Groundswollen sedition rebuilds, unblocking pent-up particulars recollecting thoroughbled aneurysm draining king-maker sport's hemophilial probity.

Legend accretion oysterizes osterized granules, reforming imperfec-tion's pearls. Overlayered officialisms authenticate prevarications, un-dercutter murmurings cube exponential multiplications explicating actu-ality's node. Videotaped head-ons, panoramas, sideway ground-viewed playbacks entrench visualistic individualisms indivisibly, arbitrating zilch.

Anticlimactic megaphoned auditions announce premio grande, some-$14,000 (155,000 peso, fluctuating agio depending) riot-shortened pick-sixshooter parlay-waylayed winners've "rightfully" earned. Feedback keens. Reradicalized banshee carpers deem recompense unjust (syndica-tors're dissimilarly agreed, calculating take-out's rapacious raking); ac-countants're pelted.

Spitball alumni wad bottlecaps, foil, wiring, thorns. Angered fingers self-lacerate hurling barbed missiles. Whitened administrators immobi-lize, invulnerably shielded blunderneath bloodily erroneous marksman-ship. Megaphony contritions nettle rage's mettle. Nettled outbursters' aiming worsens.

Laceration's espew d'corpus satirizes martyrdom: geekshow Christs abnegate soft-tissue mortifications, eliciting zounds! exclamations Shakespearean tragedians popularized, preHollywood gorefest transliter-alizations.

Terrified steward headmasters retaliate, backfiring rubberbanded pres-idents trustworthily minted, impeccably engraved. Trivial airloft diffrac-

187

tions subtract sum divisive multiples; horde-bound hornswoggled proletariat swipes bankdrafts contemptuously. High-handed cowering tossers enrage grabbers. Touchable fluff, denominatored numerically, computes worth's expirability.

Exterminated indigent's footsoldiers shotwithstanding, thereon smolders revolt's recharging ember: embittering indignity, graduating slight outflank headier onslaughts. Starvation's abominable, slavery's abolishable (polishable?); contempt's incendiary.

Disrespected gamblers cavort, upsetting Volkswagens, misappropriating halftracks supportive tankers half-heartedly fortify (corpsmen also've sustained tracksite damage's traumas). Armor-divisioned complications sidle, conjoining awesome newborn dysentery's happenings. Plagued dissenters wobble. Destructions enmire. Streetfighters swerve hotelward, claiming privilege's consummately fine commodes.

Shit-hit fanatics rout bellhop weaklings. Concierge's ever-accommodating advisements undeter intestinal destinies. Upstairs bounders flyover stairs three-at-a-time, affronting hurdles unencountered, objectors uninvolved. Number-plated doors've swung unlatched, invited intrusions.

Disinfection's porcelain defection boding ill-seated omens, yearning defecators uncover lidded mystery's Pandorama: stoppage. Dysfunctional familiarized stoppages've implosively visited remodernized nightmarishly pipedreamt inhabitation. Monstrous vibrant fecalization moves pseudopodia, assumes sci-fi blob's atomic-powered giganticism mutating once-inert matter's flushability.

Brown-stained brochade wallpaper, seeping ceilings, sogging floorboards improve filthiest leak's disastrous implication, amplifying catastrophic entropy's smelliest repercussive thumpings. Contamination exactitudes condemn exoneration platitudes disobliging "minute" inconveniences unhousebroken dogmatically unfixed quagmire exerts. Seepage refines sewer's once-grounded circumscriptions; septic-tanked augmentation annexes whole highrises.

Contagion gathering disciples coincides dung flooding. Overcivilized degeneration's fecally watered loo spellbinds doo-doo-gooders. Fantasia's aphasia afflicts crestfallen Disneylanders resurveying storybook-written tidiness's unuttered fetidity.

Styrofoamed quays unstably buoy debarkation piners. Anchorage's vessels distrustfully countersign semaphored potlatches proffering ransoms, imploring seaside's safer stateline crossing. Leper unattractiveness publicizes quarantined preconditions; upraised shriekings fascinate sickest appraised leakings. Abysmal rumor's truthful fragrance baywardly wafts.

Feudal gunfights frag hotshot capitans, fragmenting garrison units. Gangland warlords dislodge generals. Perfidious pactmen intramilitarily consume fresh-made buffeted allies, collaterally ravaging sideboard witnesses. Cornucopial gunning sates fewer murderers, inasmuchas more're annihilated.

Low-laid insurrectional columnists relishing internecine gunfought foe reduction sedulously monitor opportune strife. Seaport's quarrelsome importances concentrate netherland doom-lowering gunsights. Unofficially detained quarantinees abiding sewerside watch's profitless anguish languish. Buildings're unlivable, foods're befouled; decisively, casinos're unplugged.

FOODLESS, POLEMICALLY UNCOMMITTED, paper-rich/ penny-poor, still-uninfected straggling wanderer pogostuck merry-go-rounders reorient upward-mobilized ascendability. Remaining's unworkable. Rutted recourses, howeverlastingly redundant, outstrip stagnations.

Disorganized, desyndicated climber quorums vote bipedically. Democratic emigrations' consensus coalition braids stranded minorities. Unifying healthiness, docility, movability reenlighten Francogenerative egalitarianism, liberating fraternalization's male-ordered bridles (hermanas 2-1 overpopulating hermanos).

Resister surges press together groups predisposably riven asunder, unsentimental disaster-victimized unification preempting candied (anti-Candide) reversions idealizing brotherhood's prevalence.

Handiwork's handicaptain ouvroir ringmasters Delveccios, Eugenios, nosotros reassociate unsanctionable utopia: cloud-bound airtight unbroached heaven. Aguafirm self-sufficiency scheme's hypothesized perpetuities urforming unweanable dependencies. Bettor-built world theorem dietetically prescribes cake icing subsistences, discredited beancounter naysayers pule. Bottomed-out hayracks underscore race-stocked nadir's unsafe feedlot.

Ragtag follower tourists're amenably convinced airlifted packages'll nullify famine's consequence. Macroboosted micro transmitters've relayed S-O-Ses narrating lowlanded pestilential scourge's house-to-house fight. Warring troop divisions're usefully recounted, binding rescues' hyperurgency, rescuers' mountain-topped counterinsurgency hideaway. Downplayed upcountry jeopardy heightening sealeveled war-loving grovelers' foulness, hamster radiomen broadcast higher civility's rescue-worthy situation.

DC-3 constellation airliners purr catastrophically transoctave; rangy octane infusion refuels airshow thrill potential's unpullable dives. Wigwag wing throttlers overpass needy wayfaring bullet dodgers, airlifting nix.

"Hemp's airforce," guestimates cargo's first-class bales, unexcluding bricked coke.

"Airlanes're preempted, econopolitically. Drugdom's CIA-funded bootleggers disrelish DEA flyer hotdoggers. Airlifters'd spook'em."

Contradicted dispatches're factionally notifying DF's jefes status-quoed revistas. Magazined glosses floss teething commandantes smilingly self-promoting propagandas arraigning opposers' "criminally disruptive" maneuverings. Equipoised commissioned officer reputations stymie lording arbitrators? Darwinian corruption'd unknot treasonous entanglings; refitted superseders'll emerge government-backed; vanquished'll apperceive ignominy's slams.

Precautiously, napalming foliage'd scorch pariahs; nuking Pedroville'd unnaturally expunge treason's abashment.

Facetious reasoning's shortcoming underestimates fourth estate's longitudinal magnanimity. Intranational chauvinist mouthguard mouthpieces smelling wog capital's capitulating decay charter blimp expeditions overdrifting "strife-torn, decimated Chiapas's skyrocketing aftershock." Gondola downlookers telex corresponsible impressions redescribing historicity. WASHTON PEST, N.Y./L.A. TAMES, U.S.A. TOADY's remote operatives reassure newsroom editorialists picante uprisers're spicily newsworthy/downplayably geldable. Aghast posturings undoubtedly've pigeonholed Pedrovile's sloshed mosh piteousness. Sahara molerat's disgustingly prurient lifestylishness deflects dead-on tragedy's genocide ramifications, let alone originations "slandering" NAFTA financeros.

Sadly, lighter-than-air newshounds' prime-directive heeds Star-Trekked noninterference precept (quarantine-assisted), prohibiting AguaFir's freshened kittypool reserves replenishment. Intercepted communiques paint swank roller skyboys yearningly scrutinizing horse-coursed playground.

Racemeet greeters ecstatically repatriate undiseased peace-seeking punter assemblages. Mimeographic ceremony's bombasts (fainter, gluesmellier, blurier), remarking forecited parade huzzahs, anathematically restrain variation. Superrestricted autonomy's freedoms dwindle; terminating plagues, devolutionary warfares, pathworn retreating, recoursed horse-beating literalize, figuratively inscribe growth's stultification.

Jocks, trainer accompanists, disgracefully acquitted stewarding welshers redistribute tipsheets. Nuevo improvements concede overstressed equines' burdening; festively recreative schedulings enact predreamt apostasy menagerating Circean zoo competitor quadrupeds. Goats, ascendantly (native-accustomed constituitive staminas overcompensating interbreed quickness's impediments); mutts, ridiculously (field-filling jokers stackpiling dreks).

Unsound paper-moneyed scrips institute faith's testiness: bettings' suppliers foist tracklashed vouchers; unpayable paperbound promissories refound buildable stakehouses lathing laminated inflationary insulation.

Insularity's hermits reaffirm vices alloying metallically unbreakable penchants. Risk-taking, gaming, outsmarting (dignifiable notabilities overuse indignified) cashier nibbling, haling, outfarting (corporeal unavoidabilities underuse enveloped). Dungeon physique sporters issue bonehead conviction's pronounced renouncements, de-emphasize life user manual's unsurpassable dictum.

Despiting life-supported disruptions, horseplaying restarts.

RADIOED UPDATING IRREGULARLY redraws bottomland battlelines. Rivaling microstations transmit autocratized fiats subsuming nationalists, factionalists, neoteric nativists. Airwave treaties betroth unmarriageable entities, prepostulating coalitions yoking sworn antagonist lummoxes. Stubborn prideful strainings, devious wiles, rock-hard desperations weave contradictable coverstories palimpsestically rewriting permutation's politic diversities.

"Whoever wins'll mosey thisaway," Hanna-Margarita recites cowboy's dialect disfavoring injuns' prevailability.

"Nothing'll stay valuable," George-Matteo gibes, retrospecting W.C. Fields' riverboat's grandstand-played redestruction (himself redeploying Keaton's General's pufferbelly firebox busting): planked woods're systematically fireplaced, smattering energy's formation.

Frigidity forestalled, scavenger pigeons peck mealworms' cornflavored beetle larva privation's enterprisers dig. Cyan fingerling potatoes, sun-dried anchos, jalapeños, superabundant condiments (ketchupy sugarings Heinz misshipped, crate-stacked palettes intended forasmuch Australian palates), pozzole conglomerate cauldron mush's indisputably resurrective potpourri: simmered grubworms squirm.

Four-legged runners're refed straw, corncobs, uncomposted vegetable subsistances since-slaughtered hogs'd foregoingly snacked (exorcising coprophagic spree deviltries). Hindulike consecration shields playable feeder courseracers; competing drop-out feeders're people's fodders. Gladiator custom performability exemption overrules thumbs-down verdict.

Fortnight de los muertos viviendos pitting burgher backslider profligate fiends diametrical otherselves recasts horrorscopic frightmare exploring cannibalism. Preemulating indefatigable backtracker recidivists, Romero's roaming dead're hustling achievers; ALIVE's Andes planecrash cannibals, contradictingly, resign, consoling ruffled rectitude (need's patent remedy overturns justification's moralizing questioners). Unartistic maneaters' (need-driven subsistors) literal cannibling divagates artful abstractions autoconsuming protectorate embodies.

Nero fiddling's tradition predates doom defier antic recreations. Catalytic enhancements've precipitated ruin-enchanted revelers. Uncounted fortunes're splurged combo-betting bandylegged, monkey-jockeyed caprines, steeplechasing insolvently uncashable capricornucopias. Unkemptly maintained hoofing ground's obstacular detraction effectuates steeplechase hurdlings, sinkholes, tumbleweed actualizations. Nonmonkey horsewhippers bridle, protesting unresurfaced devastation; manhood's jeering picadors reinstall reinsman audacity's inane haughtiness, humiliate careful judicious comportment.

Round-the-clock gambler's relapses percolate synapses, filtering dreg residues dredging once-channeled singlemindedness's purebred focusing. Nonracing durations shorten. Day-littered potluck scraps reprovision contestable action-starved comestibles hourly. Off-hours kindle firesidebet chitchats propositioning screwy resolution's intercontingent multiplexes. If-then parlays weld wackily unconnectable happenstances: moonrise, eagle-sighting, megabore gunshot's staccato, thunderless raincloud inundation, mountaincat rut yowl.

Sleepless proclivity's impulsions amassing, insomniacs overdose nodozed absorptions. Climacteric deprivation's hyperreal sensationalization lends addicted horsebettors addictive delusion's superacuity. Blimped apparitional newsrooms, downunder hamlet's revolutionized nepotist rumblers, springtime rawness admix; coagulated understandings're conflictable.

Pickled mealworm diets hallucinogenerate frictionless living. Cactus alcohols' irrevocable drainages repeal prohibitions banning optionally sourced intoxicants; weedkillers, lyes, shellacs, manure liqueurs synthesize lowbrow highs. Braindamaged ravers braving tremens' "cure" erupt methanol concoctions' fiery vomits. Exhaled blazes perambulate fog-bound yardages, exhume briefest visibility's matchlight flarings. Accursed graveyards nourish friendlier neighborliness.

Humanic flamers, contranegatively, coruscate gaslamp gaiety. Staggering's consequentially powerless solace's reassuring. Corpusine flammabilities aside, bipedaling gasbags're underqualified gangbanger ruffians.

Boschian laxity co-pilots turpentine-fueled turpitude. Debasement deportment regime rules're enacted, reminiscing unsupervised oldsters' homes whereinside vulgarly admissible corridor foyers nightgowned fuckings abide unsubsided. Institutional live-and-let-love immodesties uplift dispiritedly dissipated evacuees. Civilizations crumbled crumbling beget anticivilized evacuation's unzipped socializing.

Indiscreet coitions eschewing precautional modesty revamp creche-padded sodomism's catechisms jisming crash-padded fantasy's orgy. Disinvigorated pelvis smackings outdance marathon foxtrotters' wearisome endurances. Enduring's fargone irrelevances demystify deadening's ultra endedness; numb nuts psychotronically retroprocess filmic necromancy exculpating unmannered boor licentious entropic capitulations.

Magic's realismo transpositioning bathetically undershadows august latino authors' tomed make-believes. Marquez wannabe writer types "unconsciously" typewrite bittersweet confections fertilizing entrancement literature's ground, linger sweeteningly herewhile embittered deformic acids etch trope decadences.

Orgy's organ-grinders overspill ovaled boundary's tracked wholeness. Blistering blissed consenters confabulating hump-backed jumpable obstacle annexations hypercomplicate amazing recourse's discombobulations.

Emaciated bisexuals fellate sadsack protein straws (phalluses semiconducively acceding semen). Pride-swallowing hetero sapsuckers gobble scrumptious extremities; hunger subdues omnisex appetite's openendedness. Lovelorn yodels connoting zeal's mealtimed overbite chill unetherized unwitting penilectomy patient's sangfroid. Incisored loin Hemingway protagonists brandish bookish crotchfield wounding's citations: splotchy shreddings badge cannibalistic devolvement's steak tartare barbarism, red-flagging moribundity.

Leprous delimbinations, counterphysiologically, strengthen zombies. Lightfooted being's genital liberations infer giddy superiority's fulfillment.

Oblivion embalms. Ghoulishness colonizes. Benumbed starvers misperceive Cortez's repossessional foray.

BLIMPING ARMADAS hoverbearing transglobal communication logo emblems metamorph; reporters've corresponded mercenaries, Nikon tripods Nike missile launchers, helpful smilers hellbent smirkers. Microphoned gunmen pester lesioned legions. Ulcerated amputees elucidating dissolute moral's gristliest embodiments lovingly reciprocate pesterers' consideration. Suicidally potentiated affairs've beseeched amputated lunatics desperately streaking plasm's unstaunched malady.

"Mátame, cabrón!" vaingloriously vaunts neuter empowerment.

Noncombatant interviewers deny fatality begging's contemptuous demanding.

"Describe sus pensimientos . . . piensos? penisimos?" bilingo dictionaries equipping querulous newscaster babblers precompose segueed quip.

Deliriums've confused translations. Incomprehensible request (murdering's complicity) bamboozles incontestably cheeky deadliners. Incoherent shock troop's accumulated wits misinterpret uncomplicated perorations. Monosyllabic gesticulated blurting frightens pinhole iris loons; frightening gaze rejoinders sicken squeamish newscast aggressors.

Dirigibles putter, fritter overheads billionaires disfavor. Anchorlines fasten flagpole moorages, riskily uplink diseased climbing earthlings. Amputation bodybuilders scale guywires? Rat infestation imitation's unconvincing.

Some're strong, withertheless. Bloodied ghoul flockers encrypt wolfish hiders feigning deliberately debilitated constitutions. Infirm dawdlers unpostpone post's timed intervals: theatric law's must-go-on coercion preterdominates naturalism's unwarily plodded waltz. Autistic mechanizations enmesh player/runner/rider cogs; collapses're infrequent, unconscionable.

Unjousted I-beams defining grandstand's superstructural predecessor,

197

spectator's perched lotus, squatted chameleon, scrunched flea positioning's supplanted absented pews. Reverent supplicants congregating semicircularly fence inbred thoroughbred horses, outtaken multibred nonequine replacers. Infield picnickers gorging unroasted sirloins reconcile borderless altered stateroom honeymoons' no-holes-barred libertine gormandizing. Toteboard's unscrewed lightbulb sockets electrocute aberrant infielders; bookies tally time-honored propositionings, prorating exoticism's incalculable values. Masterbeast theater outplays, disorienting arrival's unraveled rivals: rifted column's reformation clinched, celebrant soldier conquerors retch.

Spoilage spoils're undesirable. Palatially stupendous tracklands redeem Brazil's backlands, desolationally speaking. Cibolia's goldwell disappointments pale, discerning Aguafir gulch's dessication.

Harry Reasoner anchorman trainees hyperreasonably writhe. Rolex bracelets, technical outfittings, Banana Republic bushwacker fashion templates x-mark crosshaired aiming's plunderables.

Telecamera surveillance relaying courtyard's troubles satellite-to-citylight, teleprompted talking headmaster demeanors primp global-powered citizenship's invulnerability, falsifying documentary's cinema-verite terrific terroristic portrayal. Bogusly puffed bravado's goading harasses assassins. Counterinsurgers' belts swaying scalped vestige bodyparts genocidally ooze bulletins approving raza's erasure. Dripped lymph barbarity transfers savagery's memento, attesting primitivism's counterfeitters deprave tradition's tribally aboriginated engravings.

Demilitarized disciplinarians' zoning outbreak extorts obsequious courtesy. Global fame commercializes victor, victors're told; pampered upstanding fortunates're saluted, breathlessly interviewed, flatteringly indulged. Sagacious, war-weary infantrymen examine situational druthers countermandating rape: garrulous cocksuckers patently apply implied blowjobs conquerers requisition.

Cocksucking virtual lepers slaver. Stiff-legged demimonde denizen treads rehashing psychotronic splatter movie slowed inexorability stolidly ensnare meatiest well-fed prey. Soldierly muses foreshadow gunpoint's playful sacrifice: newsmen're presented, zombies're gratified.

Wary airship commanders rethink anchoring fealty? Retreat'd incur shame's damnation; bullets'd deflate heliumated bladders, upsides. Disengagement's exonerable (Nixonerable?) withdrawals kissing ass (Kissinger's?), gondola's braintrust teleflashes callback message, quoting bureaucratic popes' infallible (unintelligible) absolutions.

Extremely appeased minidespots disobey unrecognized author's blinking Morse codicil. Unfurling roperung ladders grudge distended getaways. Wind's whipping teases grounded nonzombie escapist kindred sprites repulsing suction's vortex. Smugly inviolate violators, inextricably helpless gonad donators, monsterly mobsters unify quasi-universal participation's sojourner faction, jettisoning stasis's resistant strainers.

"Outtahere!" cowled Marge's monk get-up (anti-rape ruse's religiousness unchallenged) murmurs.

Ex-associates Delveccios're genitally delved, waylaid. Porking tenderloin's surgical enlargement satisfies monomaniacal consumers. Undisguised vulvas attendantly enrapture uninhibited slurping beauties. Frisky servicemen voluntarily enjoin festivity's tireless overdriven valiance. Earthly delight's diversion intercepts watchfully hip guardian glancers. Debauching banqueters hobnob snubbed nubbin journalists, currying subalterns' riveted intensities.

Pacemaker jockeyed optimists scurry unbounded laps, closer fatalists snort unfinishable lining's moveable postponements. Engrossed, muted, chewed bookmakers recount havoc's squirming fluctuation. Suppositious wordless containment's continuable grasping apparently's giving way.

Unimpaired tagteam finalists groping ropeward grab ladder's flagellum. Tornado contortions propelling vertigo's propeller try motivation's limitability. Panoramal abnormality kaleidoscopes depth's twirled inflections. Putt-putting motor rheumatic pneumatics interwheeze fabricated hearing's prospects. Aeolian blast stretches kite-strung tails. Elevational change improves. Clicked tremor regularity transmitted intraline intimates reel's winching accrual.

Groundlings shoot somebody? Unmistaken gunmetal barrel twangs, puffy muzzle whitenesses detonate. Skeet marksmen's clay pigeon aerialists scud shuddering, appreciatively bypassed. Undershot levelings euthanize horsemeats, simians, nonhuman proteins. Final bonfire tinderboxes flare, broiling spit attachments sweepstake carrion's nightcap stretch-run close. Stricken mortals infect overlords? Genocides' contented despoilers snack subdued fat's transient feasts, eructations unrippling airways.

INTERMINABLY HANGED RESCUEES saturate stratus realm's dewpoint fluidities, seeding clouded torrents inundating budded luaus. Glimpsed earthborn episodes wink inconsistently, sundering thundercloud curtain scrims. Heavens disembodiments reenvelop misty closures; whited-out vision's peculiarity isolates absurdity's hauteur. Snug clingers adherently brainwash ourself-interested psyches, solipsisitically averting downward-looking eyes.

"Why'nt thane appalling?" windily transmutes semi-lucid gibberish, redressing uphauling rest's supposition.

Seeming hours've transited inglorious limbo, neither hereafterwards, squashed, notherwards there, dirigibly repatriated. Dragging airlifter still levitates teleposed; impassiveness's resistible distention conundrum assays goldbrick hangers, exhorting symmetrical response's paramecium aversive simplicity repeating monkeyshined ravine's screeched breakout insinuation: climb, dim-wit.

Horizontal alignment's fifty+ (km/mi) speedometer measureabilities retract climbing's uppity instigation. Subwayward peeking's rigidly airforced. Counterwind frightcrawlers budge millimeters; fatiguing skeletomuscular painstakings creakily reperceive frayed rung tie's scritched oinkings. Fatigue's congruous contemplation yearns detachment'd unparabolically catapult gravity's rainbow warriors. Pseudoscientific metaphysics (unabutting philosophers' epistemology) dream-up indefinity's unendable trip: firmamental firmness softeningly maintaining cloud-based ease! insuladermal warmness comportably transiting unheated climes! phantasmal calmness ethereally hovercoming amorphous embedding stoppages!

Intercut below, rabid infestivities overrunning settlement've judged balloonists remiss. Sharpshooting mite lookalikes counterargue gravitational contrarians: earthward salvos're unharmfully gravitated.

Mitey men've ascended megalomania's throneroom pedestaled busts.

Razed buildings, disemboweled skyscraper tombs, blasphemous plaster saint ravagings, eviler full-blooded aborigine savagings, frittered savings, lavished dreams partly established Americanized interdependence confederating scapegoats, scalawags, carpetbagger pioneers.

Microcosm's chasm receded, outstretched rung-rats crawl onward, knowingly portaging biotic scourges. Faceless, guilt-free pressbox gondoliers withhold cheering, helping's hand, await misadventure story's pat end.

Worldly bookmaker soulmates rectify unfair circumstance's recurred tragedies, ever-moving, ever-hedging shifty playabilities since chances say someone will be for ever closing racetracks.

DOUG NUFER writes fiction, poetry, and performance pieces that seem to be based on formal constraints, even when they are not. The most audacious example of his work is *Never Again*, the story of a gambler who narrates how he set out to avoid the mistakes of his past by doing (and saying) nothing he has ever done (or said) before. He is also the author of the novels *Negativeland* (Autonomedia) and *On the Roast* (Eraserhead) and the CD monologue *The Office* (softpalate), which he performs and Erik Belgum produces. He lives in Seattle, where he has had the same job (selling wine) for nearly two decades.